Valencia
and
Valentine

Valencia and Valentine

Suzy Krause

LAKE UNION PUBLISHING

Text copyright © 2019 by Elena Krause
All rights reserved.

Published by Lake Union Publishing, Seattle
www.apub.com

Amazon, the Amazon logo, and Lake Union Publishing are trademarks of Amazon.com, Inc., or its affiliates.

ISBN-13: 9781542092968 (hardcover)
ISBN-10: 1542092965 (hardcover)
ISBN-13: 9781542040396 (paperback)
ISBN-10: 1542040396 (paperback)

Cover design and illustration by Philip Pascuzzo

Printed in the United States of America

First Edition

Dedicated to Barclay and Sullivan and Scarlett.
Obviously.

CHAPTER ONE

Valencia didn't think about death too often.

If anything, everyone else thought about it too little. Too lightly. After all, there were a lot of people in the world, and every single one of them had to die at some point, no two in exactly the same way and place and circumstance. Maybe standing in line at a bank at the hands of a robber. Maybe stretched out on an operating table under bright white lights and flashing surgical steel. In a hospital bed with family standing around, looking sad and saying comforting things, or on an airplane, or in a garden, or crossing a street—maybe jaywalking.

Murdered, sick, fatally clumsy.

Oslo, Norway. Milwaukee, Wisconsin. Outer space.

She wasn't immortal, and she knew it. That was all.

The part that was, perhaps, excessive or unhealthy was the *way* she thought about death, and the way she thought about death was the way she thought about everything else: in graphic detail and at inopportune moments and in sticky, cyclical loops. She'd be walking down the street and see a speeding car, and she'd think, *That car is driving too fast*, and that was all it took; her brain would grab the thought and shut like a fist, and she'd spend the next hour or so picturing her body cracking against the front of the car like a giant egg. Afterward, she'd feel as battered and tired as if she had, in fact, been run over and into repeatedly.

It wasn't that Valencia believed she would die that way; she just couldn't stop picturing it.

And if it wasn't a car, it was a sharp edge, a high-up ledge, a flash of lightning in the distance. Every day supplied her with endless possible deaths, hundreds of awful scenarios for her brain to clutch and knead.

The only way she could get herself to stop thinking about being hit by a car or burning alive in her bed or falling and hitting her head on the corner of something was to picture—in great detail—the place where she was actually going to die: West Park Services Call Center, where she worked as a debt collector. The thought of it soothed her, not because it was a good job or because she liked it there but because it was so bland and boring that her active imagination couldn't do anything with it.

The call center was a massive warehouse full of cubicles. The walls looked beige or pink or brown depending on the time of day, depending on the way the light hit them, and no one had made any kind of effort to hang art or pick out nice curtains for the windows. The point was not to look at the walls and windows; the point was to be contained by them, to do work within them. It felt, at times, like a jail.

The only sounds in the building were shuffling feet and hundreds of hushed, one-sided telephone conversations. It smelled deceptively surface clean, like they'd only sort of made an attempt at covering up the stale air and body odor. Everyone seemed either uneasy or bored. In some ways, it was less like a penitentiary and more like a hospital; you got a feeling of dread in your stomach when you walked in. You got the sense that the people inside were all sick or dying or dead.

The cubicle walls were thin and short—barely enough to separate Valencia from the men who sat on either side of her. Even still, in the seventeen years she'd been at West Park, she hadn't ever met them, and she hadn't wanted to meet them, and they hadn't seemed to want to meet her either. One smiled slightly in her general direction to acknowledge her existence every now and then, while the other stared straight ahead at all times. They were middle aged, and they wore heavy-looking glasses and had moustaches, maybe to make up for the lack of hair on the tops of their heads or maybe because of some sort of middle-aged man peer pressure, if that was a thing middle-aged men still struggled with. They were like somewhat mismatched bookends.

Everyone else at West Park blurred together into a huge, chaotic mass when she dared to glance around, but in her mind they all looked the same as the bookend men, and they all moved in perfect synchronization. She imagined only one of them was even human, that he was the prototype for some strange corporation that manufactured socially awkward robots just to work at call centers because no one else wanted to. Robots with blurry vision and thin hair and bad breath and flat, boring voices.

So these were the people she would be looking at, and this was the place, but then there was the exact *spot* in which she was convinced she would die—a stiff but worn-out office chair. She'd be sitting in it, she thought, leashed to her desk by a phone cord, staring at the six-by-four photograph of a painting of a bird pinned to the cubicle wall behind her computer. She could imagine it happening without taking any kind of in-depth bodily mechanics into consideration, just the basics:

The day would feel very normal until it didn't feel like anything at all.

Her lungs would refuse to do what they were supposed to, and her heart would slow and stop.

She'd open her mouth, and nothing would come out except a wisp of a breath, a dainty, feathered thing (surely a person's last breath was something you would be able to *see*).

The thoughts would stop—this was her favorite part. *The thoughts would stop.*

Her head would loll forward, and, if anything, she'd feel a shot of relief that she didn't have to hold that thing up anymore. The bird picture would rush up as her eyes rushed down. A blur of beige. Desk. The person on the other end of the line would say, "Hello? *Hello* . . . ?" and the sound of the phone crashing down would be the last one to reverberate through her old, dead skull.

She would die having experienced nothing but this, having been for the larger part of her existence a prisoner in her cubicle cell. But her death would be easy, and it was easy to think about. No violent images to play on repeat. No sharp corners or spattered blood or evil people— just a picture and a chair and a computer amid a sea of weird robots. The only thing about it that wasn't easy was that it probably wouldn't happen for another sixty years or so.

Death was a thing that happened to everyone. Debt collection as a permanent occupation was a thing that happened only to the supremely unlucky, and for her it was a life sentence thrown down from the bench of a pitiless judge. She was being punished—and she deserved it. She'd only ever done one terrible thing, but it was very terrible: she'd killed someone.

How ironic, Valencia often mused, that her debt to society—to the dead girl and her family—would be paid in overseeing the collection of other people's monetary debt. It was almost poetic.

Debt: the meaning of life—not just her life, everyone's. Accumulating it and then paying it off—or, in the case of some religions, working it off, and in others, having someone else pay it off for you.

It was all about debt.

CHAPTER TWO

Mrs. Valentine absolutely thinks about death too much. It is her favorite thing to think about; she doesn't even try not to. Nor should she. It's coming—soon—and if she does anything but welcome it with open arms, she'll be miserable all the time.

She's not dying, technically, but she's old enough that if she keeps living, it'll start surprising people. She's eighty-seven years old—but she's a young eighty-seven. She's more like an eighty-six. She lives alone in an apartment in a building on the corner of Fifth and Friesen. Her face looks like a piece of paper somebody crumpled up, and her hands are rough and gnarly, but her hair is soft and a striking silvery white. She hunches forward and leans a little to the right at all times; she's like a mattress sinking into its frame with the springs poking out, the stuffing all bunched up in some places and missing in others. She limps and shuffles and wheezes. A year ago, she lost her glasses, so now everything is blurry. She has aged about as well as anyone could ask her to, but she's old. Her best friend, Mrs. Davies, lives across the hall in apartment 13 and is in the same shape—a little less hair on her head and more loose skin around her chin.

Mrs. Valentine thinks the world of Mrs. Davies. Mrs. Davies likes Mrs. Valentine back just as much and goes around telling people they're sisters because they might as well be. When you are old, you realize that rules about this kind of thing are ridiculous. You can be relatives with whomever you want. Blood is irrelevant.

The elderly women call each other by their married last names instead of their given first ones because it's a pleasant reminder of their husbands, who aren't around anymore. This started shortly after Mr. Davies passed away and Mrs. Davies moved from their acreage out of town into the empty apartment right across the hall. That vacancy felt like the luckiest thing in the world to the women, whose relationship was, for a time, reduced to phone calls. Neither one has a valid driver's license anymore.

Mrs. Valentine was over helping her unpack some things. They'd worked in complete silence for a good three or four hours before Mrs. Davies's mouth cracked open and she said, "I'm not Mrs. Davies anymore." A saline river snaked down her cheek, and she reached up to touch it with a wrinkled hand. She looked surprised, as if her identity was so shaken at the loss of her husband and home and name that she was unsure if this body could still be hers, or if she would suddenly be forced to move out of it too.

Mrs. Valentine understood completely. She hugged Mrs. Davies as hard as their frail bones would allow, trying to press her friend's spirit back into her body and hold the pieces together. She spoke firmly but sweetly into her gray hair. "You're still Mrs. Davies," she said. She hasn't called her anything other than Mrs. Davies since, and she loved it when Mrs. Davies started calling her Mrs. Valentine. A simple act of acknowledgment and remembrance—of their lost men, sure, but maybe more of each other's grief.

When Mrs. Davies was in the hospital for a couple of weeks, Mrs. Valentine started talking to herself out loud because she'd gotten so used to hearing her husband's name spoken and she missed it. "Good morning, Mrs. Valentine," she'd say. "Have a good day, Mrs. Valentine. Why don't you have a cup of tea to start off with, Mrs. Valentine?" She's never stopped, even though Mrs. Davies has recovered as much as she's going to and is back across the hall. It feels eccentric, but this makes her happy—someone once told her that eccentric people live longer than everyone else. She likes proving that person right by staying alive.

Mrs. Valentine tries to find joy in little things, since most of the bigger things are getting too heavy and slippery for her to hold on to. She likes sitting on her balcony and watching the kids of the apartment complex play soccer. She enjoys eavesdropping on the couple living directly below her, who also like sitting on their balcony in the evenings. She has a recording of a favorite piano piece that she lets play on repeat day and night—Rachmaninoff's Étude-Tableau in G Minor. It's familiar and comforting. She turns the volume up every so often as she gets used to the music and it starts to fade into the background too much. It blares through the narrow hallways of the building and presumably seeps through the paper-thin walls into other apartments, but the neighbors have never complained. Maybe it comforts them too.

On occasion, Mrs. Valentine amasses a small amount of credit card debt. Mrs. Davies lectures her about interest rates and fiscal responsibility, but what Mrs. Davies doesn't understand is that Mrs. Valentine does it on purpose—so she can visit with the debt collectors. She looks for social interactions in unusual places these days. She has to. She's exhausted all the usual ones.

"Carla has been having such a rough time," she'll say to Mrs. Davies as they sip tea on a rainy afternoon. "Her little boy has been acting up at school, and she hates her job. She wanted to be an architect, you know, but then she got pregnant with Jimmy, and her husband ran away."

Mrs. Davies will look confused for a moment, and then Mrs. Valentine will laugh and nod. "Oh, I'm sorry, Mrs. Davies. Carla was my debt collector today. She's such a sweetheart; we spoke for half an hour, and she sounded near tears the entire time. We're going to talk again tomorrow."

Mrs. Davies will shake her head, but she won't say anything— this isn't unusual; she hasn't said much since her hospital stay. She still manages to make it clear that she doesn't approve of Mrs. Valentine's strange hobby, but she understands her friend's desire for companionship, her need to be needed as her world squeezes in around her.

Mrs. Valentine has traded in her spot at the community garden for a single basil plant on her windowsill. She doesn't paint anymore—her hands just *won't*—and she's given up on any kind of spontaneity, having rediscovered instead an old affinity for scheduling.

There's a piece of paper taped to the wall by the fridge upon which she has drawn shaky lines and letters: the days of the week across the top, underlined, the hours of the day down the left-hand side. Every single time slot is filled with a name or TV show or small chore or activity or just the word *nap*, written a little darker than any of the other words and underlined twice, because she doesn't like to take naps but knows she needs them. She is very stern with herself on this point. "Now, Mrs. Valentine," she'll say into the empty room, resisting nap time like a three-year-old, "you need a nap. You know you do. When you wake up, you can have tea." Bribery works best, she's found— another way she's like a three-year-old. Sometimes she feels like she's two people in one: a stubborn child and its harried mother. She exasperates herself but still tries to be nurturing and understanding. Old age, after all, is hard. She prides herself on her empathy.

She doesn't need the paper anymore; she can recite her entire daily program forward and backward and standing on her head (an absurd thing to imagine, considering her porcelain bones and stuck joints), but she still checks it every half hour. Sometimes, when she's alone in her small apartment, it can feel as though time has slowed or stopped. The minutes get empty and endless, and it's comforting for her to see that the days are still chugging forward in half-hour increments and that when the next one arrives, she will not be in danger of floating off into the expanse of it like a balloon without a string. Something to do is her tether, even if that something is to lie down on the couch and sleep for thirty minutes.

She knows the things in the boxes on the schedule are not important by anyone's standards, but these are the things she is capable of, and these are the things that make up her hours and days. Important is a very hard thing to nail down anyway. Maybe Important is contingent on Ability. Maybe the simple act of being alive doesn't seem all that important until it stops feeling involuntary and starts feeling like something you have to work at. She doesn't just live anymore; she *accomplishes* living. After all, she could do something fantastic in the morning, but if she doesn't live through the afternoon to tell anyone about it, the fantastic thing won't matter at all. Better to live through the whole day, even if you don't get much else done. So she gives herself a very tiny little bit of wiggle room and grace on the visiting and cleaning, but she is strict about the living and hasn't yet missed a single day.

This week, however, she needs to make a more substantial edit to her schedule. Mrs. Valentine has hired a girl to do her housekeeping once a week. It's debatable as to whether she needs someone else to do her housekeeping—she could probably continue getting by on her own. But she needs to meet this particular girl.

Everyone has ulterior motives. When an evil person has ulterior motives, it's called scheming. When a good person has ulterior motives, it's called planning.

Mrs. Valentine is planning.

CHAPTER THREE

Valencia's birthday was three months away, in August. She didn't care about birthdays, had no friends to celebrate with anyway, but she felt herself caring about this one—physically caring. She cared so much it made her vomit.

She cared about thirty-five because she could remember her father at thirty-five. Her father at thirty-five had a house and a career and a family—a child and a wife. He had a beard and looked old to Valencia. There was a furrow in his forehead that was deep like a ditch and coarse gray hairs above his ears. He worried about everything, all the time, and his knees ached too much to go on walks with his daughter. She remembered thinking, as a ten-year-old, that thirty-five was the end. It was the age at which you stopped caring about anything and became fretful and achy and didn't smile at your kid anymore.

And look at her: she didn't even have a kid to stop smiling at yet.

She wondered sometimes if she had inherited her father's sadness. She'd been a sad and anxious child, but no one had noticed until she'd grown into a sad and anxious teenager, and then they'd always said, "It's just a phase." It wasn't; she was a sad and anxious adult, too, one who became sick to her stomach whenever she thought about turning thirty-five.

Her therapist, Louise, who passed out psychiatric labels like she was Oprah Winfrey giving away cars (*You get an anxiety disorder! And you get OCD! And you get depression!*), thought thirty-five was a dumb thing to be afraid of. Valencia could tell. She seemed to like it better when Valencia was afraid of death or apartment fires.

When, at her last appointment, Valencia had said, "I keep throwing up every time I think about turning thirty-five," Louise had stopped what she was doing and tilted her head to the side like a puppy, her chandelier earrings jangling noisily against her neck. Her hair, however, had not moved at all; it was cut short and styled into a rock-hard, flamelike shock on top so she resembled a candle. Valencia had always admired this subtle act of bravery, the short hair. Louise had nothing to hide behind. Valencia never even tucked her hair behind her ears.

Louise had been trying to refill her stapler, and Valencia thought at first that she wasn't going to respond to her confession, but at last there was a click and a snap as Louise brought the arm and base together and fired a single silver staple onto the floor. "What're the next things?" Louise asked, setting the stapler down and picking up a stack of papers.

Valencia didn't know if Louise was a good therapist or a bad one because she had no one to compare her to. She was kind but often seemed like she wasn't in her head. Like her mind was a helium balloon bumping around the corners of the room while her long body swiveled back and forth in the chair across the table doing busywork that had nothing to do with her client. Her office smelled like flowers—not any one flower, but all of the flowers at once. "The next whats?" Valencia asked, confused, looking into the corner of the room where Louise's mind was.

"The next most scary things. If turning thirty-five's at the top of your list of things you're afraid of at the moment, what're numbers two and three?" Louise was trying to straighten the papers now, bringing them down onto her desk loudly, repeatedly. If Valencia were an assertive person, she would have asked Louise to please stop that; it was distracting. But she was not, had never been, an assertive person.

"Airplanes," she said over the noise of the papers cracking against the desk. "And then highways."

"You're scared of airplanes, or you're scared of flying?" asked Louise. Thwack, thwack, thwack.

"Oh, flying," said Valencia, feeling stupid. "I'm not afraid of . . . of the airplanes themselves. Just of them falling out of the sky. With me inside." She knew it worked, somehow, that planes could fly with people inside them and get where they were going and even land without exploding into flames. But if she were aboard, everything that usually worked would fail because she deserved it. She wondered if it was a point of vanity, of self-importance, to think that her very presence could alter the laws of physics or override the mechanical workings of jumbo jets.

"Have you ever flown?" asked Louise, and Valencia thought it was impressive how much she didn't seem to be paying attention but could still ask relevant questions.

"No."

"Well, Valencia, I think you should. Maybe if you tackle number two on your list, number one won't seem so frightening. Maybe you'll learn you're brave enough to do things you're afraid of." Louise had the corner of the paper stack in the mouth of the stapler now, and she was standing beside her desk pushing down with all her might, but the stack was too thick. She frowned, split it in two, and started banging the top half against the desk again. "Sorry, what was I saying?"

"You were saying I should fly somewhere."

"Oh yes. You should."

"Where?"

"Doesn't matter. You could fly to Saskatoon or Tokyo. A shorter trip would be easier, but a longer one would be more effective, in my opinion. Is there anywhere you've been wanting to go?"

Valencia wanted to go everywhere. She often borrowed travel books from the library and drove to the airport, where she'd sit for hours, drinking airport coffee and eating stale, expensive airport muffins and watching the planes land and take off. It was, to her, like visiting an aquarium. The airplanes were like sharks, with their sleek gray exteriors and their sharp fins, slicing through the air without moving, somehow.

She shrugged. "No."

"Think about it," said Louise. "Plan a trip." She stapled the first stack of papers and then the second, joined the two with a paper clip, and set them down in front of her. "There," she said. "That was annoying."

Valencia nodded meaningfully, but Louise wasn't looking at her.

"And then highways, you said? You're scared of highways, or—"

"Yes." Valencia felt an indignant tremor in her voice and tried to smooth it out. "Driving on them. I'm not scared of . . . of *roads*. I'm scared of driving on highways. Or, or, or . . ." She had to swallow and wait for her words to catch up with her brain. "Or being a passenger in a car on the highway. Leaving the city."

Louise chuckled, as though this were ridiculous. As though she hadn't probably just had some other patient in here talking about a fear of cotton balls or something like that. As though car crashes were not an actual thing that could hurt a person. Valencia frowned into her lap.

"When's the last time you drove on a highway then?"

"It's been a few years," said Valencia. "To see my mom and dad. They live in Saskatoon."

"You haven't seen your parents in a few years?"

"They come to me. They know I don't like highways."

"Ah." Louise loved saying *ah*. Maybe she had entered this profession just so she could bang things on desks and say *ah*. "Well. One at a time. Let's do the airplane thing first. You might talk to your doctor about adjusting your meds as well," she said, obviously giddy at the thought, like she were a scientist and Valencia her experiment. She opened the drawer by her right knee and started digging around in it. "Thinking about your birthday shouldn't make you vomit—at least not until you're my age." She chuckled into the drawer, like she was saving herself a little laugh for later. "Might just need to up your dose."

The thought of upping her dose also made Valencia want to puke. She didn't want to need medication at all, let alone more of it. Louise was probably right, and this was probably yet another sign that she did, in fact, need to up her dose. Again.

She had taken Louise's advice, as she always did, and now her pills were blue instead of red, and thirty-five was still terrifying, no matter what color the pills were. But perhaps Louise had been onto something with the trip, because when Valencia had woken up the next morning, she'd been thinking about that instead of her birthday. And when her stomach had turned over and emptied out, it had been because she was picturing a Boeing 737 plunging into the Atlantic Ocean, one claustrophobic space being swallowed up inside of another. *It worked, Louise,* she'd thought as she leaned over the toilet bowl.

And that was how she'd begun to plan her trip—or, more accurately, to obsess over it. She'd had a horrible feeling in her stomach, which at first she'd thought might be her appendix bursting or the early sign of a liver disorder or something like that. Upon careful inspection and introspection, however, she realized that it was actually some kind of anxiety-diluted—or sharpened—excitement. It had been so long since she last felt such a thing that she'd mistaken it for pain.

A new dosage of anxiety medication always felt like a heavy blanket on Valencia's mind for the first week or so, before her body became accustomed to it. It wasn't necessarily a bad sensation—it just wasn't conducive to productivity of any kind. She wanted to curl up under that blanket and sleep. She went to work in slow motion and didn't have to try so hard to ignore her fellow coworkers—they existed in her periphery, shadows moving around and speaking in murmurs. She only saw what was right in front of her, and even that was shrouded in a strange kind of mental smoke.

It was out of this fog that he came, like the lead singer of a rock band emerging from a cloud of dry ice: the perfect man.

He appeared as though he'd been breathed into existence and thrown at her. She'd been seated at her desk. She'd stood, turned, headed for the coffee maker, and then she was on the ground. He was on the ground too.

They stared at each other for a moment, winded and bewildered. He leaped to his feet, and she looked up at him.

The first thing she noticed about him was that he looked sorry. His face was fire-engine red, and he shook his head and held out his hand to help her up, expressing his regret and self-loathing. He looked around to make sure no one else had seen and looked at her as though he'd full-on bodychecked her instead of bumping into her by accident. She avoided his hand and pulled herself to stand using her office chair. *Don't be offended*, she wanted to say. *I just generally avoid touching anyone, ever.* Instead, she said nothing at all.

Now that they stood at eye level, she noticed a second, more out-of-place thing about him: he had hair. Normally this wouldn't be noteworthy, but he might have been the only man with hair in the whole building, and that meant he was automatically the only man with hair in her insular world. It was nice hair, too, even though it was pressed flat down against his head like he'd been wearing a hat or a helmet.

Beneath the hair was a handsome young face, unobstructed by a moustache or thick glasses, and it was now trying to smile at her, despite also looking like it was going to crack into a million other expressions. She smiled, too, but at his feet, and mumbled something about him not feeling bad and about her being clumsy and about not being hurt at all (though afterward she wondered if she'd only imagined herself saying those things) and finally speed walked past him to the little coffee station on the other side of the room.

She took her time filling a Styrofoam cup and turned to head back to her cubicle but noticed that the mystery man was seated at a desk across the aisle from where she sat, drumming his long fingers on the armrests of his office chair and looking right at her. At least this explained how he'd come out of nowhere like that; he'd been walking to or from his chair, and she'd stood up right into him. This made the whole thing worse—it had been her fault.

She realized two things then: one, that she was still moving toward her seat without even thinking about it, and two, that he intended to speak to her when she got there. Her brain began to shoot emergency adrenaline to the rest of her body, begging her legs to stop or redirect, but they kept propelling her forward. She felt like an insect being washed down a sink drain.

"Hi, I'm Peter," he said when she arrived, standing to greet her and taking the few silent steps across the oatmeal-colored carpet to her desk.

She smiled at him, or tried to, and set her coffee cup down, looking longingly at her chair.

"Again," said Peter, who either didn't see the meaningful glance or didn't understand what it meant, "I'm really sorry about that. I honestly just didn't see you until it was too late." His voice shook, and his smile was genuine, but tentative. He was either sunburned or embarrassed. He stuck his hand out to shake hers, which, unbeknownst to him, was a mistake.

She did not want to touch anyone's hands. They were dirty. She could almost guarantee it. Panic sprang up inside her when anyone tried to shake her hand—or hold it (this hadn't actually happened since high school, but that was another matter altogether).

Unfortunately, though no one was trying to hold her hand these days, people did try to shake it, often when they were also trying to make a good first impression. Louise had wanted to. Also one of her dad's friends, whom she'd bumped into on the street once. And now this man—Peter.

She acted like she didn't notice his intention, sitting abruptly, picking up her telephone headset, pretending to untangle the cord. This was a science she'd practiced and perfected: the art of avoiding handshakes without—she hoped—offending people.

He held his hand out for an embarrassing amount of time. An artist could've painted his portrait. She smiled at him, her eyes avoiding the hand until it dropped back to his side. He was still standing; his hand had been level with her face. But she was resolute.

She didn't want him to think she was rude and realized she should say something, like someone who wasn't rude would. Like a normal person would. Was this terribly deceitful of her, to pretend to be normal? She tried to think of what polite, normal people said. *What do normal people say? What do I say normally? Do I normally say things?*

At that moment, she couldn't remember the last time she'd had an in-person conversation with someone who wasn't Louise, someone she didn't know and who didn't know her. Someone handsome.

Her mouth opened, and she felt a rush of panic, not knowing or having any control over what was going to come out. "Welcome," she said, and her voice echoed in her ears. Had she shouted?

She thought she was going to say a whole sentence, one with four or five words, but that one was all that came out. *Welcome.* Like she was a big wooden sign at a national park. It was disappointing but not surprising.

She tried to remember how to meet people. *Names, smiles, pleasantries.* Had she told him her name? *No.* Blood rushed to her head, and she thought she might pass out.

Peter looked uncomfortable but no less friendly. He sat back down in his chair, scratched his knee, and pointed at the picture of the painting pinned to the wall behind her computer. "Did you do that?" he asked.

She shook her head. "My grandma did." She tried to make her voice bright—not neon-pink bright, or even pastel. More *mauve*. She attempted a smile and felt like she was trying to sell him a used car. A real lemon.

The bird picture had been an attempt at happiness. Her grandmother had painted it years before, but recently it had sold in a local charity's art auction. Her mother had taken a photograph of it and sent it to Valencia before taking the original to the community center. It was part thoughtful gesture, part guilt-trip—Valencia had not been to visit her ailing grandmother in a long time.

Valencia had brought the picture to work and stuck it to the wall with a pushpin, centered and square. It was shame, initially, that motivated her to do this, but there was also the thought that maybe because she liked the painting and its painter, the picture could bring her joy. Sometimes she stared at it, listening for her insides to affirm that she was feeling anything resembling happiness, but always she was met only with guilt.

The failed attempt at normalcy and happiness was discouraging but not surprising: the bird was entirely ineffective. It did not keep her happy; it just kept her company and reminded her of her failings— much like Louise, who existed less to help Valencia with her problems than to catalog them and nod at them and match names to them.

"Wow," Peter said. She could tell he was impressed. "She's really good. It's good."

"She's dying, my grandma. It's a bird," said Valencia. This was not going well. Or was it going great? She had nothing to compare to this encounter. Maybe they were flirting? Maybe she should tell him about her trip. Maybe she could tell him about therapy and Louise? *She's dying, my grandma. It's a bird. I'm so sorry; I'm afraid of airplanes and my birthday, so I'm on pills that make my brain feel like Silly Putty.*

She noticed then that her mouth was open. Had she said all that out loud? In high school, she'd always worried that she said all of her thoughts out loud without realizing and that everyone pretended not to notice to spare her feelings.

She noticed then that Peter's hands were shaking as much as hers, and that made her feel a little better. Maybe everyone's hands shook when they met new people. He examined the dying grandmother bird, nodding in approval. He didn't look at her when he spoke again. "So, how long have you been working here, Valencia?"

Before she could answer, there was a loud snap, and Peter crashed to the floor at her feet, limbs flailing like a rubber windmill. He'd been leaning his lanky body backward in the cheap office chair, and it had broken in half. The robot clones around them looked up and then back at their computers in perfect unison.

Valencia froze. Would he be offended if she laughed? Would he feel awkward if she didn't laugh? Would he be embarrassed by any acknowledgment at all? He looked like he was working through a similar set of questions in his head. His whole face was the color of tomato sauce. This was the second painting in a series. She pictured a row of them in an art gallery, an exhibit on her life, with a cute little plaque that read, "Bad at People: A Study in Embarrassing Social Interactions."

Her body began to make decisions for her brain. She felt herself nodding and excusing herself, saying she needed to ask Norwin, the manager, a question, as though the question was so pressing she couldn't lean over and help Peter to his feet first. As she walked away from him, she realized that this was, socially speaking, the wrong decision, but it was too late. The story of her life. *Bad at people.*

She paused and glanced over her shoulder and saw him looking after her. "I, uh . . . ," she began. She shook her head and smiled apologetically; then she was moving forward again, faster than a person should walk in an office. There was a man with a stack of papers, and then someone said, "Oof!" and then the papers were fluttering to the ground, and she was only vaguely aware that it was her fault.

She had said she needed to see Norwin, so she headed to Norwin's office and knocked on the door. She wasn't sure what she'd say to him when she got in there, but if she was going to be inventing excuses, she would at least follow through on them so they would not also be lies.

"Come in."

She pushed the door open, using a Kleenex from her pocket to turn the knob so she wouldn't have to touch it. Norwin was seated behind his desk, smoking a pipe that created billows of smoke around him so he looked like a cumulonimbus cloud with a couple of arms sticking out of it.

"Yes?" he mumbled as the smoke dissipated. He was just like all the other men at West Park, except that he was secluded in here all the time and had begun to look rumpled and wild and wildernessy, like a hermit living in a cave.

Valencia cleared her throat and began to fiddle with the ends of her hair, running it through her fingers and examining it like she'd never seen it before. "Um," she began. "Oh, never mind—I had a question, but I just remembered the answer."

Norwin grunted, but his eyes smiled at her, and she smiled back, thankful for a manager who didn't care for talking. She'd always suspected that he appreciated her for the same reason. She sneaked back to her desk a few minutes later when Peter, seated on a chair he'd taken from an empty cubicle, was on a call.

After that, whenever he saw her, Peter smiled and nodded, and Valencia smiled and nodded, and they became stuck in a quiet rut they dug for themselves with all their up-and-down head motions.

He looked at her over his shoulder a lot, though.

At least his face would be one of the last things she saw before she died.

CHAPTER FOUR

Anna stares at Mrs. Valentine's apartment door. Hanging just below eye level is a lightly stained wooden sign with a heart cutout at the bottom and stenciled lettering.

> COME IN, COME IN
> TO MY LITTLE PLACE
> I WANT TO SEE
> YOUR LOVELY FACE

It sounds kind of witchy, like the cannibalistic old woman in the gingerbread house from "Hansel and Gretel." Anna doesn't want to be here today, and this isn't helping.

Old women make her uncomfortable. They're unpredictable; it's hard to know what to expect or what's expected of you in their presence. Growing up, she was never close with either of her grandmothers—her father's mother was crotchety and cranky and seemed almost more like a badger than a person, in both physical appearance and personality. She made people feel small and horrible, and she smelled like vinegar.

Her mother's mother had simply been heartbroken, to such an extent that there was nothing else *about* her. There was hardly anything you could say that wouldn't make her intensely sad, and then there was nothing you could say to console her. So, despite her sweetness and the fact that they'd always gotten along fine, Anna avoided her with the same diligence as she avoided her mean grandmother. She never knew what to say to someone who was so old and depressed. What do sad old people want to talk about? Fine china? Medication? Potpourri?

Both of her grandmothers are dead now; they went within a few months of each other—three heart attacks between the two of them. *Too many heart attacks*, Anna's mother said, in a heartbroken attempt at a flippant joke.

Now, Anna stands at the door of another old woman who could fall over and die at any moment. She relayed this worry to her mother, protesting the housekeeping job, saying it made her feel uneasy, but her mother pressed her lips together into the straightest line Anna had ever seen and said bluntly, "Anybody could fall over and die at any moment. But we'd all still like clean houses to live in while we're here." Anna's mother doesn't like stupid excuses.

Anna hopes Mrs. Valentine has a healthy heart and eats a lot of garlic. She hopes the old woman won't be mean, but even more than that she hopes Mrs. Valentine won't sit in the corner and cry the whole time. Tears are harder to deal with than anger.

She finally knocks. She has to at some point.

The door swings inward without hesitation as though Mrs. Valentine has been standing there, waiting with her hand on the knob. Maybe even watching through the peephole. Anna tries to raise the corners of her mouth peaceably. She realizes at once that this apartment is the origin of the loud, tinny piano music filling the hallway.

"You're the girl?" asks Mrs. Valentine. She doesn't look witchy—or nervous, or sad, or angry. She looks nothing. She looks like she's waiting to look anything until she knows for sure that Anna is the girl.

So Anna nods. It does the trick, and the old woman's face explodes into a million little furrows, beginning at her lips and spidering up to her eyes like the cracks in a busted windshield. Her smile ripples out and moves everything in her body. Everything in the room. Maybe the neighbors can feel it, even if they don't know what it is.

Before Anna knows what's happening, she is encased in Mrs. Valentine. It's a lot less like a hug, a lot more like falling into a beanbag chair. A beanbag chair that has been stored in an attic for many years. An attic full of lavender.

The hug lasts for a very long time, and when it comes to an end, Mrs. Valentine grasps Anna by her shoulders and pulls her into the apartment. Now they're standing just inside the front door, like Anna has passed the first test and will have to pass another before she gets to come the rest of the way in.

"You're here!" says Mrs. Valentine, looking amazed, almost reverent, as though Anna's presence is some great thing. "This is wonderful, uh . . ." For a moment, Mrs. Valentine looks lost, and Anna realizes the old woman has forgotten her name.

"Anna," she says. She can feel her face reacting involuntarily to Mrs. Valentine's crinkly tissue paper grin, the corners of her own mouth stretching as far as her younger skin will let them go.

"Anna," repeats Mrs. Valentine, and now her mouth slides all to one side of her face in an expression Anna can't read. "Yes. Of course. Of course you're Anna." And then she beams, like she is so, *so* proud of Anna for being Anna.

They stand there for a moment. Then Mrs. Valentine reaches out and taps Anna on the top of her head like she needs waking up. "You have the most beautiful red hair, dear. Is that natural?"

"No," says Anna, surprised by the physical contact.

"I've always wanted to do that. Dye my hair." Mrs. Valentine eyes Anna's head appreciatively. "I should probably do it sooner than later. I'm eighty-seven! I know there's never going to be a better time. I don't want to be one of those ninety-year-olds who looks back on her eighties all full of regrets about the things she should've done when she was still well enough to do . . . anything." She begins to fluff her hair up with her bony fingers; it's thin and fuzzy, and Anna imagines it floating off down the hall in clumps like dandelion seeds.

"This white stuff will take color very well, won't it? I wonder why more old, white-haired people don't dye their hair all kinds of crazy colors," the old woman continues, more to herself than to Anna. "You know, I should—I'm going to leave a note for the mortician asking him, if I haven't gotten around to it before then, to dye it before he sticks me in the coffin, so I'll at least have red hair for my funeral. More people will see me there than here anyway—people fly for funerals, not coffee! Which is stupid." As she speaks, she moves back into her apartment, bustling around the living room, digging in the couch cushions and peering under stacks of junk mail, evidently searching for a pen. Anna takes a tentative step after her. "Good grief," sputters Mrs. Valentine, her big voice almost lost in the music blasting from behind her, "this place is a mess—but that's what you're here for anyway."

Anna cringes. It feels intrusive, watching Mrs. Valentine bumble around, seeing her clothing protest as she bends to look under things, hearing her faint wheezing as she stands. This Mrs. Valentine is a kind of old person Anna's never encountered in real life; she's like a caricature of an old person, but it's her personality that's been tweaked and stretched instead of her nose and mouth. It's her essence, not her head, that is too big for her body.

It occurs to Anna then that she's watching a performance. Not that Mrs. Valentine isn't lovely, isn't hilarious, isn't genuine and outgoing and sweet—but *she* is the one doing the tweaking and stretching and widening. It has a kind of desperation to it, like the girls at school who are not popular but wish they were. In fact, Anna probably wouldn't recognize it here if she hadn't seen it there first. Mrs. Valentine wants Anna to like her.

Mrs. Valentine finally spots a pen, snatches it up, and writes on the back of an unopened envelope. "Here, just let me get this down. *Mortician—dye hair.* There. No one wants to show up at her own funeral looking plain. You want the people to cry because they miss you, not because they're bored to tears." She huffs and coughs and taps her throat, and Anna worries that this particular funeral is imminent, but Mrs. Valentine regains her composure and smiles warmly. "That mortician will get it done, too—he is just the nicest young man. Mister, uh, Mister . . . *Baker*, maybe?" She seems horrified at her memory lapse. She looks hard at Anna, who shrugs.

"I'm . . . I'm not sure?"

"Good grief, of course you're not sure. What need do you have of morticians? But I really should know his name by now. He's taken care of quite a few of my friends. I have him over for coffee sometimes—oh, dear girl, you should meet him even though you don't need him; he tells the funniest stories, but he spends all his time surrounded by cadavers. It must be hard to work at a job where your sense of humor goes completely unappreciated by your, eh, *clients*." The old woman laughs, and it's like a shot ringing out. Anna jumps.

Mrs. Valentine studies her carefully, and then her face falls into a theatrical kind of wistfulness. The next act in her strange play. "When I was your age, Anna, I always said I'd do everything later. I can't tell you what an odd day that was, when I woke up and realized it was later. And now I'm living in the part that comes after. There's a part after later, where almost everyone else is dead and you're just killing time, and it's . . . *odd*."

"Oh," says Anna. It's more escaped air than an intentional word. She's still standing by the door. She could turn around and walk home if she wanted to—but then her mother would chase her right back here. She's trapped between the two women.

It's not that she doesn't like Mrs. Valentine—she likes her very much, pities her a little, feels protective over her in a way that seems ridiculous for having known her for all of five minutes—she just doesn't like talking about death. She doesn't know what to say to someone who's talking about death, especially their own death, especially as though it's going to take place right here and now with no other witnesses.

Mrs. Valentine motions for Anna to follow her farther into the apartment, and she does, feeling the awkwardness that always comes with entering someone else's personal space piled on top of the awkwardness that comes from having been made to picture someone you've just met in a coffin. Mrs. Valentine leads her to the kitchen, where a messy little table is set with two cups of tar-black coffee and a plate of Oreo cookies. "Sit down, dear—do you drink coffee?"

Anna does, but only coffee with lots of flavored syrups and cream and sugar and only, when it comes right down to it, coffee that doesn't taste anything like coffee. She likes coffee for the sake of saying she likes coffee. She thinks of her mother, forces a smile, and picks up a stack of cards from the seat of one of the chairs so she can sit. "I'd love some." She looks down at the cards; another elderly lady smiles up at her from the front of the one on top. Funeral pamphlets. Of course.

"My friends," says Mrs. Valentine lightly. She plucks them out of Anna's hands and plops them on top of the refrigerator.

CHAPTER FIVE

"Hi, Mom." Valencia stood in the middle of her kitchen with the telephone receiver tucked between her shoulder and head, wrapping the cord around and around her arm, unwinding it, wrapping it again. It left little white indentations on her skin.

"Valencia? Are you okay?"

"Yes, why?"

"Honey, it's five in the morning."

"I know." But Valencia hadn't registered what her mother said, only the way she'd said it. She sounded upset.

I knew it. Moments earlier, Valencia had woken from a sound sleep to worry sitting on her chest like a stray cat—she hadn't been able to tell where it came from. It peered at her knowingly, waiting, pressing down on her. Something was wrong. Somewhere. She'd instinctively called her mother to make sure it wasn't her who was sad or in trouble, and now she heard the fear in her mother's voice and knew she had been right to worry. This feeling was so rarely indicative of actual trouble, but she'd always been sure that if she ignored it she would miss the one time it really meant something.

"Are you okay, Mom? What's happened? Is Dad okay?"

"Nothing has *happened*, honey. I'm fine. I really am." Her mother still seemed upset, but also like she was trying to sound soothing. She was trying too hard; what was she hiding? "I was just . . . asleep."

Valencia stopped playing with the phone cord. *Of course. Five in the morning.* She'd gone straight into emergency mode, where things like time and sleep didn't matter, barely even existed. "Right, of course, I'm so sorry. I didn't mean to wake you up. I'm so sorry, Mom."

"No, no, don't be sorry. It's good to hear from you, Valencia. I always like to hear from you." Valencia's mother spoke like she was inching across cracking ice, coaxing Valencia to follow her to safety. Saying her name too much, saying it too tentatively, repeating phrases and speaking slowly, as though trying to hypnotize her. "I love hearing from you . . ." Even the silence between her sentences hummed with a familiar blend of worry and reassurance. "Valencia, I know you don't like it when I ask—"

"Oh, Mom—"

"Honey. I just need to know—"

"Mom. I'm *fine*."

"Are you still on your medication, Valencia? Are you still seeing Louise?"

Valencia swung the phone cord like a jump rope, repeatedly smacking it against the side of the counter. "This has nothing to do with . . . that. I'm fine. I just had that feeling I get sometimes." Valencia's mother would know what she means when she says "that feeling." This was a phrase that had been in use between them since Valencia was a little child. "I just wanted to check on you. If you're fine, I'll let you go back to bed."

Silence on the line.

"Well, actually, Valencia, there is something I was going to call you about anyway. Since I have you here . . ." She paused, waiting for permission.

Valencia stiffened. "You just said nothing was wrong."

"I said your father and I are fine. But . . . your grandmother's not doing well, Valencia."

This was the elbow of every conversation Valencia had with her mother, the place the subject turned sharply away from wherever they'd been going and started toward its usual destination. Her grandmother had not been doing well for a long time; it was starting to seem like she had not ever done well, like her default setting was "dying."

"I know, Mom." But her mother was not telling her this because she didn't know it; she was telling her this because she wanted to give weight to her usual request.

"You haven't seen her in such a long time. It would mean so much—"

"I know." Valencia wanted the conversation to be over. Her mother knew better. Or should.

"She'd sure love to see you before . . . before she, you know . . . she's really not doing well."

"Well, I'd love to see her too. I work a lot. It's hard to get time off. I'll see. I have to go. I'm going to be late." Her go-to line for getting off the phone with her mother, regardless of the day or time.

"Valencia—"

"Love you, Mom." Valencia hung the phone back on the wall and sat at the table. She was the worst daughter ever, the worst granddaughter ever too.

She reached for the yellow legal pad that lived on the table. She kept these everywhere—in the car, in her purse, by the bed, on the coffee table. It had been one of Louise's better ideas. "You like writing?" she'd asked in their very first meeting.

"Yes," Valencia had said automatically, even though she hadn't written a thing since high school. She'd wanted to please Louise back then.

"Good," Louise had said. "We're going to do something called a cognitive behavioral therapy diary. A CBTD!" She'd laughed at herself, and Valencia had laughed too. Because she'd wanted to please Louise.

The idea of the CBTD, Louise had explained, giggling again as though things that rhymed were automatically funny, was to train Valencia's brain to pay attention to itself, to show her what was going on in there, to change the way it worked things out. But now Valencia just used the growing collection of notepads to record inane essays and lists, and she'd found it was much more soothing than trying to describe what she was thinking or feeling. She was even becoming a little dependent on them, like she couldn't process thoughts without seeing them on paper. Sometimes this struck her as hysterically funny: Louise, in attempting to help reduce her compulsive behaviors, had introduced yet another one.

But what else was a person to do when she didn't talk to other human beings on a regular basis? And it was helpful for remembering very basic English rules and providing an opportunity to use words like *thus* and *furthermore*. Other people got to use those words at cocktail parties and fancy dinners with mayors of cities and heads of committees.

Valencia sat back in her chair, looking around the dimly lit kitchen. Kraft Dinner in this chair was as fancy as her dinners ever got, but she didn't feel sorry for herself. Did she deserve fancier dinners?

The essay on the kitchen legal pad was about Peter, a recurring theme as of late, though she never came right out and said it. It was cleverly disguised to look like an essay about cyclists. At the top of the page was the title of the work, underlined twice: "The Positive Attributes of Cyclists." Seeing as Peter was the only person she knew (in the loosest sense of the word) who rode a bike (at least, she assumed he rode a bike, because of the helmet she'd seen sitting beside his computer monitor), it might as well have been called "The Positive Attributes of Peter."

Interspersed with the attributes were place names, places she could fly on her therapy trip, which she'd been picking at random from travel magazines. She had been going back and forth between the essay and the list, switching when she became blocked or overwhelmed, and now

30

she picked up her pen and bent over the page again, reading what she'd already written so she could add to it.

1. Bikes are slow. Wind is crazy. Roads are awful. Thus, cyclists are patient and resilient and strong.

Bogota, Colombia

Zurich, Switzerland

Limerick, Ireland

2. Motorists hate cyclists, pedestrians hate cyclists. They choose underdog status. Thus, cyclists are humble.

Kowloon, Hong Kong

Chicken, Alaska

3. Furthermore, people who ride bikes do it because it's good for you and it's good for the environment and you take up less room in the parking lot. Thus, cyclists are good, disciplined, thoughtful people.

Salar de Uyuni

Valencia had never given this much thought to bikes or the people who rode them. She filled several pages with praise for the man she had interacted with exactly once, disguised as praise for thousands of complete strangers. Peter, by virtue of being a cyclist, sounded like an amazing person. This was a drastic leap in logic, but Valencia was very good at this kind of leaping; it was her only claim to athleticism.

Of course, she wasn't basing her entire opinion of him on the one hobby she knew about; he had, at that point, been at work for a few weeks, and in that time she'd noticed other things about him. It was like she had some kind of built-in Peter-sensor. The hair on her arms stood straight up when he was near, like she'd rubbed a balloon against them, like they were tiny receiver antennae waiting at all times for his radio transmissions. She noticed how he smiled at everyone equally. She noticed how he laughed easily. She noticed his good posture, for a tall person. And she noticed his nice face.

She could fall in love with a man like that, easy as sledding down a hill. Maybe she was already in love. She hadn't realized the process could be so expedited, caught through that first brief exposure like an airborne illness.

The last and only other time she'd fallen in love (or infatuation, at least) had been in the twelfth grade. The guy's name was Don, and he drove a Jeep and told her he thought her "idiosyncrasies" were "quirky," and that dismissive language should've been her cue to ignore him forever. He didn't understand that her compulsions were not cute, that they consumed her.

The falling itself had happened quickly, but not this quickly, and it hadn't ended well. It hadn't middled well either. It had barely even *begun* well, because on the first date the unthinkable had happened: Don had wanted to hold her hand.

Of course he had. She had wanted to hold his hand, too, but the difference was that she only wanted it abstractly. She wanted it in the same way she wanted to swim in a pool full of butterscotch ice cream— a fantastic *idea*, the kind you daydream about in math class. But when it comes right down to it, no one who has given it any thought really wants to swim in butterscotch ice cream. It would be sticky, and you wouldn't be able to stay afloat; you'd sink and suffocate. At the very least, you'd eat too much of it, inhale it, get it in your ears and nose, and you'd hate it by the end of the whole ordeal.

She wanted to hold Don's hand so much, and she also did not want to touch him at all. It was a confounding paradox, so much more than a "quirky idiosyncrasy."

She'd spent most of that night, most of every date and interaction from then on, trying to figure out ways to keep him from touching her. Every time he reached for her hand, she'd shove it into her pocket. If he tried to put his arm around her, she shrugged or ducked out from under it. Once, he looked at her like he was going to try to bypass the unsuccessful hand-holding and go straight for a kiss, so she stood up. They'd been sitting on a park bench, and her shoulder met his nose, hard. There had been blood.

When at last he'd finally dumped her, he'd said it hadn't ever felt like she'd really been all that into him. And what was she supposed to say to that? Which was worse: admitting you were one of those nutcases or denying yourself a chance at love—or, at the very least, physical affection? She'd shrugged at him, though her heart was breaking into a million pieces, and said he was right. Said she hadn't been. Went home and cried and cried.

It was all a dead end for someone like Valencia. The sled would find a tree halfway down that hill. She couldn't shake a man's hand, couldn't hold it while they watched a movie. Couldn't eat food prepared especially for her by those hands, couldn't ever live in an apartment where they touched the doorknobs and flipped the light switches.

And even if all that were a nonissue, how could she ever come clean about killing Charlene to a potential love interest?

> Char, Char, hit her with a car
> Throw her in the water, where all the fish are

Some thoughts could be pushed away with other thoughts, with essays and lists. Some could be snuffed out as easily as a tiny fire burning on the end of a candlewick. But when Charlene came barging into Valencia's mind, she could not be put out without physical action. Valencia shut her eyes and pushed the block of yellow paper away as though it were Charlene herself. A dish full of old food smashed against the floor, but she barely heard it. She stared down at the mess, overcome with exhaustion. If no one cleaned it up, it would just stay there. That was fine. She could step around it.

A dog barked outside the window, and it was only then that she realized the sun had risen while her head was down. She checked the time and wasn't surprised to see that she was late for work.

She flew around her apartment, searching for her keys and purse and shoes. A stack of books and papers toppled as she rammed against the little table by the fridge; she swung around to catch a potted plant before it crashed to the floor, and her elbow made contact with her favorite coffee mug, which had been balancing precariously on the edge of the counter. She stepped around the broken shards of pottery that now sat in a murky coffee river and made sheepish eye contact with the disapproving face of the wall clock.

She made it out the door, fumbling to lock it, scrambling to open it again when it clicked shut on her purse strap. She tripped over her feet all the way to the bottom of the stairs before realizing she'd forgotten to double-check that the stove was off. It was like a curse, her inability to go anywhere without checking two or three times that the stove was off, whether or not she'd used it recently. She tried to remember if she had been prone to this particular quirk before Charlene passed away because this was the kind of question Louise would ask.

She didn't think so.

That's interesting. That's what Louise would say, and she'd write it down in her notebook while Valencia watched the rings on her knobby fingers clunk together. And it *was* interesting—Charlene's death had nothing to do with stoves. Louise would probably have some kind of weird assignment for her to complete before they saw each other again. The assignment would be something idiotic and impossible, like, *leave the stove on all day and all night, and if you don't burn to a crisp in your bed, you'll be cured of this particular obsession.*

She paused for a second, key in hand, leaning against the heavy glass door of the apartment building, glancing up the stairs she'd just come down.

I need to check.

No. This was not rational, but it also wasn't uncontrollable; it was nothing more than a bad habit. *So there, Louise.* She felt a rush of bravery. She pushed the door open and headed for her car.

She drove to the call center. She worked her shift. And when she arrived home, she was barely surprised to find her apartment surrounded by emergency vehicles and flashing red and blue lights.

All day she had wondered, but now she was blisteringly aware that she'd made the wrong decision in the stairwell that morning. All day she had pictured this, and now those unrelenting mental images leaped out of her brain and into the real world. She stood in the glow of her blazing apartment building with 164 other newly homeless people watching firefighters rescue a delirious old woman from the third floor. Ashes fluttered down from the sky like ticker tape, and a weak cheer went up as frail feet clad in ratty slippers touched the ground. But the celebration was swallowed up in a collective gasp of horror when the woman passed out cold into the nearest pair of arms.

It was all Valencia's fault. She should've gone back. It would've only taken a minute.

A young couple to her left looked like they'd been getting ready to go out for dinner when the fire alarm had sounded. The woman wore a dress but no makeup or jewelry, and the man's feet were bare. They made desperate and unsuccessful attempts to console their screaming baby, who seemed to grasp the severity and hopelessness of the situation better than anyone else. Next to them, a teenage girl stood with her arms clamped tightly around two children; one of them whimpered loudly. Something about a cat.

To her right, a scruffy man sobbed onto the top of his television set. Valencia recognized him; she'd seen him sometimes, leaving or entering the building with a guitar case. Once, years ago, he'd invited her to a show he was playing at a nearby coffee shop, but she'd felt that his invitation was more because he wanted her to see him and less that he wanted to see her. She'd turned him down, and he'd never spoken to her again. The fact that he saved his TV instead of his guitar from the fire spoke to the state of his musical career.

She closed her eyes so she wouldn't have to look at these people, then opened them again because she didn't deserve to look away. She'd evicted them and incinerated their homes, endangered their lives and the lives of their pets and children and grandparents and television sets.

She took note of each one, adding them to her already substantial list of things to feel awful and anxious about, attempting to subliminally bore her apologies directly into their minds, but averting her gaze anytime someone caught her looking at them. In that moment, like most others, she regretted her very existence. She was, unquestionably, the worst.

She turned away from the disaster, and there was Peter, witnessing it all. Across the street, he stood beside his bike, staring—not at the flames but at her. *He knew.* He knew this was her fault. How did he know?

He looked repulsed and afraid. "How could you do this?" he asked, and though he wasn't yelling the words, she heard them with perfect clarity, over the noise of the fire and the sirens and the crying.

"I didn't mean to," she said in a voice as quiet as falling ash. "I didn't start it on purpose."

"You made the choice not to check the stove," he said. "It's the same thing." He turned away, mounted his bike, and rode off down the street without a second glance. When she turned back to the crowd, everyone stood pointing at her.

It wasn't a daydream so much as a narrative, like a little play in Valencia's head as she left her apartment for work each day. In her mind, she saw the characters, and she saw herself—but it was a twisted version with sharp, ugly features. Peter was a recent addition to the story.

Sometimes it came as she turned the key in the lock; sometimes it didn't start until she was down the stairs or across the street. Sometimes there were a few more adjectives used to describe her or none at all. The words were mean but not spoken meanly; the voice that said them was cold and matter-of-fact and spoke with just a hint of condescension, like its owner didn't care for her but also didn't care enough *about* her to spend any extra energy disliking her. The stories always ended in disaster, and the disasters were always Valencia's fault. The voice described her as naive but dangerous, and the voice was hers, though it came on without any precognition on her part, like someone was using her mind as a puppet.

The first clear memory she had of her inner narrator was from the second grade; she had been taking a math test. She'd loved math. She'd been very good at math. The class had only been half over, and already she had been nearing the end—she'd probably finish before anyone. The last question had been easy, and she had felt smug.

Question 20: 4 − 2 = __

But as she'd put pencil to paper, smiling to herself, thinking, *That's easy, two*, the voice inside her head—which was not actually a voice, but she hadn't had the vocabulary to describe it in another way—had begun to talk about her mother.

Her mother, said the voice, would be disappointed in her daughter for being so show-offy. She was always saying that—"Don't be a show-off, Valencia." If her mother knew what Valencia was thinking and feeling, she would probably even be angry.

Or, said the voice, maybe something might happen *to* her mother. Maybe when children did bad things, bad things happened to people they loved. No one had ever told her this was the case, but it made sense. Maybe even as Valencia was writing that perfect two, just the way Ms. Nilofar had taught her, with the tiny loop and the tail that curved up like it belonged to a kitten, her mother was at home turning white and clutching her chest and stumbling around the kitchen.

She'd looked at the page in front of her, at all of the correct answers printed in straight light-gray letters, and it had gone out of focus as tears came to her eyes. She was always passing in her tests and assignments first, with that smile on her face like she was so much better than everyone else. *I'm not*, Valencia had thought, talking back to the voice, trying to make it stop. *I'm not better than anyone. I'm bad at everything.*

She would prove it.

She'd erased the two and had written a shaky four, but when she saw that the lines were crooked, she'd felt a crackling deep inside her head. She'd erased it and written it again, but now there were faint smudge marks all around the erroneous four, and it was still not straight. She'd ruined her perfect math test; she'd felt panic rising inside of her. But at least no one would think she was showing off. *But that four* . . . She'd erased it again. She'd drawn it again. Erased it again. She'd needed two directly opposing things: a clean, perfect page, and one that was blatantly *im*perfect. One would calm her insides; one would keep her mother alive.

After that, math was no longer easy, and things as small as straight lines had enormous consequences. The voice was there to stay, presenting her with impossible decisions; her only recourse was finding ways of making enough noise in her head to drown it out.

And just when she'd started to wonder if the voice was wrong about her capacity to cause harm, she'd killed Charlene.

Now she existed only as much as she had to and often felt like even that was too much. While other people aspired to be great and memorable, she longed to be small and inconsequential. After all, her story had already been written; it ended in tragedy.

That, all of that, was why these thoughts had the ability to stop her short like a vaudeville hook and cause her to immediately double back and do unnecessary and time-consuming things—like checking and rechecking the stove—no matter how late she was running or where she was going or how far she'd gotten. She knew that if she didn't listen the first time, she would spend the next however-many hours hearing dire words and seeing disastrous scenes play out again and again and wondering if this was the day it would all happen for real. She recognized the ridiculousness of it and sometimes made weak attempts at reason and logic, but she found these attempts to be but a mouthful of spit on a blazing apartment building fire.

As the sound of sirens and the smell of smoke and the sight of pointing fingers faded from her mind's eye, she trudged up the stairs to her apartment. She let herself back in and headed to the kitchen. As though her eyes alone couldn't be trusted, she placed her hands on the burners, held them there long enough to really *know* they were cold, and spoke into the empty room: "Off. The stove is off. Everything is off." So the memory of her voice, her actual, out-loud voice, would be available later and hopefully louder and more convincing than the imposter one—because even after checking the stove, she still couldn't shake the thought that if she were not in her apartment, it would absolutely be on fire.

"*I'm* off." She said that out loud to the stove too. It felt fitting. She felt like a crazy person.

The stove did not reply. As though it agreed with her but was too polite to say so.

CHAPTER SIX

Mrs. Valentine, not a woman often given to embarrassment, is choking on it right now. Her kitchen table is an atrocity: store-bought cookies and two cups of cold coffee sit amid stacks of papers and dirty dishes and used Kleenex. She could've at least thrown those away.

She used to be the kind of person who would clean and—more importantly—bake when she knew someone was coming over. She made glorious cinnamon buns and offered different kinds of tea and juice, warm coffee, cream and sugar. The basics. People's eyes used to light up when they came into her kitchen; they didn't have to pretend to be impressed, and it was all of utmost importance to Mrs. Valentine, a quick and easy way to be hospitable, to make company feel at home in her small apartment. The more company felt at home, she always thought, the more company she'd have.

Now she doesn't even have flour in the house. She doesn't have the energy to bake. She doesn't have juice, she's fresh out of tea and milk *and* sugar, and her coffee is cold.

It hadn't crossed her mind to feel embarrassed until she sees the girl move the stack of funeral pamphlets so she can sit, and then it flashes through her—what is it, shame?—and now it won't go away. She feels acutely aware of how long it's been since she had someone new over.

The mortician is a man, and she doesn't think men care very much if there are used Kleenex on the table they're eating off of. Mrs. Davies doesn't judge either; she practically lives here. She's used to it. Yes, the girl is here to clean the house, but Mrs. Valentine really could've gotten it all to a manageable place, especially since the girl is not *actually* here just to clean the house . . .

Anna—whose hair and clothing and makeup are, as far as Mrs. Valentine can tell with what's left of her vision, perfect, denoting a person who notices imperfection—surveys the small kitchenette and sips her coffee politely, following each delicate swallow with a bite of her cookie. She's probably thinking about how much work she has to do. Probably regretting the decision to come here. Mrs. Valentine doesn't want her to regret this, any part of it. She tries to look even more friendly, smiles an even bigger smile, presses forward with small talk.

"Are you and your family enjoying your new place?"

"Yeah." Anna shrugs and swings one of her long arms around to scratch a spot on her back. "I was hoping they'd buy somewhere closer to the river, though. When I graduate, I'm going to get an apartment down there in one of those cute old buildings. Somewhere more vintage, you know? Like here."

Mrs. Valentine smiles. "Stay anywhere long enough, and it'll become more vintage."

Anna's big brown eyes rest on the fridge, the one mostly clean surface in the kitchen. It's bare except for two pieces of paper, attached with Scotch tape. They're silly drawings, caricatures, one in pencil, one in ink. One a man, the other a woman.

"Is that supposed to be you?" asks Anna, pointing at the woman. Mrs. Valentine nods, feeling ridiculously proud that she could still be associated with the young woman in the picture, even if it is just a cartoon. Anna's finger moves to the picture of the man. "And your husband?" There's a noticeable silence, which starts almost before she's finished saying the last word, and her cheeks flood with color. She has most likely put two and two together, considering that if the man is not here, now, he probably isn't anywhere anymore.

"That's him," says Mrs. Valentine, sensing a chance to talk about her husband. It came sooner than she'd thought it might. She tries to look a little sad, but not overly so—more thoughtful. "Or, rather, that was him over fifty years ago. Those were done before . . ." She's trying to sound cryptic. She doesn't get to talk about Mr. Valentine much. She wants to, though. Needs to. When you're eighty-seven, everyone forgets you were ever eighty-six, even if you look it. They forget, even more, that you were ever seventy-six. Or forty. Or twenty. The few friends you have left (alive and in their right minds) know everything about you that they care to know. Like Mrs. Davies—Mrs. Davies knows all about Mrs. Valentine. She doesn't ask anything anymore, is too far under her own emotions anyway. These days she comes for coffee and sits across from Mrs. Valentine, nodding and whispering unintelligible things to the air, getting quieter and quieter.

Anna doesn't know anything about Mrs. Valentine other than her name and address, and she seems like the kind of girl who would be a good listener, but Mrs. Valentine knows she can't come right out and say, "Let me tell you about me and Mr. Valentine and all of our adventures and what happened to him." No kid wants to listen to an old woman tell stories about an old man. She has to be sneaky about it, or her captive audience will escape. She has this part down to a science.

She can tell Anna is thinking. She's trying to think of a good way to change the subject without coming across like she doesn't care—that's what the good mortician (Mr. Baker?) attempted. And the mailman. And the girl Mrs. Valentine hired to do her gardening a few years ago, before she gave up on gardening altogether. Mrs. Valentine knows that people don't want to talk about heartbreaking things, for your sake or theirs; you have to trick them into it. You have to lead them to the conversation and trap them in it.

"Before he went missing in Bolivia, forty-eight years ago," she says after a carefully timed pause, watching Anna's face for the desired reaction. "I don't know where he is. No one does. They all think he's dead, but I don't think he's dead. I imagine he'll come back someday with incredible stories to tell me."

She tries to say it all matter-of-factly, but not flippantly. Not like she isn't bothered by it, but not like she's too bothered by it to talk about it. It requires a little bit of good acting, which is a hard thing to accomplish with such old and used-up facial muscles.

Judging from Anna's reaction, however, she's done the job well enough. The girl takes a sip of coffee without remembering to take a bite of cookie after and doesn't seem to notice. Her eyes are a little wider now; her forehead has a crease in it. "Missing? For forty-eight years?"

"It's a long story," says Mrs. Valentine. This is a classic bait line, a good thing to say when you want to tell someone a long story. You shouldn't outright ask for permission—a lot of people can think of an excuse about why they don't have time for a long story if you give them a chance—and you shouldn't just start telling it either—the person might become uncomfortable, possibly offended, about your infringement on their time. If you say, instead, "It's a long story," as Mrs. Valentine did, you will be able to tell quite quickly through verbal and nonverbal cues if your audience would like you to continue or shut up. They might even, out of politeness or curiosity or both, urge you to go on and feel like it was their idea to hear the story instead of your idea to tell it. People always enjoy their own ideas more than yours.

Anna, it seems, wants to hear the story. Mrs. Valentine will have to oblige. She takes a huge breath, as though that air will have to last the entire time. She will have to lose him again, but it'll be worth it because she'll get to be with him again in the telling.

CHAPTER SEVEN

She's crazy. I heard—
> *Who?*
> *Valencia.*
> *Crazy? In what way?*
> *In every way.*
> *I don't like them letting people like her work here.*

The office clones' bald heads reflected the stark fluorescent light as they turned mechanically, back and forth from desk neighbor to desk neighbor, relaying information as it was received or made up. Perhaps this was why they'd all grown moustaches—so they didn't have to cover their mouths when they told secrets. She wished she had the ability to grow a moustache—a beard, even. Like a small tree in front of her face all the time.

> *Valencia? That girl? The quiet one?*
> *Yeah! The one with the shifty eyes. I heard—*
> *Now that you mention it, I've noticed her talking to herself sometimes.*
> *See? She's a loon. I heard—*
> *Who?*

Valencia imagined the whispers, and she knew it. Didn't matter.

> *I've never seen her before in my life. Is she new here?*
> *Nope, been here at least ten years.*

I heard she killed someone.

She's looking! Shh . . .

"You want what, now? You want me to give you my date of birth and credit card number over the *phone?*"

Valencia came back to reality, thankful for the interruption even if the voice doing the interrupting was as unkind as the ones in her head.

"Yes, ma'am," she said to the person in her ear. "To verify your account." She pulled a disinfecting wipe out of the stash under her desk and started sanitizing her computer keyboard—it was almost as involuntary an action as blinking her eyes. At age ten, she'd watched some television show about the accumulation of dead skin cells on everyday household and office objects, and it had been like being conscripted; she'd gone to war against the unseen bacterial world at once. She couldn't articulate why she was so averse to the idea of dead skin cells. She wasn't sure she had a choice not to be. Maybe it was a reaction to stress more than a reaction to uncleanliness; she felt soothed as she cleaned, like she was wiping down the inside of her head, wiping the voice away for a moment.

As her mind settled, she felt eyes on her and was sure they were Peter's. She could picture the look on his face, too, because it was the way everyone looked at her: a combination of fascination and amusement, sometimes concern or alarm.

She was the only one in the office who used a full pack of disposable disinfecting wipes before lunch. She was not wrong, nor was everyone else smarter for letting their possessions pile high with whatever they happened to slough off onto them, but she was weird because she was the only one doing what she did. This was unfair, but she'd never cared before.

She cared now. She didn't want Peter to think she was weird.

But maybe he could think of her as quirky or fascinating, like a character in a movie who had the cute kind of OCD, who liked things to be straight and counted steps and kept a clean kitchen. It was adorable Hollywood mental illness. And helpful too. They could marry, and he'd never have to worry about crooked pictures hanging on their walls.

But that kind of OCD only lasted 90 minutes, 120 at most.

What would he do, for example, the fourteenth time they had to drive all the way home from wherever they were to make sure she'd unplugged the toaster? Her mother had told her once that she didn't have to unplug the toaster, but Valencia unplugged everything, always, as soon as she was finished using it. She'd heard a news story when she was six about a house that burned down with a dog inside it because someone had forgotten to unplug something, but she could never remember what the thing was that had been forgotten. A toaster? A lamp? An electric blanket? All she knew was that she now shouldered the great responsibility that came with knowing that story. If she left the toaster plugged in and it burned down the apartment building, she would be culpable.

Peter could not possibly love someone so neurotic—and should not have to. He deserved a girl who'd shake his hand and laugh at his jokes and leave all the burners on with complete disregard for anything else. He deserved someone so carefree she would one day burn his house right to the ground. He deserved someone who didn't have blood on her hands.

Valencia sneaked a peek at him, but his back was to her. He hadn't been looking at her after all—was she relieved or disappointed?

"You want my credit card number? My *credit card number*?" The voice, enunciating more than necessary, was repeating itself and growing louder. Valencia forced herself to concentrate.

"Yes, ma'am."

"Would you also like my children's names and birth dates? And our address and the name of their school?"

"Pardon me?"

"And would you like me to send you all of my banking information and my debit card as well? How about I just make it easy for you and mail you a nice big check? Or would you like cash? My car? The food out of my mouth? I'm eating a sandwich, lady, you want *that*?"

"I'm sorry? I just need some basic information to verify your identity—for your, for your own security—" Valencia's tongue began to trip up on the syllables.

"Yeah, right," said the voice, faster and sharper. "I'm not stupid— but *you* are if you think I'm going to fall for this. Take me off your list, or I'll call the police. Don't call again." The dial tone buzzed in Valencia's ear. Instead of moving ahead to the next call, she pulled off her headset and took a sip of coffee. She was tired. She looked at the bird in the photograph painting.

The bird's eyes mocked her. Like it thought her existence was stupid. Like her grandmother had painted it specifically to send a message to her granddaughter in the future. *Dear Granddaughter, your existence is stupid.*

Sometimes, when Valencia's life felt especially meaningless, she couldn't help but think about what Charlene's would have been like.

Charlene, when she'd still had hope of being anything at all, was going to be a physical therapist. This fact was mentioned in her obituary, that she'd wanted to be a physiotherapist when she grew up so she could "help people like herself"—people in wheelchairs, people who needed help moving. Valencia had, of course, taken these words personally at the time—Charlene wouldn't have needed help moving if it hadn't been for Valencia. She had wanted to stand up in the middle of that funeral and scream, "It was my fault!" She'd wanted to burst into tears, not because she had more tears that needed crying, but because she'd wanted Charlene's mom to see them. She'd wanted everyone who cared about Charlene at all to see them. She'd wanted to wear her apologies on her face and down the front of her shirt.

Instead, she'd sat there in silence and plucked every single hair out of the back of her arm in a patch that grew to resemble the back of the head of the man seated in front of her.

A physical therapist. How fulfilling and life affirming and altruistic. Valencia was just a debt collector, not a surgeon or a social worker or a volunteer at an important charity.

Dreg, said the bird's eyes. *Noun, the least valuable part of anything, origin: 1250–1300; Middle English, Old Norse dreg yeast. Example sentence: Debt collectors are the dregs of the working world.*

The bird was right. Valencia's job was to call people, tell them how much money they owed their credit card company, and collect a payment from them. Her mother thought she was a telemarketer, and Valencia had long since stopped trying to explain the difference between a telemarketer and a debt collector—the difference between chasing people down to sell them useless junk and chasing people down to charge them for useless junk they already had. It was an important distinction to her, but it wouldn't be to anyone else.

The main thing that debt collectors and telemarketers had in common was that everyone hated them, and maybe that was all that mattered anyway.

She glanced over her shoulder at Peter, who was on a call. What possible explanation could there be for his presence here? Had he dreamed of being a debt collector as a little kid?

She watched as he scratched his neck and stretched one of his long legs. He looked like he could be on his way to so many different places. He looked smart and calm, like he spent all of his time working to better himself and the world and rested easy in his life choices. He had a group of moles or freckles on the side of his face that looked like a connect-the-dots picture. She pictured herself marching over to him with a Sharpie marker.

That was something a confident woman in a movie could get away with, drawing on a coworker's face. "Peter," she'd say flirtatiously, perching on the edge of his desk, "you have a constellation on your face." When he looked confused, she'd lean forward and join the freckles, never breaking eye contact. He'd be struck dumb, so she'd move to his hand and write her phone number there and then saunter back to her desk, leaving him awestruck and covered in marker ink. And he'd be so taken with her beauty and self-assurance that he'd love every minute of it.

The thought of doing those things in this body, with this face, in this frumpy cardigan and these khaki pants was depressing. He'd probably fall out of his chair again trying to get away from the crazy lady with the Sharpie. Beautiful, fashionable people had different rules.

She needed to stop looking at Peter so much. At least that was one good thing about Louise's crazy airplane assignment: if she were on an airplane, she would be *forced* to stop looking at him.

She didn't have a destination nailed down yet, but she had picked a date for her trip the night before: August 3—an important date for a lot of people because it was the anniversary of Charlene's death. That day was always hard enough; why not spend it in the sky breathing into a paper bag?

Valencia placed the headset back over her ears and moved the mouthpiece into position, taking a breath before she connected to the dialer. The computer screen blinked to the inbound screen, and she exhaled. Inbounds—when the customer called in to pay off their debt—were so much easier than outbounds. She didn't have to convince them that she wasn't a telemarketer or a scammer, she hadn't caught them off guard or at an inconvenient time, and they actually wanted to pay off their debt. They'd called *her*. She'd always thought it wouldn't be such a bad job if all the calls were inbounds—at least she wouldn't spend all of her days wishing she were not at work and all of her evenings and nights dreading all of her days.

"West Park Services, this is Valencia. How may I help you today?"

"Hello. How are you?"

"Fine," said Valencia. "And you?"

"Not great," said the man on the other end. "I'm in debt."

"Well, I can help you with that," said Valencia. "Did you receive a letter in the mail?"

"Yes. From my credit card company—it said to call this number." He had a quiet voice, and he sounded young and nervous. She felt sorry for him. She wished she could tell him she hated talking on the phone too. She recited her lines, but her voice cracked unexpectedly when she spoke.

"Yes, I can help you with that." *How can I help you? How can I help you? Yes, I can help you. How can I help you? Help you. Help you. Help you.* She was like a monk or a parrot or a broken record. Her mouth was sick of saying these things, but they were part of her penance. "First, I just want to let you know that this call will be recorded for quality assurance purposes. I need your name, credit card number, and date of birth, please."

"Oh, okay," said the man.

But he didn't offer any of the information she'd asked for. Maybe she'd spoken too fast.

"Sir? Your name?"

"Oh, James," said the man. He sounded embarrassed. "Mace, James. James Mace."

"Okay," said Valencia. She typed it in, and his account came up on her screen. James Mace, New York City, New York. "And your credit card number and date of birth, please."

James Mace was quiet for a moment; there was a shuffling sound in the background, and then he spoke again. "Yeah, I just realized I don't have my wallet with me—I wrote down the number to call and then forgot I'd probably need my credit card number to access my account. I'm so sorry."

"Oh no, no problem at all," said Valencia. "Happens all the time. You have our number. You can call back again. You'll continue to receive phone calls from here, too, every day until your account is closed. You can settle it with any one of our account representatives. Just remember to pay at least the minimum payment by the date mentioned in your letter, or there will be more fines added to your account. We can set up an easy payment plan, or you can pay in one or two transactions; whatever's easiest for you."

"Very good, thank you," said James Mace. He sounded distracted, and she was sure he hadn't heard any of her much-rehearsed speech.

"Any other questions, Mr. Mace?"

He paused again. "Well, okay, sure."

"Yes?"

"What did you say your name was?"

"Valencia."

"Valencia," the man repeated. "I hope it's not rude to ask, Valencia—I mean, I hope you don't think I'm being rude in how I ask it. I was just wondering—well, a name like that, I haven't heard it before—"

"Oh," said Valencia, "no, it's not rude. My mom grew up in Germany, and when she was a kid, they took a family vacation to Valencia—over in Spain—and it's just always been her favorite place. So."

"Ah," said James Mace. "That's cool. Have you been?"

"Oh, I haven't been . . . anywhere," said Valencia.

"Me neither, really," said James.

"But I actually mean *anywhere*."

"Oh."

The pause in the conversation was the thing that made Valencia aware that a conversation was being had in the first place. She wasn't usually one to have not-debt-related conversations at work. She wasn't one to have not-debt-related conversations ever, except for with her parents or Louise. And that one awkward one with Peter. It was a wonder she knew how anymore.

"Anyway," she said. "I'm so sorry; I should let you go."

The man laughed. "*You're* sorry? I was the one who started it," he said easily. He was very good at conversation. He sounded like he practiced every day on actual people. "So I should be the one letting you go. You probably hate it when the people you're trying to collect from start talking your ear off."

"They don't usually," said Valencia. "Unless it's to scream or say they want to kill me. This is a nice break, to be honest."

"They say they want to kill you?"

"Well. Yes. I'm a debt collector. People don't really like debt collectors."

"Huh," said the man. "That's brutal. I'm sorry."

"It's okay. But this is nice."

"Oh, well, cool," he said. "And I've got nowhere I need to be. I mean, I won't keep you forever, but you're welcome to sit on this call for a few minutes if you need a breather before your next death threat."

"I actually do. Thank you." Valencia felt something climbing up her throat and realized it was a genuine laugh. She swallowed it.

"Cool," he said. He sounded pleased. "So, Valencia . . . let's see . . . okay: What do you do? For fun? With friends? Hobbies? You into cars? Pets? Ceramics?"

He meant well, but it was a depressing question. Did she have hobbies? Friends? She didn't do much more than work. Read. Watch movies. Exist and passively consume entertainment.

Alone.

She'd kept in touch with a few friends for a while after high school, but they'd all gotten married or had big careers. They'd moved, some of them. They'd ditched her for better friends.

No, none of that was it—after all, they'd managed to stay friends with each other after all of these big life changes. The truth: she didn't like to have people over, because of the germs they brought with them, and she didn't like to go to people's houses, because of the germs they kept there and would send home with her. Friendship, like love, couldn't survive in her sterile world.

She *read*, she *watched*, she *existed*. Only one of those things felt like an acceptable answer. "I read? I read a lot."

"Awesome," said James. "I read too. I'm on a biography kick at the moment, but I usually really like sci-fi. How about you?"

Small talk. Everyone else in the world probably engaged in it every day. They had no idea what an absolute luxury it was. And this man made it so easy.

"Mm, I like biographies," she said, nodding. "Memoirs. Short story and essay collections. Literary fiction. Sometimes genre fiction—like Agatha Christie; I like her. Who doesn't like Agatha Christie, I guess. I mean, I think. Um . . . textbooks. I like flipping through them, not reading them cover to cover. Magazines—travel magazines, mostly." She paused, thought. She had been speaking very fast. "Not in that order," she added quietly, hoping that her answer had been thorough enough.

"Wow," said James Mace. "*Wow.* So when you say you read, you mean you really *read*."

"Yes," she said, because she wasn't sure what else she would've meant.

James chuckled. "Cool," he said. He said that a lot.

It felt like fresh air was blowing through the call center. The man's voice and quiet manner were more soothing than bleach wipes. She wished she could sit and listen to him talk for the rest of the day. He could say anything he wanted. He could count to a billion. He could recite boring old poems about flowers. He could say the same word over and over and over until it didn't mean anything to either of them anymore. *Cool. Cool. Cool. Cool.*

"I should probably go," she said then, even though she didn't want to. Part of her wondered if she were subconsciously trying to exit before she said something stupid. "This was nice, though. Thank you."

"Okay," said James Mace. "What'd you say? If I don't settle up my bill today, you'll call me tomorrow?"

"Yes. Well, maybe not *me*, but someone from our call center will. Your number is in our dialer. You'll get a phone call from a representative in twenty-four hours."

"Cool."

"All righty," said Valencia. All righty! She'd said *all righty*. Definitely out loud. *All righty.* Her celebration of her not completely stagnant conversational skills had been grossly premature. "We'll hear back from you soon then. To make your payment. Have a good day." *What*, she thought, *you're not going to also call him buckaroo?*

"Wonderful. I hope the rest of your day is good as well," said James.

"You too." *You, too, buckaroo.*

For the first time in her entire career as a debt collector, Valencia was sad to hang up the phone.

She almost didn't notice the dialer thumping and clicking along to the next call, an outbound. A ring sounded as the system pulled up the name and account information on her screen so she could see who to ask for and how much they owed.

"What?" a gravelly voice growled at her.

"Hello, this is Valencia calling from West Park Services. May I please speak to Harold?"

"No."

"Uh—"

"You can hang up, is what you can do. And then you can not call back." The man on the phone had a thick British accent; he sounded like John Cleese, and she half expected him to say something outlandish and hilarious next. Unfortunately, he was almost certainly only going to insult her.

"Uh—"

"Uh. Uh. Uh," said the voice like a mocking ten-year-old. "Is that all you know how to say?"

Valencia knew it was a rhetorical question. She really did. "No."

"Uh. No. What a vocabulary. You speak like a bloody idiot. I'm not wasting any more of my time! And you know what else? You sound *fat*."

The dial tone buzzed in her ear for only a moment; then the computer dialer clicked loudly as it moved her along to the next available outbound—business as usual. The dialer had no sympathy. She disconnected before anyone could answer and slumped back in her chair. It creaked loudly and made her jump.

"Everything okay?" Peter called across the aisle, his headset around his neck; he looked at her over his shoulder with concern. He leaned back in his chair only a little, cautious and untrusting of its sturdiness. Or maybe cautious and untrusting of her.

She nodded, trying to maintain her composure. She'd managed to avoid speaking to Peter for more than a month now. He was like a celebrity, someone she saw a lot of and admired from a distance but didn't interact with. Having him speak directly to her was paralyzing. "My," she said, "um . . . my computer. Froze? I need more coffee." She held up her mug, which was still half-full, and hot coffee spilled over the side into her lap. She flinched and set the mug down on the desk.

Peter nodded too. "You know you're in Canada when your computer freezes in June," he said. He looked pained as he said it, and this endeared him to her even more. She knew the inside feelings that went with that outside face. "Dad joke," he said, then added quickly, "Not that I'm a dad. I'm not." He had eyes that smiled even when his mouth grimaced, like he knew a secret way to be embarrassed without letting it eat him alive.

Valencia wanted to throw her head back and laugh just to make him feel better, but her heart was in her throat, and she feared the laugh was going to be more like a sob, so she held it in. She managed a smile. He started nodding again, faster and faster, taking a deep breath.

"I should probably . . . ," he said, pointing at his computer, still nodding.

Valencia realized she was nodding, too, and her hands were clasped in front of her like she was praying. "Oh," she said, as though an important thought had suddenly come to her, "I forgot something. I have to . . ." She was desperate to have forgotten something. She pointed behind her, rising from her chair. Was she still nodding? She felt a rush of sadness override her humiliation as she hurried away. Where was she going? It didn't matter. Peter would surely never speak to her again. Maybe no one would ever speak to her again. Maybe cashiers at grocery stores would eye her warily while they rang up her purchases and nod at her instead of wishing her a good day, and her acquaintances would give her patronizing smiles when they passed her on the street instead of inviting her over for coffee, and Peter would never again swivel his chair in her direction, and she would spend the rest of her life wondering if she were deaf or just ignored.

CHAPTER EIGHT

I met Mr. Valentine on my birthday.

Before I'd even opened my eyes that morning, I remembered it was my birthday, so I kept them closed. When the day officially began, I'd be alone in my apartment, and then I'd have to go to work, and it being my birthday wouldn't mean anything. (That's how it is when you're in your thirties; birthdays aren't important anymore because everyone has gotten over the initial excitement of your basic existence. You're old news. But there's this nostalgic part of you that still remembers—maybe longs for—a time when people were excited.)

Problem was I didn't even know if *I* was excited anymore.

This thought made my eyes pop open. I looked out the window by my bed and saw an airplane cut through the sky, leaving two little white lines behind it. I thought to myself that, with the possible exception of those on business or headed to someone's deathbed, everyone on that plane was going somewhere better that day than I was, somewhere new or different—a young couple on a honeymoon, a little boy going to a theme park for the first time, a woman moving to a new city for an important job. All excited about their trips, presumably their lives. I was envious of them all.

There was something scratching at my consciousness, something from the day before that hadn't quite made it through the mesh of sleep into this one yet. Something sad.

Right, the funeral.

My grandmother's. I'd been one of her caregivers, and she'd been very sick, very ready to go at the end, so it was a bittersweet thing. The funeral had been nice; lots of relatives I hadn't seen in a while, some lovely stories about her—a celebration, really, of a life well lived.

I looked up at the sky just as the plane disappeared into the clouds. My heart jerked in my chest as though trying to chase it, and I rolled onto my back, deciding. Thinking about my responsibilities, my relationships, my job, my bank account. It would all be fine, I realized. Nothing that wouldn't keep without me, nothing too precious to spend. My family, surrounded by friends and aunts and uncles and cousins who had come for the funeral, surrounded by casseroles and flower sprays, surely wouldn't notice my absence. My grandmother didn't need me to read to her or help her out of bed anymore. I spoke out loud in my empty bedroom, to my heart. I said, "Go for it."

(That's what hearts want to hear. Of course, whether or not you should always tell a heart what it wants to hear is another matter entirely. Hearts are like two-year-olds who often want to do very stupid things like suck on steak knives or belly flop down staircases.)

I packed a bag, called in sick to work, and drove to the airport. It was that easy. It reminded me of a game I'd played as a child, a little box with a plastic cover containing a maze and a tiny ball. The object was to get the ball from one side of the maze to the other by tilting and tipping the whole thing, guiding the ball with gravity. That day, the world was the box, and I was the little ball, being guided along without much say and moving my feet only to keep from falling over as the ground dipped and propelled me forward. It wasn't bravery so much as obedience.

I walked into the terminal, looking around like someone was going to jump out and drag me back to work. Like the police car out front was there for me. But my paranoia was, of course, just nerves; I was a young woman walking into an airport. No one cared where I was going. It was a big deal to me, but not to anyone else. I was so unused to being out of my routine that it felt *wrong*.

And then it was just exciting.

I imagined I was the main character in a movie, that this was the first scene, one with no words, only music—a frantic score with loud, heady percussion written to capture the frenzy of activity in the airport that matched the wild banging of my heart in my rib cage.

It made sense for this to be the opening scene. I had been alive for thirty-four years, and nothing had ever happened to me. I began to wonder if I'd actually even existed before this. Isn't that a wild thought? That maybe the earth isn't old at all? Maybe it all just kind of popped into being that day, with characters and settings in place who all had their histories written but were only then brought to life. That's what it felt like.

Mise en scène. I pictured the camera angles as they captured quick, close-up shots of my white knuckles around the shoulder straps of my bag, the departure board flipping letters and numbers, a shared smile with a stranger as we stepped around each other. There were people in business suits carrying briefcases, a high school sports team lugging heavy duffel bags to the baggage check. Stewardesses in high heels headed to their gates, their steps short and staccato, hurrying but appearing laid back all at once somehow. Everyone moved in time with music only I could hear.

I stopped for a moment to take it all in, and the imaginary camera pulled back to show how small I was in the context of the city's busiest transportation hub.

A small city, a small transportation hub, but *still*.

I approached the ticket counter with a sense of accomplishment, knowing I had already completed the part of the journey that keeps most people from making it in the first place. I had decided to go.

The lady behind the counter was wearing a striped red-and-white tie and had her hair pulled back so severely that it seemed to pull her forehead taut. I pictured her taking out her ponytail at night, hair cascading around her shoulders and forehead skin sliding down her face like an avalanche, piling up in layers just above her nose. She looked injured by my existence.

"Yes?" she said at last, sighing as though I were keeping her from her job, as though I were not, at the moment, part of that job. My background music cut out, and I felt injured by her existence.

"I'd like to buy a ticket."

She raised her eyebrows but didn't say anything. I couldn't stop looking at her hair, straining to hold up all of that forehead. I'd never flown anywhere before and suddenly realized I might appear suspicious, wanting to fly just any old place as soon as possible. Like I was running away from something. Not that it was any of her business. On the other hand, maybe she would appreciate the chance to speculate.

"Here's the thing," I said, leaning in and lowering my voice. "I just need to get away. As soon as possible."

"Where to?" she asked, clearly annoyed.

"Doesn't matter," I said, looking back over my shoulder. "Just anywhere. Fast."

She rolled her eyes at me. I smiled back at her.

She started clacking away on her computer with nails that looked like glittering talons, moving slowly and looking inconvenienced. I must not have looked interesting enough to have something to run from. "This isn't a very smart way to fly," she said in a condescending tone, as though she were my financial planner or my mother. "You're going to pay much more than you would've if you'd booked ahead of time."

"Money's not an object," I said dully, and she pretended not to hear me.

"New York," she said. "Flight through Toronto, leaves in one hour."

"Good," I said, in one last attempt to pique her interest. "They'll never catch me."

She pretended, again, not to hear me.

I bought a book and a chocolate bar from the duty-free gift shop to fill the time. I normally didn't buy myself chocolate bars, but it was my birthday. I ate it slowly, taking only one bite every ten pages so I could savor it. It was a thing I had to do often back then: remind myself to slow down and savor things. (It's a science I've perfected, as you can tell by how slowly I do everything now.)

At LaGuardia, I found myself standing at the sliding glass doors as people rushed around me like I wasn't there. I heard quiet trumpets in the deep squeak of the doors on their tracks, and my heart kicked up a beat again.

I hoisted my bag to my shoulders, zipped up my jacket, and stepped out into the New York sunlight. It felt more special than the sunlight I was used to. People wrote plays and songs and movies about the things that went on under this sky. The people who lived under the sky I had at home just existed.

Looking back, I'm not sure what I found so distasteful about the idea of "just existing," as though existing were not an incredible miracle in and of itself. Falling in love, swimming in hotel pools, jumping on trampolines, eating good food. When I was young, none of that was enough. What I wouldn't give now to be able to jump on a trampoline without all my bones crashing together and disintegrating inside me like pieces of chalk.

I had a map. I'd found it by an information desk on my way through the airport. I unfolded it and unfolded it and *unfolded* it. I thought I would be there for the rest of my life, unfolding that map. A woman appeared at my elbow. "Where're you trying to get to?" she asked. She was eating a sandwich and wore a vest that said something about transit on it. She already seemed to know that whatever I was looking for, I would not find it in the endless unfolding of that map. How very philosophical of her.

"I don't know," I admitted. "I guess I need to find a hostel or something. Someplace cheap?" The woman raised an eyebrow. "Cheapish?" Was she smirking at me? "Or just . . . available?"

She *was* smirking. "That bus, the M60, will take you down to the West Side," she said. And like magic, a bus appeared. She gave me the name of a hostel and its address and told me what stop to get off the bus at and wished me luck. She took a bite out of her sandwich and winked at me. She reminded me of the unctuous alligator in a children's book I'd read all the time as a kid. I winked back, because I didn't know what else to do. It felt very strange. I decided not to wink at anyone ever again.

I got on the bus and sat down in the only empty seat, next to a middle-aged man wearing brown shoes and thick glasses. He had a moustache and a book on his lap. He looked smart to me, but only because he was wearing thick glasses and had a book on his lap. What's that saying about seeming smart until you open your mouth?

"Where are you from?" he asked, barely looking at me but somehow knowing I wasn't from New York.

"Saskatchewan," I said, smiling.

"Oh. Is that in Europe?" he asked.

"No, Canada," I said gently.

"Oh. Huh. I've never heard of it," he said, like things he'd never heard of didn't matter. He turned the book over in his lap. I didn't want to assume he did this so I could see he was reading *A Tale of Two Cities* and think he was smart even though he'd never heard of Saskatchewan, but I felt like that might have been the case. "I mean!" he added in a flustered voice. "I've heard of Canada. Just not that city. The one you're from." I nodded. The conversation was over. He picked up his book and started reading again. I noticed he was on page three. I felt awkward, the way you feel when you see an elegant old woman trip and fall on her face and you simultaneously feel the need to help her up and pretend you didn't see it happen to preserve her dignity all at once. I looked up and noticed that the man across the aisle from me was dressed the same way as the one beside me, right down to the moustache. Like a clone. He was also reading a book. They turned their pages in unison.

The bus went over a couple of bridges and past a tollbooth and through Harlem, and I arrived at the hostel on the Upper West Side about forty-five minutes later. It was almost full, but there was a bed for me as long as I was willing to share a room with three strangers. Normally, I wouldn't have been, but that day I was. Because I had no other options, or because it was a day of doing things I wouldn't normally do, or because I was still making decisions the way a rock falling down a hill would—crashing ahead, bouncing off of things, and letting gravity do its work.

I left my bag in the room in one of the little lockers. I stuffed my wallet into my purse and raked my fingers through my hair. All the traveling had thrown me off a little; I had no idea what time it was now. It was still light out, though, and hot too. Midafternoon probably.

When I'd gotten on the plane that morning, sat down next to a stoic teenage boy with safety pins poked into his jean jacket, and tucked my backpack under the seat in front of me, my only goal had been to travel, to go. My destination didn't matter. The trip's duration didn't matter. The going was what mattered, the proving to myself that I could go. At least, that was what I had thought right up until I stood in my tiny hostel room combing my bangs down over my eyes so that I couldn't see the dirty walls and realizing that I had not arrived at the end of the maze yet.

Gravity was still presiding over my day. It propelled me down the stairs of the hostel, and the earth seemed to lean slightly to the right as I exited the building, so I went that way. I stopped at a small pizza place where a teenager who was either sweaty or, perhaps, drenched in airborne pizza grease served up face-sized slices for $1.25. The pizza had the same oily sheen as the teenager's forearms, which made it a little hard to eat.

I took it to go because I could not stand still. It was dizzying. The ground sloped and tipped; I zigzagged down streets and alleys, past basketball courts and parks and coffee shops and apartment complexes. It was strange to think I'd woken up in my own bed that morning.

I found the subway, went underground, headed south. I emerged again in a new place with a flood of other people. They all seemed to be in the same state of perpetual motion as me. No one stood still, not even for a second. I had felt, up until this point, that the momentum was only mine, but maybe this whole city was tilting and shifting; maybe everyone felt the ground rolling.

I looked up and around. The tall buildings, which I'd thought might feel imposing and cold, were instead comforting. They even felt protective. Music floated through the air from the musicians on the street corners, everything from brassy saxophones and out-of-tune pianos to nicked-up drumsticks on overturned garbage cans. There were flowers for sale on every block. People on bicycles wove in and out of yellow taxis and black limousines. I took a bite of my pizza.

Were I actually a little silver ball in a labyrinth game, I would stop rolling forward when I got to wherever it was that I was supposed to end up—and so it was that I came to a halt on a busy street corner where a busker with wild black hair was playing "Ruby Sees All" on his acoustic guitar. I felt no more propulsion, so I figured this was it, whatever "it" was. The stop was so sudden that it almost threw me off my feet. It was then that my brain kicked in, and I began to think.

When you're in motion, it's hard to think. Or it's easier not to think, which is a different thing entirely, I suppose. Reality kind of trails behind you like it's tied to your ankle, and if you're going fast enough, you won't even notice it for a while—this was true for me anyway. I'd been in motion for hours and hours, and now as I stood on the sidewalk in the middle of Manhattan, what I'd done caught up to me all at once and almost knocked me over—how much money I'd spent, how far I was from home, how no one in the whole world knew I was here. It was completely irresponsible, maybe even dangerous.

I gently put it all behind me again. I'd deal with it, if it needed dealing with, later.

Now the busker's song was my soundtrack. He had a stretched, raspy voice that made me wonder if all he ever did was stand on street corners, singing as loud as he could, bouncing on the balls of his feet, grinning at strangers. He caught my eye as he sang the words, and it felt like he was reassuring me, singing about me, falling in love with me. I smiled back and let him, even though this was probably just a smile he gave to everyone, hoping for bigger tips in his guitar case.

Everything melted away, and I was left there with just exactly what was happening at the moment: the busker singing me a song, the skyscrapers leaning over to hear, the sun on my shoulders. I almost ruined the perfect moment by worrying I'd never have another like it ever again. Could this be the thing I had come here for? One perfect moment?

There was an elderly gentleman standing to my right, beaming at the musician. Maybe he was having the same kind of day I was. Maybe he'd woken up in Toronto or Nantucket or Miami that morning, called in sick to his job, jumped on a plane, and rolled all the way here on adrenaline and providence the same as I had. I decided that this was the truth about him because it made me happy. I hoped I would do things like that when I became an old person.

(I don't, but that's okay.)

That was the end of my perfect moment because I was almost killed in the very next one.

A pickpocket was discovered in the crowd, caught in the act by a shrill old lady who started hopping up and down and yelling, "I've been robbed! I'm *being* robbed! He's here! He's right there!" And she must have been right about it, because the man she was pointing at bolted in my direction. He was like a bull; he would trample me. I jumped to avoid him, backward onto the street, like being run over by a gigantic pickpocket would be worse than being run over by a taxicab.

In the end, I was lucky: it was a bike, not a car, that ran me over.

I found myself lying on the ground with my ears ringing and my eyes struggling to focus. Parts of me started to throb and ache, slowly and gently at first, but with increasing intensity. Pain ripped through my head, and I winced. I heard horns honking. The tall buildings moved from their foundations; they came close and lifted me onto the sidewalk and bent over me with concern. And as my eyes sorted things out, they morphed into a little crowd of people.

"I am so sorry," came a voice from off to the side—a man's voice, and its accompanying face appeared above me a second later, earnest and contrite, with large, serious eyes that I thought were probably serious even when he wasn't apologizing. "I am so sorry," he said again, reaching to help me up. "Are you okay?" I took his hand and stood, and standing hurt. I took a few breaths, and that hurt too.

"I think so," I said, and a woman beside me reached out and patted me lightly on the shoulder before turning and walking away, satisfied that she had done her part. A few others left with her. The pickpocket had presumably gotten away in the scuffle, and the lady who'd had her pocket picked was taking it up with a policeman who just happened to be walking out of a nearby shop.

The busker was standing before me now, too, the body of his guitar resting on the top of his shoe, his fingers drumming habitually on the head. "*Seriously*," he said, as though this were a sentiment that made sense all on its own.

I smiled at the remaining people: the busker, the man who was sorry, a couple of ladies with garment bags slung over their arms. "I'm fine," I said, though I felt like I might throw up.

"Guy hit you with his bike," observed the busker unnecessarily, and the man who was sorry looked even sorrier. The ladies with the garment bags moved away without saying anything.

"I am just . . . ," the biker said, "so, *so* sorry. I honestly didn't see you—"

"You were going pretty fast, though," said the busker.

"I'm so sorry," said the biker.

"No, of course you were going fast," I interrupted. "You were on the street. I was the one who jumped back into you—my fault. Completely my fault." I smiled at him as reassuringly as I could, trying to focus my eyes. "There was just this, this *huge* guy, running at me—"

The busker slung his guitar easily over his shoulder and grinned at me, cutting me off. "All's well that ends well," he said. He nodded at the man with the bike, dismissing him. "Keep an eye out, *bud*."

The three of us stood there for a moment, and two of us were surely thinking about that last word, the poorly disguised insult.

The busker seemed to think it had gone over everyone's head. He stuck his hand out to shake mine. "I'm Conor," he said, and his voice sounded just as stretched when he spoke as it had when he'd been singing, but the beauty of it was gone now. "So, hey, I was just going to walk over to that pizza place"—he pointed at a little storefront half a block down the street—"and grab a slice before I go home. I think my day is done. Want to join? My treat."

I looked at the other man, the one who had knocked me flat on my back. He seemed like he was wishing for gravity to suck him right through the concrete into the sewer below, and I felt bad for him. But he, his eyes still serious, just nodded. "Sorry again," he said. "If you're sure you're all right, I actually have to get going—work."

"Oh," I said, and I realized I was disappointed. "Okay, of course. I'm completely fine. Thank you for . . ." I had begun the sentence without any real direction. Thank you for what? For the concussion? "For stopping to make sure I was okay," I finished, and he smiled.

"For sure," he said. He looked like he was going to say something else, but the busker—Conor—interrupted again.

"Shall we?"

And so, even though I never actually agreed to it, I found myself following the busker to the pizza place and gingerly feeling a cut on my cheek with the tip of my ring finger.

Mr. Valentine always tells me—told me—that if I'd looked over at him as I walked away with Conor, I would've seen him looking after me, clutching his bike helmet, wishing desperately that he'd had the nerve to ask me out instead.

Mrs. Valentine glances at the clock. "Good grief, we've been sitting here talking for half an hour. I mean, I've been talking for half an hour. You haven't made a peep."

Anna smiles. "It's okay," she says. "I like love stories."

"This isn't a love story," says Mrs. Valentine matter-of-factly. "Remember? He disappears at the end."

"Right," says Anna, who doesn't know what else to say. "I just mean it starts out like a love story."

Mrs. Valentine smiles, pleased. "Yes, and there's love all the way through. But it's just not a love story."

"Right," Anna says again. Mrs. Valentine is a little bit ridiculous.

CHAPTER NINE

"You're going to die," said the bird. It was not somber; it laughed at her. It thought she was stupid. "What a vocabulary," it said. It sounded like a humorless John Cleese. "I'll call the police!" It flew from the painting and out the window of the call center, and when she looked after it, she saw that the sky was black. It was like looking into a bottomless pit, but one that went out sideways instead of down—or was she looking up? Was the room sideways? It was raining hard, and the rain was coming straight in as though the window were on the ceiling.

There was a stove in the corner of the room, and it was on fire. There was a bed by the stove, and her grandmother lay in it, papery and small. "Valencia?" she called, her voice crackling like the fire. "I'm really not doing well . . ."

"*I'm* really not doing well. I'm dead." This voice belonged to someone else whose face was hidden. A female voice, coming from a wheelchair facing away, inexplicably not in the same room as her grandmother, but not in a different room from Valencia. Her shoulders were hunched like the rain was pushing her down. Her short hair clung to her slender neck.

In spite of the torrential rain, the flames moved to the walls, grasping at them, climbing them, crawling across the ceiling toward Valencia.

"You should have checked." The bird's flat voice floated back inside, like it had perched on a branch just outside the window to taunt her without being seen. "This whole place is going to burn to the ground, and you're going to die, you're going to die, we're all going to die . . ." Then the room started falling, and it was on fire, and the building was an airplane. "Don't be afraid of turning thirty-five," said the bird. "You won't live to be thirty-five."

A shuffling sound in the kitchen woke her up. Valencia bolted upright. Silence.

She'd always had very vivid dreams, but in the days after Charlene's funeral, they had, for a time, become unbearable waking nightmares with such a real quality to them that she'd worried she was either seeing demons or going crazy.

In these dreams, the dead girl's body, now freed from its wheelchair, stood in the center of Valencia's bedroom. Just stood there, decaying. Sometimes, it would nod its head, hard, up and down, and its whole jaw would come unhinged and clank together with an unbearable shattering noise. Sometimes it would suddenly have moved closer to the bed. Sometimes it would disappear altogether, but she'd still be able to hear it moving all around her. It seemed to make the thing happy that it distressed Valencia so much. It would eventually shuffle off, out of the room, getting quieter and quieter until at last she couldn't hear the sound of its wretched, crunching body.

Valencia would lie there long after the last noise, frozen, on her back, unable to scream or cry, unable to differentiate between dream and reality. She would wake up to her alarm clock, gasping.

These dreams had subsided over the years, but the fear of them was still there. It was like Charlene—that awful ghost version of Charlene—was in the kitchen every night. And every once in a while, Valencia would wake up and think she heard it moving in there.

No one's in the kitchen. Nothing's in the kitchen. Charlene, especially, is not in the kitchen. Then she worried that the thoughts would make their opposites come true, a punishment for feeling safe, a trigger. *Something could be in the kitchen*, she thought, to cancel out the first thought, and then worried that this thought would somehow cause something to be in the kitchen.

She tried to clear her mind, to take back all the thoughts and train her brain on something else entirely. She made up a rhyme in her head, something her mom had taught her to do as a child when she'd had a hard time falling asleep.

> Airplanes are the safest way
> The safest way to go
> Better to be way up above than on the ground
>   below
> Airplanes are the safest way
> The safest way to go
> Better than car or van or Jeep or truck or train
>   or boat

She pulled her legs into her chest, held her breath, and listened, waiting for a shuddering breath, the scrape of a foot on the floor. She knew no one was out there, knew it absolutely, but knowing didn't help at all. Knowing felt dangerous.

So she ran. She dressed in yesterday's clothes, straight from the laundry basket, and raced through her apartment like something was chasing her, down the stairwell, and out to her car, heart pounding. She had not been able to check the stove on her way past and would now have to choose the lesser of two irrational anxieties: Ghost Charlene or Stove Catching on Fire.

The bird's voice followed her out of the building.

"You're going to die. You're going to die. We're all going to die . . ."

"Airplanes are the safest way, the safest way to go," she countered under her breath, hoping no one would hear her. "Better to be way up above than on the ground below . . ."

A crisp, rattling sound came from behind her as she bent to unlock the door; she gasped and spun, and a dry leaf skittered across the parking lot.

Let it all burn.

The dash clock in her car glowed 5:30. She didn't have to be at work for more than two hours, but going back into her quiet apartment was unthinkable, so she put the keys in the ignition. She drove to work, drawing deep breaths, taking her time on slow side roads, trying not to worry about whether she would get into an accident, whether there was or was not someone in the back seat, or whether her apartment was currently engulfed in flames.

Even on terrible mornings like this one, Valencia half enjoyed the easy drive to work. She liked having the road to herself, liked being in motion, liked watching the world pass by without expecting anything from her. She drove up Thirteenth to Rae Street, taking Fourteenth to Elphinstone, took the unnamed back road beside the small creek that wound up toward the airport. This part of town was old, and the roads were lined with bright, elderly trees that bent over the road comfortingly. She turned the radio on and spun the volume knob to the right. A familiar voice, low and clear, filled the car, and Valencia wished, as she often did, that there was someone in the passenger seat. She'd turn to them and say, "Who is this? I recognize the voice, but I don't know the song . . ."

There was never anyone in the passenger seat. But was there someone in the back seat? She glanced nervously in the rearview mirror and turned the volume up even more.

She pulled into the lot at 6:45, still early, parked in her usual place, and got another legal pad out of the center console. The essay in progress was, again, about Peter but not *about Peter*. It was also a little bit about the man she had spoken to on the phone the other day. He had, she reasoned, shown her that she had it in her to speak to people—and that was something she had been wondering about for a while now.

How to Speak to People

1. Greet

    a. Hi. Hey. Howdy. (Probably not *howdy*.) Etc. Casual; not too excited but not like you're mad.
    b. Keep your eyebrows down. Surprise is not an appropriate emotion here.
    c. Don't do that thing you do.
    d. Smile without teeth.

2. Ask One of the Following Questions:

    a. How are you?
    b. What's up?
    c. What's new?

3. Tell a Funny Story

    a. (May have to make one up.)
    b. WHY DON'T I HAVE ANY FUNNY STORIES?

4. Have Actual Exit Strategy

    a. Say you have to go.
    b. Smile.
    c. Don't be such an absolute idiot about it.
    d. Seriously, Valencia.

At last, she saw the secretary pull up in her light-blue Cavalier and unlock the front doors, and she hurried inside after her, eagerly anticipating the presence of other people.

When she got to her desk, she eyed the computer warily, remembering her nightmare. The memory of the dream was, somehow, more vivid and tangible than the memory of the previous day, and for a moment she second-guessed herself, as though she were looking into a mirror wondering whether she was the person or the reflection of the person.

She put on her headset, and the dialer clanked to life. It was the usual lineup—a woman from Maine who had apparently never heard of herself, a man from New Jersey who burst into a string of expletives before slamming the receiver down, and a little girl from Rhode Island whose mother could be heard in the background coaching her to say, "I'm home alone. You can't talk to my mom." Then a smooth drunk who proposed marriage, a supposed psychic who threatened physical harm to Valencia's husband and children if she didn't quit her job by the end of the week, and someone with an acidic-sounding voice who seemed to derive great pleasure from his colorful description of what debt collectors "deserved to have happen to them." Calls like these had once been shocking, but now they just made Valencia feel heavy and sad. Bored, even. She could come up with *much* worse torture methods than these telephone hacks—because she practiced thinking of torturous things, against her will, all day long. Things involving, for example, fingernails. Scalps.

After twenty outbounds, she looked down at the paper in front of her. It was covered in tiny sad faces. This was a dubious coping mechanism she'd invented after her first few months at West Park, when she'd finally understood that verbal abuse was going to be a consistent, unrelenting part of her job. She drew a sad face every time she felt herself making one, and when the paper was full, she allowed herself one square of the chocolate bar she kept in her purse. She was trying to use sugar to trick her brain into enjoying abuse—it probably wasn't a healthy tactic, but it was necessary if she was going to be there for another sixty years.

She peeked inside the silver foil and realized there was only one square of chocolate left. It wasn't even lunchtime yet—she'd set a depressing personal record.

A woman answered the next call. "Yeah, hello? I have about five minutes—talk fast." She already sounded suspicious.

"Hello, this is Valencia from West Park—"

"Yo no hablo inglés."

Valencia rolled her eyes and sighed. She wasn't sure what people thought would happen to their debt if they put off speaking to the collectors like this. It didn't just disappear. "Ma'am," she said, "I need to speak with a Mrs.—"

"Yo no hablo inglés! Yo no hablo inglés! Yo no hablo inglés!" The woman's voice rose to a childish shriek, then there was a click and the dial tone.

The office was muggy; the air was wet. Valencia's fuzzy brown hair stuck to her face and neck, and she bunched it together and held it away from her back for a moment of relief. She disconnected from the dialer and pulled her headset off. She was feeling sick from the combination of sugar and heat and annoyance. What was the point of being professional? She wished she had it in her to be unprofessional, to yell back or quit or throw her office chair across the room. This last thing was something she often imagined herself doing, and she was worried about wearing that particular pathway in her brain down so much that one day her body would act the thought out without her conscious permission.

Is this how ordinary people end up doing unthinkable things? She laced her hands together and clamped them firmly between her legs. How much control did anyone really have over their movements? She couldn't stop her body from pumping blood or sweating—what if it wanted to throw her chair across the room? It would. There would be nothing she could do to stop it, and it would be just like the daydream, which always ended with someone taking her chair to the face. The reel always caught at that part, and she had to watch it over and over until she could jerk her brain into forward motion again.

She realized she was breathing fast, too fast. She closed her eyes and pulled on the thin white hairs on the backs of her arms. (*Trichotillomania!* Louise had observed with more excitement than concern. *You seem to do that when you're having a hard time calming down. Would you say that's accurate?*) She reviewed what she knew about voluntary and involuntary movements, reminding herself that if she lost her job, she'd have to find a new job somewhere else. For the moment, it was enough to keep her from doing anything rash, even if it didn't make her feel any better. *Breathe! Blink!* She tried to coach herself. *Don't throw stuff! Try not to wreck anything! Stop pulling your hair out!* She blinked a few extra times to remind herself that she was in control of her body. She could blink exactly eighteen times if she wanted to—no more, no less. Voluntary movement. *One, two, three, four—*

"You okay?" said Peter. He stood beside her chair, one hand in his pocket, the other holding a steaming cup of coffee. He looked terrified but casual, like a catalog model in a horror movie.

"Uh, yes," said Valencia, unlike any kind of model in any kind of movie. This was the second time he'd asked her if she was okay; either she was noticeably unhinged, or he was obsessed with her. Could he hear her heart? Did she look sweaty? Then, a terrifying stream of thoughts: Had she been coaching herself out loud? Had she uttered the words *don't throw stuff* in her actual out-loud speaking voice? Had she yelled it? Was that why he was checking on her, because she'd been sitting in her chair hollering, "Don't throw stuff!" at her computer? All too likely. It could also have something to do with all the blinking. "I'm fine," she said. She visualized the sound waves that made up her voice, trying to steer them, straighten them out. "You know how it is. Just talking to horrible people. On the phone." His nice face smiled at her. Was she blushing? Was she shaking? Was there an earthquake? She realized that his mouth had been moving, and now he looked expectant. "Sorry, what did you just say?"

"Oh, I said, there are a lot of those. Horrible people."

She nodded. She was, after all, one of them. *Pull yourself together!* "There are, but I should be used to them."

Peter shook his head, shifting all of his weight from one side of his body to the other. "I think it's good you're not, actually. Awful people are the ones who are used to people being awful to them."

"That's probably true."

A successful interaction. She felt better, and Peter looked like he did too. She thought she saw his shoulders settle.

"Do you need a coffee?" He held his out toward her.

She did, but not one he'd touched. "No, thank you."

"That's cool," he said, looking embarrassed. He nodded at her empty cup. "I see you've got one there."

"Thanks, though. For offering. I just. You know. Caffeine! And . . ." Those were the words that came out of her mouth, in that order, and then hands flew around in her peripheral vision, like birds—her hands, she realized. She crossed her arms and nodded and suddenly felt very close to laughing, or maybe crying.

But Peter smiled. "I know," he said. And it seemed that he did know, and she liked him even more than she had before. "If I have too much coffee, I feel a little bit crazy too."

"Crazy?" She didn't mean to bark at him or to give him such a dirty look, but she had, at first, thought he was calling *her* crazy—actual crazy. *Crazy* crazy.

"Oh, I don't mean . . . ," he said, faltering.

"Sorry," she said. She forced a cough, frowning more intentionally. "I had something in my throat." He looked relieved. "Yes"—she delivered one more piteous cough for dramatic effect—"yes, caffeine makes me feel that way. Crazy. Just literally insane. Like I'm going to throw this chair clear across the room."

He laughed like she'd told a great joke instead of admitting an embarrassing secret. *Interesting. I could confess a lot of things if I pretended I'm joking about them. Hey, Peter, here's something bizarre: I'm afraid to fall in love with you because I'm sure that if I do, you'll be struck by lightning, just because I love you. There is a layer of me that actually believes that, just directly under the layer that knows it's impossible. Isn't that hilarious? Louise calls it magical thinking, but there's nothing magical about it. It's just torture.*

"But wouldn't that be so satisfying sometimes, especially at a job like this?" Peter looked at her chair as though he were considering it. "I sure felt like chucking mine across the room when it snapped in half on me. Kind of a bad first impression."

"I . . . I didn't think it was," she said, surprising herself. She had been concentrating so hard on keeping her voice steady that she had no leftover energy to worry about what she was saying. If she had more air, more nerve, more old-fashioned *gumption*, she'd laugh in a flirtatious way and say, *You know what? I think the whole point of a first impression is to be memorable. Otherwise we'd just call it a first meeting, and I'd have forgotten your name already.* Maybe she'd push on his shoulder as she said this, because that was a thing that women did in rom-coms. It looked silly, Valencia always thought, but men seemed to love it, having their shoulders pushed on by women who were also laughing flirtatiously. And then he'd laugh and she'd laugh harder, and she'd kiss him, even though this was an office and even though they hadn't even verbally established the existence of a mutual attraction. And it wouldn't faze her, because in this daydream she could be one of those people who didn't care about germs. Like, I'll see your gross mouth germs and raise you mine.

Maybe she *could* say and do all of that. Why not? She opened her mouth. "No," she said dumbly, "it wasn't. A bad first impression."

"Thanks," he said, and his smile broadened. They stood there for a moment, and it felt okay not to say anything. "Anyway. I should probably get back to work. Good luck with the awful people."

"Thanks. You too." She turned back to her computer, pressing the palms of her hands together anxiously. When was the last time she'd exhaled?

Reluctant to connect to the dialer, she decided to clean her cubicle instead. This would buy her at least five minutes; her desk was a mess. She crumpled up old chocolate bar wrappers and deposited them in the garbage can at her knees. She rounded up over a dozen pens and placed them, one by one, in a neat row beside her computer keyboard, using a piece of paper to nudge the ends into a perfect line. Lastly, she gathered all of the lined yellow papers into a stack and banged them against her desk like Louise had done. It felt kind of nice to be so thoughtlessly loud and obnoxious in the quiet office setting, until she remembered Peter at her back. The thought of him thinking of her as loud or obnoxious silenced her immediately. Her face burned, and she looked down at the stack of papers in front of her; the one on top was the ever-growing list of places for her trip. Her eyes flicked over the now-familiar foreign words. Svartifoss. Trolltunga. Eilat. She didn't know where these places were exactly, but she felt certain they weren't in Canada. Would she have the nerve to travel out of the country? She picked up her pen and added Winnipeg to the bottom of the list. She needed at least one easy destination on there. The flight would be an hour, tops. She wouldn't need a passport, and she could be home by August 4.

She couldn't procrastinate anymore; she connected to the dialer, and the inbound light flashed.

"West Park Services, Valencia speaking; how may I help you?"

"Valencia! Hello! You're the one I talked to yesterday, right? How're you doing today?"

Valencia recognized the kind, quiet voice and smiled. "Fine." And she was, all of a sudden. "And you?"

"Terrible!" said James Mace cheerfully.

She smiled at her computer. "What can I do for you?"

"Well, I'm wallowing in debt and despair, as usual," said James. "So, that, first of all."

"Okay," said Valencia. She recited her lines mechanically but faster than usual. "I can help you with that. First, I just want to let you know that this call will be recorded for quality assurance purposes. I need your credit card number and date of birth, please."

"Hmm . . ." He cleared his throat softly, the same way he did everything else. "Huh."

"You don't have it?"

He hummed. "No," he said at last. "I can't find it."

"You can't find it? Your credit card?"

"I can't. Hmm. That's so strange; I could've sworn it was right here in my wallet . . ." He clicked his tongue and hummed some more. He was like the old space heater Norwin brought to work in the winter. "Actually, to be honest, I was just calling to see if you wanted another break."

"Oh," said Valencia. "Really?"

"Well, yeah," said James Mace. "I couldn't get over it, after we talked yesterday, that you get death threats at your job regularly like that. The way you said it was so casual. I feel like that would really *affect* me if I were you. Maybe it's an obnoxious thing for me to call you like this—and tell me if it is, please—but . . . yeah. I just wanted to."

His voice trembled the slightest bit as he said this, and it saved him. Valencia had at first been on guard and then had rolled her eyes at what felt a little cheesy. But then his voice trembled, and she realized he was nervous. She was like a person who had once gone hungry being asked for food. She would not deny a self-conscious person affirmation.

"Thank you," she said, trying to get her sincerity across, trying to put him at ease. "I would really love a break."

"Cool," said James, and she could tell he was smiling. "So, okay. Here's the topic of conversation for today: I'm doing a crossword. I'm stuck on this one. It's six letters. Starts with *h*, ends with *t*. Of rain or rainfall."

"I . . ." Valencia was bad with unexpected bends in conversation. She was bad with unexpected anything. She wished she knew a six-letter word that had something to do with rain and started with the letter *h*.

"*Oh*," said James, sounding smart. "Here's the thing. I had six *down* wrong, so the actual last letter is *l*. *Hyetal* fits." He gave a self-deprecating laugh, as though, *of course*, anyone would've guessed *hyetal* if they'd had the right information to begin with. She could imagine him sitting at a desk in a dark-brown study with his hands tented in front of him, nodding his head with his eyes closed, pleased.

"I wouldn't have gotten that," she said truthfully, without shame. This was probably why it was easy to talk to him when it wasn't easy to talk to anyone else—she didn't have to worry about impressing him. He was only a voice, not a whole person that a voice came out of. He was someone who could cease to exist for her when the phone call ended.

"Oh, but I bet there are a whole bunch of questions on here you'd get that I wouldn't," he said. "That's the great thing about loving words, loving books. There are so many of them. We don't all know all of them. We just all know some of them. Which is also the great thing about doing a crossword puzzle with someone else."

"Yes," said Valencia. "That's true. Okay, give me another."

They worked through ten more questions before Valencia reluctantly said she needed to get back to work. James Mace sounded disappointed but said he'd call again, if it was okay, and Valencia said it was, surprised to feel a shiver of excitement run up her spine.

There followed a considerable silence, and it felt rich and full and promising, like a forest of feelings. A jungle. Anything could come charging out of it.

"Cool," he said. "Talk to you soon."

"Okay," she said, feeling more than a little disappointed that the silence hadn't produced anything other than that.

CHAPTER TEN

The clouds have been gathering while Mrs. Valentine shares her story, but the kitchen seems to darken all at once. The window beside Anna is open just a few inches, and suddenly her shirtsleeve is wet. "Oh," she says, surveying a growing puddle on the kitchen floor, "should I shut this?"

"No, it's fine, dear," says Mrs. Valentine. She's lost in thought and doesn't seem to even know what Anna's talking about.

"Okay, but there's quite a bit of rain getting in—"

"It's fine," says Mrs. Valentine sweetly. "You'd better get to work, though—the day's getting away on you. It's dark out already!"

"Oh, sure, sorry." Anna stands, quietly pushing the window down with one hand. Her foot has fallen asleep, folded up underneath her.

"Nothing to apologize for, dear girl. I'm the one who can't shut my mouth. Once I get going, you know. That's it. You'll be like this, too, when you're older."

"If I don't take after my grandma Davies." Grandma Davies, the sad, quiet grandmother. Anna knows that her grandmother and Mrs. Valentine were close friends for a long time, and now, having met Mrs. Valentine, it makes perfect sense why their relationship worked. Mrs. Valentine must have talked and talked and talked while Anna's grandmother just sat there and listened and listened and listened.

Anna's mom used to go on and on about how good it would be for her mother to have such a friend living so close, but neither she nor Anna ever gave much thought to the woman left behind when her grandmother passed away.

"You'd be lucky to take after your grandma Davies," says Mrs. Valentine, almost indignantly. "She's an amazing woman. In fact, I really doubt you've ever met your grandmother if you're going around saying things like that."

Anna is confused by two things: the present tense used to speak of her dead grandmother and the insinuation that she never met the woman. Only the latter seems broachable; the former must have been a slip of the tongue. "What? Of course I met her. Knew her."

Mrs. Valentine's face moves, just her mouth, just the faintest bit. "I mean," she continues, still seated, arranging the things on the messy table so they're in neat rows, "you haven't met the Mrs. Davies that I used to know before your grandfather died. She's just going through a very long rough patch. Grief can really shut a person up—but she didn't start out like this, and she's not going to finish this way either, I don't think." Mrs. Valentine raps on the table with her knuckles like she's giving a motivational pep talk to Mrs. Davies via her granddaughter. "People like me and you just need to keep at her. Someday, she'll find some part of her old self again, and when that happens, I'll introduce you for real. I think you'll find you actually have so much in common. Okay! Come on."

Anna is bewildered, but the bizarre moment passes before she can say anything. Mrs. Valentine has moved on to the work assignment. The old woman pushes her chair back, and it screeches across the linoleum. "Floor." She points at the floor, which crunches beneath her feet. "Counters, dishes, uh . . ." She pauses in the middle of the room and turns. "That alone might take up this whole afternoon, mightn't it?"

Anna nods, her eyes wide. "It could," she says in a small voice.

"No bother to me if that's all you get done this week," Mrs. Valentine says quickly. "And no bother to me if you don't finish even that today. I think you've noticed this place hasn't been cleaned in some time. At this point, it's more like you're cleaning it for whoever lives here next, you know?"

"Uh-huh," says Anna, sweating. There's that talk about death again.

Mrs. Valentine leans against the counter, smiling to herself. "Oh, *speaking* of your grandmother, she's coming over in about fifteen minutes."

Anna freezes. It wasn't a slip of the tongue. What was it then? Her grandmother Davies has been dead for quite some time. She's most certainly not coming over in fifteen minutes. She opens her mouth to say this, but nothing comes out. Mrs. Valentine doesn't even notice. She's looking around the messy room, as though saying goodbye to the clutter and the crumbs. At last, she smiles at Anna and nods encouragingly. "You stay as long as you like, do as much as you want, and let yourself out when you're done, all right? Your money is there on the counter." And it is, neat stacks of coins on top of a pile of magazine and newspaper clippings. Mrs. Valentine smiles at Anna and disappears down the hall.

Anna feels sick. And curious. The sick part of her wants to go home and tell her mother that Mrs. Valentine is either crazy or hasn't been informed of her best friend's death. The curious part of her wants to see what will happen in about fifteen minutes.

The curious part wins.

She crosses the room to the coins and newspaper clippings—there are dozens of them, arranged into messy groups, words and paragraphs and pictures cut from articles. She picks one group and fans its contents out on the counter. A headline reads "Tour Bus Crash En Route to La Paz." It's cut away from its accompanying article. There's a picture of what appears to be a giant, ultrashallow lake, with people standing on top of it, captioned, "How to Find the Right Tour Operator for Your

Trip to the Salar de Uyuni." A paragraph from an especially old, yellowing paper details a Jeep getting its wheel stuck in a hole and flipping over, killing everyone inside. A strange little group of clippings to hang on to, Anna thinks. She can't tell what they all have in common, doesn't know the names referenced in them, but she gathers all of the groups of papers together in a neat pile and sets them on top of the fridge along with the funeral pamphlets Mrs. Valentine put there earlier.

She fills the sink with water and starts on the dishes and soon hears Mrs. Valentine back in the living room, chattering away. She pauses to listen; it's hard to hear very well with that piano music blaring.

"She's such a sweet girl. She looks *just like you*! I couldn't believe it! I think this arrangement will work out fine. She's in there now, cleaning up the counters. I don't care very much when it's just me here, but it will be nice, just the same, to have people over and not feel ashamed of my mess." Mrs. Valentine is quiet for a moment, and Anna strains to hear another person talk, even though she knows she won't. Mrs. Valentine speaks again. "Well, yes, you know, I did start telling her the story, but then I decided I didn't want to bore her with the whole thing. I felt sorry for the girl. Her eyes were glazing over. Like a couple of doughnuts." Mrs. Valentine bursts out laughing, but the visitor makes no sound, of course.

Anna realizes she's standing with both hands in the sink, leaning slightly toward the living room. She grasps the dish towel and tiptoes to the table, a vantage point from which she'll be able to see into the living room. She wants to see the silent guest. Her grandmother.

Mrs. Valentine is seated on the couch, speaking enthusiastically and gesticulating wildly—laughing and then sobering and then laughing again—at a chair across the room. The music swirls around her. The song is fast and sad and loud.

The chair is empty.

CHAPTER ELEVEN

Valencia was trapped in the bathroom again.

Trapped more mentally than physically, but just as stuck either way because the door was shut and she couldn't open it. There might as well have been multiple deadbolts—and if there had been, she wouldn't have felt so dumb about the whole thing, as though a barrier had to be physical and tangible in order for it to also be legitimate. In this instance, however, there was nothing between Valencia and freedom but an unlocked doorknob. A metaphor for her entire existence. If she had her notepad, she could write an essay about it—and she probably would, later. It would be called "Nonexistent Locks: A Memoir."

The doorknob was a shiny metal bulb that did nothing but turn when you turned it. The problem was Valencia couldn't turn it. She hadn't touched a bathroom doorknob in years, though not without a lot of careful planning and the occasional inconvenience. She usually relied on the fact that with the hundreds of West Park employees, it was unlikely she'd be the only one in the bathroom at any given moment. After washing her hands, she'd stand in front of the mirror and pretend to fix her hair until the door opened, and she'd rush to it, trying to look casual, and stick her foot in its path to hold it open like that for whoever was walking through. Everyone probably thought she was so polite. She liked that. Maybe people called her sweetheart behind her back.

But here she was, alone in the bathroom. All of the stalls were empty. If any part of her touched the doorknob, she would spend the rest of the day tracing the germs' travels in her mind—from her hand to her computer to her purse strap, and to the pen on her desk to her house keys and into her house, then onto everything she touched in there. It would become an uncontainable problem; she would start to forget which things she'd touched, which ones she hadn't. She would have to clean everything.

Everything.

It would take days.

She really didn't think she could touch the knob, just as she didn't think she could amputate a limb if she found herself in one of those crazy mountain survival stories where a person got an arm or leg stuck under a rock and had to choose between sawing it off and dying. This felt almost as extreme, almost as hopeless, if not as cold or imminently dangerous. There was nothing to do but wait.

Her rescuer, who did not show herself for a melodramatic forty-five minutes, was a skinny, happy woman who must have been wearing an entire bottle of perfume and three vats of teal-blue eye shadow. Valencia stuck her foot in the path of the door before it could shut and held it open for the lady, smiling just as calmly and kindly as she could, as if she hadn't just spent almost an hour trapped in a bathroom staring at a doorknob on the verge of tears. And wasn't she so polite for holding the door? *That Valencia. What a sweetheart.*

Flustered but, she hoped, not visibly so, she returned to her desk, slid into her chair, and looked around at her office mates. They were all intently focused on their screens and their calls. Only Peter seemed to sense that she was looking at him and glanced over his shoulder, offering a smile.

She spun her chair away from him, thankful she didn't have to explain her prolonged bathroom break to anyone—she'd realized long ago that she couldn't explain anyway.

It all felt like a ridiculous little game that she'd made up and played alone. Sanity saving and crazy making. Harmless and hopeless. Complicated. She lived in a state of balancing impending disaster and damage control—like the people of Tornado Alley. Those people were probably asked sometimes why they didn't move out of Tornado Alley. They probably shrugged their shoulders and said something about how it just wasn't that easy.

She took a deep breath, connected to the dialer, and exhaled when the inbound line lit up.

"West Park Services, Valencia speaking; how may I help you?"

"Hey, Vee." It was James Mace, calling her *Vee* like they were old friends. She hadn't been Vee since high school. People who knew her back then had called her Vee—her ill-fated boyfriend, her best friend, her teachers. Had they used the nickname out of tenderness and familiarity, or had it just been easier to say? A nickname supposedly meant someone cared about you, but she'd always worried that in her case it was actually a shortcut. So they'd have to spend even less time on her than they already did. Three fewer wasted syllables. *Vee.*

But hearing it now, spoken into her ear like this, Valencia felt like she was a mug being filled to the top with warm tea. Somehow, he cut syllables without sounding rushed. Her abbreviated name sounded longer, even.

"I have to tell you, Vee, I still can't scrape together that money." He said it like it was an inside joke.

"Okay, that's no problem." She smiled into her coffee cup.

"How's the day going?"

"Oh, it's . . . it's going," she said. Her dad always used to say that, and she'd always found it hysterical. Now, as an adult, she'd come to realize that everyone said it, and it wasn't actually all that funny. It didn't even mean anything.

"How long have you been a debt collector, Vee?"

"Sixteen . . . no, wait. Seventeen years."

"Wow, long time. You must like it? Death threats and all?"

"No, no. No. Not at all." She snorted. "No."

"Are you looking for a new job then?"

"No." She struggled with this question. "I just . . . don't know what else I'd do?"

"What do you wish you could do?"

"It changes." She looked up at the wall clock hanging at the end of the row of cubicles. It was identical to a clock that had hung above Mrs. Gerard's desk in fourth grade, a white chunky one with bold black numbers. "I used to want to be a teacher, an elementary school teacher." This wasn't at all true, but Valencia had already said the lie by the time her brain acknowledged it was one. Guilt gripped her, and she started picking at the hairs on her arm again. She wasted so many white lies on situations that didn't call for them.

James Mace sounded interested, which made it worse. *Here! This is why you avoid people.* "So, why not? Why don't you do that?"

Valencia felt sadness wash over her at this question. *Why don't you . . . ?* She'd asked it of herself so many times back in her twenties. Why not go back to school? Why not give something to the next generation? Why not enjoy her life or be passionate about something? Anything?

The answer, of course, was that she didn't deserve to. And didn't know how to. She felt tempted to tell him about Charlene and Ghost Charlene and the bird on the hat. About that night in high school that had changed everything and the second night a few years later that had changed everything again—permanently. Maybe it would feel good to tell him. But probably it wouldn't.

"I guess . . . it feels too late to go back to school?" That could be a common, rational reason.

"Too late? You don't sound old."

"I'm almost thirty-five." She flinched as she heard herself say it and wished she had thought to lie about her age. That would've been a fine place for a white lie.

He scoffed at her. "You have plenty of time. All the time in the world."

"Well. I guess. What do you do?"

James Mace coughed. "Computers."

"Selling them? Fixing them?"

"Yeah, just working on them."

"Do you like your job?"

"No. But I'm not going to be doing it forever. I'm only thirty-three. I've just finished my schooling, and I have to save up some money, and then I'm going to start my own business—which I'll tell you about another time."

Valencia was overjoyed to hear him say the words *another time* but worried it meant he might be getting ready to hang up. She didn't want that yet. "I'm going on a trip," she blurted out, even as she realized it didn't make sense in the context of their conversation. "I just mean, on the topic of age. I'm going on a . . ." Here was another tough spot; she couldn't very well tell James she was going on an airplane for the sake of flying so she could overcome her fear of a number, could she? "A birthday trip." Genius. That was a very normal thing to do, a very normal reason to do it.

"Really?" James was interested; her atrociously clumsy segue had worked.

"Yeah. Yes." Maybe the trip could be a fun thing to talk about if she didn't let herself actually think about it at the same time. Maybe talking about it like it was something she wanted to do would be the thing that gave her courage to do it.

"Where to?"

"I haven't decided yet. I'm making a list of possible places."

"That's awesome," he said. She felt him leaning into the phone, or imagined she could. "Good for you." His encouragement was like sun shining through the phone lines. She basked in it.

"It *is* good for me," she said. "Any suggestions?"

"I'll think on it," he said. "Maybe I'll make a list too."

"I've never even been on an airplane," she said. "I have a fear of"—it was like listening to someone else talk; the words just seemed to flow without her saying them—"flying." Humiliated, she examined the ceiling above her head. Why wasn't it on fire when she needed it to be?

"My mom has a fear of flying too," said James, like it was not that big of a deal, just something that people happened to have, like freckles or food aversions or limbs. "My uncle's funeral was in Toronto, and she drove twenty-seven hours to get there because she refuses to get on an airplane."

"*Oh*," said Valencia, surprised. It had never occurred to her that she might not be the only person crippled by the fear of something. It took all of her strength to keep her mouth from saying that James Mace's mother was still a step ahead of her; Valencia would not have made it to the uncle's funeral since she was also afraid of driving on highways.

"That makes it even cooler that you're doing this. Facing a fear is a big deal."

She realized she was beaming at her computer screen. *Cool.* He thought she was interesting *and* cool. Her heart soared. "Thank you," she squeaked.

"Anyway," he said. "You have a job to do, and I don't want to get you fired. *Although.* Maybe getting fired would be the best thing for you right now. Then you could go do something you actually want to do. Maybe I'd be doing you a favor."

"They won't fire me for talking on the phone," she said hopefully. "They gave me the phone; it's my job." *Please don't get off the phone*, she said silently.

"I should still let you go. But. Can I call you again tomorrow? I mean I should put something down on my account." He sounded hopeful too. Maybe he was also saying things silently.

"Yes," said Valencia. "Please do."

CHAPTER TWELVE

Anna hasn't mentioned the incident to anyone, not even her mother. She meant to; in the moment, the whole thing terrified her, and she had to fight the urge to run out of the apartment and never come back. Instead, for reasons she never was able to fully explain to anyone, she crept out of sight, back to the sink, and furiously started washing dishes.

She left the kitchen spotless, slipped out of the apartment as stealthily as she could, yelled, "See you next week, Mrs. Valentine," and ran down the hall.

And now, here she is again. True to her word. The creepy poem still hanging on the door, the piano music blaring behind it. She isn't afraid anymore, only curious—her mother always gave a speech about how fear of other people could turn into hate if you didn't try to understand them. She said you should lean into frightening people. She always followed up with a confusing counterpoint about trusting your gut and running away from men if they asked you to get into their cars. In short: don't run away even when you feel like running away, but also, always run away when you feel like you should.

Anna is beginning to understand that there are very few rules that don't have confusing counterpoints.

Mrs. Valentine is excited to see Anna. If she noticed Anna's quick, silent exit the week before, she doesn't seem to think anything of it. She welcomes her in and shows her where she keeps the vacuum cleaner. "This is all I need from you today, just a quick vacuum, here and in my bedroom. Oh, and maybe you could do the bathroom, if that's not too much trouble? You're so fast! You did such a wonderful job in the kitchen last week; I've just been standing in it and looking around and touching everything . . ." She's drawing out all of her words. She takes a big breath through her nose and rolls her eyes back into her head. It is, Anna thinks, a terrifying display, but she understands what it means and is happy to know she's pleased Mrs. Valentine.

Anna takes a breath, too, and summons the words she practiced on her way up the stairs. "When I'm done, maybe you could tell me the rest of your story?" she asks. She hopes it doesn't sound rehearsed, even though it is.

Mrs. Valentine places both hands over her heart. "Of course!" she cries, delighted, as though the thought never even crossed her mind. "I'd love to, if you really want to hear it."

"Of course I do." Anna hears her voice reaching to match Mrs. Valentine's.

"I'm visiting with my son in the kitchen just now," she tells Anna. "But he can't stay long; you probably won't even see him."

I'm sure I won't, if he's anything like Grandma. There's a pause; Mrs. Valentine seems to be waiting. "Okay," says Anna.

"Okay then, vacuuming first, and then the bathroom, if you don't mind. Bless your heart, and thanks again. Money's on the kitchen counter, same place as before. I should get back to the kitchen."

Anna begins her chores. She hears the apartment door open when she's vacuuming the bedroom, but by the time she finishes cleaning the bathroom and returns to the living room, Mrs. Valentine is lying on the couch, not talking to anyone, not even talking to no one. The music has been turned up, the same piano song as the week before, still on repeat.

Her eyes flutter open as Anna enters. "Done already?" She laughs from deep inside her chest, and all of her many chins puff up around her face. "And still wanting to hear the rest of that story?" She looks so hopeful and ridiculous that Anna feels heartbroken.

"Absolutely," she says.

"Okay. So, where was I then?"

"With Conor, the busker," says Anna. She has to talk loudly to be heard over the music but is sure it would be rude to ask to turn it down.

"Bless you, dear. That's exactly where I was."

CHAPTER THIRTEEN

Working at West Park felt like walking around corner after corner, expecting someone to jump out and attack. And someone almost always did.

This time, it was an old lady whose voice was sweet and cheerful at first, but only because she thought Valencia was her granddaughter.

"How's school lately, Bridget? Why aren't you at school today?"

"Oh, sorry, ma'am, this isn't Bridget. My name is Valencia—"

"Va-who-sia?"

"Sorry, my name is *Valencia*, and I'm calling from *West Park Serv*—"

"You have the wrong number. Goodbye—"

"No, actually, this is the number you supplied on your credit card application . . ."

And that was all it took. That was all it ever took. Valencia held the earpiece away from her head as the woman's shrill voice streamed through.

She had made five trips to the coffee station already; it was only ten a.m., and her heart wasn't pounding so much as shaking. Vibrating. She could feel it in her fingertips. She could not possibly subject her body to another shot of caffeinated sludge. The dialer clicked over to someone's answering machine; they'd let a young child record the message.

They probably thought they were really cute, but the whole thing was unintelligible.

She disconnected before the beep and closed her eyes, rubbing her temples. She got a headache if she didn't drink coffee, but she also got one if she drank too much, and the window between none or not quite enough and too much was really more of a crack. A slit. A sound caused her to open her eyes, but even as she did she wasn't sure she'd actually heard anything at all. She looked around and spied a crumpled-up piece of paper on the desk in front of her. Had that been there before? She looked up in time to see Peter swivel around in his chair. A note? From Peter?

She smoothed it out, overcome with nostalgia. When was the last time someone had passed her a note? Sometime in high school, more than a decade before, when the senior class of Balfour High had been untouched by any real tragedy and didn't feel guilty talking to each other about meaningless things. Charlene had been alive and no one cared—because no one had known that Charlene being dead was an option. Valencia had sat in the exact middle of the classroom, counting tiles on the ceiling, more often than not trying to distract herself because she had to use the bathroom but, even back then, couldn't bring herself to use a public one. The notes passed were more for something to do than to garner any actual information, which could easily be gotten between classes or on the phone later that evening. *Are you mad at me? Do you think he likes me? Do you think he likes her? What are you wearing to the party? (Were you invited?)*

But this wasn't that kind of note; it was an exceptionally well-done caricature of Norwin. Not spiteful or mean, just accurate enough to be hilarious. He had a plume of cigar smoke around his head and a plaid shirt that rumpled in the armpit areas and stretched tight across the belly.

Peter had drawn this for her, but what was it exactly? Did it mean they were friends? Was it just meant to cheer her up? Or . . .

The dialer beeped at her that a call was incoming, and she cleared her throat, still smoothing the wrinkles out of Paper Norwin as she answered. "Hello, West Park Services, this is Valencia speaking."

"Llanfairpwllgwyngyllgogerychwyrndrobwyll," said the person on the other end.

"Pardon?" she said.

"It's a place in Wales." It was James.

"Okay."

"It's *very* hard to say."

"So I've heard. Why—"

"For your list. Of places to go."

"Oh. Are there things to do . . . there? That place you just said? Is that actually a place, or are you playing a joke on me?"

"Why would I do that?" James asked, sounding genuinely confused.

"I don't know," said Valencia. "People do that."

"To you?"

"No," said Valencia. "I mean, they have. You know. Just back in school. It was always my least favorite feeling, being the butt of a joke. People tricking me for fun."

"Huh," said James. "How about this: I promise I won't try to trick you. You can just assume everything coming out of my mouth is true, that I'm not trying to make you feel dumb or anything like that. Put your guard down for a few minutes."

"Okay," said Valencia. She wanted to ask him how she could be sure that the promise itself was not a trick, but she bit her tongue. What did it matter? This was a person who would one day pay off his credit card debt and never speak to her again. It was a good opportunity to practice some self-discipline with no real consequences. Louise would cosign that.

"Yes," James continued, "it's a real place, and as for things to do . . . I have no idea, but I've been practicing saying it all day. I think I did a good job."

"Sounds like it."

"Well, write it down anyway. It's a place, and it has a cool name, so when people ask you where all you've been, you can say, "Just here and Llanfairpwllgwyngyllgogerychwyrndrobwyll." People will definitely forgive you for only having been two places if one of them is Llanfairpwllgwyngyllgogerychwyrndrobwyll."

What people? she wanted to ask him. People never asked her where she'd been. People never asked her anything. "I'll write it down," she said.

"Liar," he said.

"What? I will."

"If you really meant to write it down, you'd have had me spell it. You can't possibly know how to spell Llanfairpwllgwyngyllgogerychwyrndrobwyll off the top of your head."

"Okay," she said. She obediently pulled her list from her purse and poised pen over paper. She adopted what she hoped was a light, jokey voice. "Please spell it. I have a feeling you're going to slip it into the conversation as many times as you possibly can, regardless."

"Of course I am. I didn't learn to say it so I could only say it once and have that be the end of it." He spelled it for her. Then she tried to say it, and he laughed, and she wished she had more things to say that would make him laugh. He had a great laugh. Her heart started vibrating at an even higher frequency. The combination of caffeine and conversation could actually be the death of her. The thought crossed her mind that it might be more than the small talk that made her heart beat like that. Which would be okay, she thought suddenly. This might just be a good opportunity to let a little crush bloom in her mind. She could enjoy it, and when it was done it would not break her heart. Because it wasn't *real*. Because he wasn't *here*.

Not like Peter, who was far too *here* to be comfortable. She glanced down at the drawing, and her heart fluttered again. This, she thought, was not okay. Could you do that? Organize your feelings into *okay* and *not okay* piles and get rid of one?

"So, question," said James.

"Okay."

"Is there a particular reason you're afraid of flying? Or is it just abstract? Or is that the kind of question I shouldn't ask my debt collector?"

"No, that's fine," she said, even though it really wasn't a question a person should ask their debt collector. Though most people probably wouldn't refer to the person who called to collect money as *theirs*. And having never really been anyone's anything before (besides her parents' daughter), she found herself settling into the title a little defensively, as though someone were waiting on the phone lines between them to take it away from her. Another debt collector or someone. She was James Mace's (debt collector).

There was a pause, and Valencia suddenly realized she had already been asked the question in question. "Oh," she said, "sorry. You asked why."

"Only if you want to say," he said.

She did want to say. She'd only ever talked about this with Louise, and was Louise even listening, except to dab squares in her weird little mental illness bingo game? "Well," she said slowly, like she was dictating something for him to write down, "I guess the reason I'm scared of flying is that I'm kind of scared of everything."

"Okay," said James, considering this. "How come?"

He didn't seem put off, and that gave her courage. She would say it like jumping into a frozen lake. She would let everything out before she could think about it; she would be fully immersed before it even registered that she was about to die of hypothermia. "So . . ." She stopped. This was not as easy as jumping into water. "Okay, so . . ."

James waited patiently.

She remembered one of her first conversations with Louise, when she'd talked and talked, thinking she made no sense at all, and then Louise, like a mental magician, had been able to condense the rambling, repeat it back to her, and name the thing she'd described so sloppily. Valencia had been amazed at this.

"My therapist explained it to me really well once. About, about my brain. About the way it works. She said my brain 'catches' images or thoughts and won't let go of them until my body does something to help it release them. And sometimes it's something almost . . . expected? Or, um, *ordinary*? Like, lots of people might be afraid of a plane crashing. But the thing that's different is that my fear is rooted in something very unnatural, unexpected—like, I might become consumed with the idea that the plane will crash because of something I've done or haven't done or have done but didn't do the right way . . ." And this, she thought, was the part where she drowned under the ice, her mouth making shapes, bubbles spewing out. James would now say goodbye to her and never call back. It had sounded so acceptable when Louise had said it, but coming from her own mouth it didn't anymore.

She paused, and James said, "Mmhm," like he wanted her to keep going, so she did.

"So then . . . to make the fear go away, I have to do the thing I didn't do or make up for the thing I did or . . . or sometimes I can't make the fear go away, and I have a panic attack, because the thing is too big; I can't do anything about it. Is this . . . ?"

"Yeah," said James. "That makes sense."

"But it doesn't, though," said Valencia. "Right?"

"No, it really does," he said earnestly. "I have a cousin who has OCD."

She felt her shoulders drop from where they'd been hunched up under her ears. He'd named it; she didn't have to say it out loud.

"It sucks for him," said James. "It's hard. People don't take him seriously about it."

Her mouth dropped open. "Right," she said. "Definitely."

"Sorry," he said. "I don't mean that I know everything about it or that I don't want to hear about yours. I just mean I at least have a reference point. I'm not like, 'Oh, OCD, where you get mad if stuff isn't in straight lines.'" He laughed.

He neither pitied her nor feared her and even seemed to be very close to understanding her. It was a miracle. Valencia wanted to cry. Here was a perfect person. The most perfect person she'd ever met. And she'd probably never get to actually meet him because he lived in New York, and they both had things keeping them in their respective cities and countries: for her, a fear of flying, and for him, thousands—maybe hundreds of thousands—of dollars in credit card debt. And besides, would he want to meet her? She was getting ahead of herself.

"Sorry," he said again. "I hope I'm not making you uncomfortable. It's such a 'people' thing to want to immediately relate instead of listen. I'm sorry. I do that."

"No," she said. "You're really nice to talk to. And it *is* nice, with something not a lot of people understand, to meet someone who gets it."

"Well," said James. "Good. I'm glad I can be that person for you."

Her whole head felt warm, like someone had lit her hair on fire. "Thanks." Her voice suddenly sounded loud in her ears. She cringed and looked around. Norwin was walking toward her, looking as though he meant to speak to her. "Sorry. Um, I should go."

"Okay," he said, used to her abrupt goodbyes. "Bye, Vee. Talk soon."

She disconnected from the call just as Norwin paused by her cubicle. "Valencia," he said, wheezing slightly from the walk over, "do you know where Murray went?"

Valencia raised her eyebrows at him. "Um . . . Murray?" She didn't know anyone named Murray.

Norwin nodded.

She shook her head. "I don't . . . ," she started, but he'd already turned to the man seated beside her and repeated the question, and this time he received an answer, then trotted away.

"Hello? Hello?" Her dialer had still been rolling along in the background, and someone picked up without her noticing. "*Hello?*" the voice said again, irritated.

"Oh, sorry, West Park Services, Valencia—"

"Yeah, West Lake whatever whatever. I know. You guys called me yesterday, asking for money, and I just wanted to say: I'm onto you. You're a bunch of ugly freaks hiding in a basement somewhere trying to scam people out of their hard-earned money. And guess what? I'm not giving my hard-earned money to a scammer. You wanna know how much I don't like scammers?" He began to tell her exactly how much he didn't like scammers.

Valencia was used to this, but this time she didn't feel like taking it. She wanted to be assertive. She would ask the person to hang up. She would threaten to call the authorities. She would say to the authorities, "A man called me."

And the authorities would say, "You work at a call center."

And she would say, "He called me an ugly freak."

And they would say, "Well, you are."

And she would say, "He said he wanted to kill me."

And they would say, "Honey, if you don't like death threats, maybe you shoulda gone to college and *become something*."

And so, as usual, she did not stand up for herself or alert any kind of authorities; she said nothing until the man finally hung up. She felt a sharp pain in her jaw and realized she was clenching her teeth again. She'd developed a click in her jaw in recent years, and at her last dental appointment Dr. Wojcik had asked her if she'd been particularly stressed out lately. He'd said she needed to focus on relaxing her jaw. "How?" she'd asked, staring at him.

"Well, just, let the muscles relax," said Dr. Wojcik, who had looked at her like she was the dumbest person he'd ever met. "Take a big, deep breath and relax. Try to let your mouth relax."

Relax. Just relax. This word is very self-explanatory. You are very dumb. I can't think of another way to explain this to you. Just relax.

It had never occurred to her before that her body was tense all the time. Relaxing it was hard, and it felt strange. It felt like a lot of work for something that was supposed to be natural.

But she'd worked on it every day after that. She hadn't seen much improvement, maybe she was even getting worse, and she wondered if all of that relaxing just wound her up even tighter. Like trying to open a jar but cranking the lid the wrong way for ten minutes until the thing was virtually unopenable. That thought made her feel panicky. Was it possible to get so tense that your body wouldn't be able to take any more air in? Could she suffocate trying to relax?

She remembered the way her shoulders had settled, just for a moment, in her conversation with James earlier. Too bad she couldn't do that on purpose.

She pulled out her yellow legal pad, but instead of writing an essay, she started to draw. It was a caricature like the one Peter had done, but of the man sitting to her left—of all the men at West Park, really. It was good; she'd always liked art, always been good at it. She just hadn't had any reason to do it in recent years. Peter's caricature was like a challenge, a stick poking at her comatose creativity.

She waited until Peter had gone for the day before nervously tucking the finished picture under his keyboard. She checked herself as she walked away. Was she being flirtatious? She decided she wasn't. Flirting was something you did for another person. It was a lot of things, really: a display, a show, an initiation, maybe an invitation. This was two things, and two things only: a distraction and an act of great bravery. But if he happened to be impressed, so be it.

CHAPTER FOURTEEN

Conor.

Conor was a big jerk, and I knew that going in. Honestly, though, there was a sense of exhilaration, after a day of traveling and wandering alone, of being out on a sort-of date in a strange city. I felt as though my soul had jumped out of my body and into someone else's, like the shell of me was still back home, living and working and carrying on its business as usual, doing all of the regular things that, it turns out, it didn't actually need a soul to do. Meanwhile, my soul was having an adventure—it didn't matter in the least who was sitting across the table from me. The point was not who was there; the point was that someone was. The most important thing was that I was.

Conor seemed interested in me at first and told me I had nice hair and a beautiful smile. He asked me a few preliminary questions about who I was and where I'd come from, but in retrospect I don't think he was even listening to my answers because when I told him I'd gotten up that morning, skipped work, and hopped on the first airplane out of Saskatchewan all on a whim, he just nodded and said, "Oh. I'm from Kentucky."

"I've never been there," I said. I guess I was, maybe selfishly, both-ered at having the only interesting thing I'd ever done glossed over like that. I tried to let him know by making bothered faces at my pizza. That was when I realized he wasn't paying much attention to the look on my face either. Instead, he was looking past my face, at the faint reflection of his own in the stainless steel of the pop machine behind me. He must have found himself fascinating; he couldn't look away. There was a pause in the conversation as he admired his bone structure, and then he launched into his life story, as though I'd asked for it by admitting that I'd never been to Kentucky.

"The thing about Kentucky is . . ."

It didn't surprise me very much. I found myself tuning out, not caring in the least what the thing about Kentucky was, imagining how I'd tell my friends at home about this bizarre evening. Describing the bike incident and the pizza parlor, the middle-aged man sitting just behind Conor who looked like a retired soap opera star whose name I couldn't remember, the cheese on Conor's chin, the way he ended every other well-rehearsed sentence with a brow furrow and a head tilt, like he was trying to appear as though he didn't know what to say next. I wondered if he'd practiced this speech in the bathroom mirror, pretending it was a TV talk show interviewer or a pretty girl who couldn't resist a New York musician. I pictured him leaning into his own likeness, like he did as he spoke to me, lowering his voice and smirking with smug satisfaction. I tuned in for a second. He was telling me about a girl he'd dated in high school. He had a gross half smile on his face; he talked through it with his eyebrows raised, shaking his head like he was constantly impressed with his eloquence.

"You look like her. Is it weird to tell you that? I mean, it's not like it matters; that was a long time ago. But I wrote all my songs about her back then. They were really good, even though I was, like, fifteen when I wrote them. Usually, fifteen-year-olds write really dumb love songs, you know? But, I don't know, I think these were good. They were so heavy."

It took him a while—he felt the need to delve deep into his angsty teen years for some reason—but his story eventually caught up to us, here in the present, eating pizza. He was playing a lot of music, had made some important connections, was recording. "Yeah, just, you know, recording a demo." He sniffed as he said it, stretched in his chair, and slung an arm across the back of it and shrugged. I could tell he wanted me to think that he thought it was no big deal, but I could also tell how much he liked saying those words.

"Recording a demo. Recording a demo. Just, you know, recording a demo." Into the bathroom mirror, combing his hair just so. I had to suppress a laugh, and he seemed to think I was smiling at him. He seemed to think I was impressed.

I bet the mirror never said, "Well, thanks for the pizza. Nice to meet you, but I've got to run." Judging from his reaction, not many girls did either. I left him there, sulking a little, after at least ninety minutes of one-sided conversation. He did not offer to walk me to the subway station. I did not care.

It was well into the evening by now, but the streetlights and crowds fooled me into feeling like it wasn't that late. I'd always thought it would be frightening to walk alone in New York City at night, but it wasn't. I'd been on my feet for hours, but I wasn't at all tired. These were the kinds of things about that city that made it so surreal. It was a city of this-should-be-happening-but-it's-not and this-shouldn't-be-happening-but-it-is and I-should-or-should-not-be-feeling-this-way-but-I-am-or-am-not.

I found my way back to the subway and rode it just as far as Times Square. I didn't feel like going to bed; and I didn't feel like being alone. I was not wrong in supposing that I wouldn't be alone in Times Square.

I walked up one sidewalk and down another. I was overwhelmed by the mass of people pressed into me from every direction and the flashing billboards that lit up the night sky. Costumed performers tried to get my attention as I walked past; groups of giddy showgoers and tourists poured in and out of the buildings, trickling along the sidewalk and pooling into happy little clusters on the streets. The atmosphere was beyond festive; it was hysterical. I watched the people in their circles, laughing too loud and yell-talking at each other. I was a complete outsider. A knot of girls to my right wore little black dresses and matching frantic looks on their faces. They seemed desperate to have fun.

(I'm sure Times Square can be fun when you're on the inside of the right group, but from my perspective that night, it felt cold and commercial and robotic.)

I was content to be invisible.

A drunk girl in trippy toothpick stilettos lost her balance and fell into me from one side, but it barely broke my stride. Maybe because she wasn't really there. Did having a million people around me count for anything if I wasn't connecting with them in any way?

I decided no, it did not.

I spotted a woman leaving one of the restaurants nearby. She appeared to be heading home from a late shift, still sporting a uniform and slipping into a jacket. I stopped her and asked what her favorite thing to do at night in New York was, and she gave me a tired smile and told me to take the train to Brooklyn and walk the bridge back into Manhattan. This was probably not her actual favorite thing, just the thing she kept in her back pocket for tourists when asked. But I was a tourist. So I did it.

After the roar of Times Square, I thought I'd be part of a great herd crossing the bridge, but I was wrong this time. I passed a few couples and a group of teenagers, but that was it.

I walked for a few minutes in silence and stopped to see what was around me. The view from the bridge was beautiful. The city skyline rose up; the lights from millions of windows hung like water droplets in a spiderweb. Traffic rushed past on either side just below my feet. A fire truck blasted its horn, and I could hear dogs barking from the city. The famous statue stood across the water to my left.

I felt sorry for her. She was an icon of freedom—her name was Liberty—but she wasn't free. Her feet were made of copper and stuck forever in a mass of concrete. I wondered if she was brave, if she'd go somewhere if she could, or if she enjoyed the excuse to stay put.

I stood with her for a long time in comfortable silence. I think she appreciated it.

After a while, I looked over and saw another woman about ten feet away. She had short dark-brown hair and wore a long green jacket. She was alone, like me, but she didn't seem to notice me standing there. She buried her head in her arms and leaned forward against the railing. I watched her back rise and fall and realized she was sobbing. At last, she looked around and spotted me staring at her. She sized me up for a minute with huge brown eyes and then scowled and went back to her crying. I didn't know what to do, so I just walked on.

The thing about New York is that it's like a fishbowl, except everyone is the fish, and everyone is also on the outside looking in. When you see a distressed person in a small town, you feel compelled to go to them, to ask what's wrong and if they're okay. When you see someone sobbing on the Brooklyn Bridge, you kind of take it as part of the scenery—why shouldn't there be some beautiful person crying on the Brooklyn Bridge?

Or at least this is what I've said to myself every day since, to make myself feel better for not stopping—that anyone passing by would've done the same as me.

It was the wrong choice; I know that now.

Mrs. Valentine examines her hands; she touches each finger on her right hand with the pointer finger on her left, and then reverses hands and repeats the action, like she's checking to make sure they're all still there.

"Oh my," she says, glancing at the clock. "It's getting late, and I told your mother I wouldn't keep you over supper." The sun is setting behind some smoke-colored clouds, and a tree branch begins to tap on the living room window as the wind picks up. It looks and smells and feels like it might rain again this evening.

"It's fine," says Anna.

"What I mean is," says the older woman, "I don't have any food here for you."

"Oh, I didn't—I wasn't wanting you to feed me. I wasn't expecting that . . . but if you have no food here, what are you going to have for supper?"

Mrs. Valentine looks unconcerned. "I'm not very hungry. I have some bread in the freezer."

Anna gapes at her. "You can't just have bread for supper."

"Precious girl, I often do; it's fine! I get up to so little in a day—I don't need much fuel for it."

But Anna is halfway out the door, saying she'll be right back. Her pockets are heavy with change.

She returns forty-five minutes later with two small grocery bags. The rain came while she was out, and she's soaked through. "I'm not a cook," she calls into the apartment, "but I'll make you noodles! I have some other stuff here, too, milk and eggs and some veggies." The grocery haul cost her more money than she'd made in her two visits combined, but she doesn't care. She can't stand the thought of old Mrs. Valentine, alone in an apartment, eating freezer-burned bread, talking to the chair across from her. "Where's your pot? You have a pot, right?"

Mrs. Valentine makes a half-hearted objection, but then she points to a cupboard full of pots and pans and goes and sits at her table, still staring at her hands.

"While I'm making this," says Anna, "you could keep telling your story."

"I can't remember where I was," says Mrs. Valentine.

"The bridge," says Anna. "The girl crying on the bridge. What happened to her?"

Mrs. Valentine sighs, becoming fascinated with her fingers once again. "She jumped."

I was walking away, and I heard an inhuman wailing sound, like wind blowing through a cave. I turned in time to see something drop into the water below, and the noise stopped as abruptly as a light switching off. It took me a moment to realize that the sound had been a scream, and the thing in the water was the girl.

The rest of that night is mostly blank in my memory. I remember that moment and know with some certainty that people came running, and other people ran away—to find a phone to call for help—and there was a lot of yelling and elbow grabbing and pointing down at the dark water. *There she is! No, that's just a log. There she is! That's not her either.*

Someone was crying, maybe more than one person, maybe me. The police came, and I'm sure I talked to someone and tried to be as helpful as I could be, but the next thing in my mind that I remember with any clarity is walking down a quiet street in the Upper West Side at four in the morning, shivering and trying to find the magic that had been there earlier that day. They hadn't pulled her from the water yet, as far as I knew, but I couldn't see anyone surviving that kind of fall. I couldn't help but imagine the conversation we would've had if I'd asked the girl why she was crying. At some point, the numbness subsided just enough for a healthy fear of the quiet, dark city to set in, and I found my way back to my hostel.

My roommates were asleep, so I moved around the room carefully, dumping my jacket in the locker and slipping into bed with all my clothes on, my purse clutched protectively against my stomach. You would think it would be hard to fall asleep after such a night, but it was as easy as simply closing my eyes. My mind just stopped. As abruptly as a light switching off.

CHAPTER FIFTEEN

The phone rang, and Valencia scowled at it. She was not at work; she should not have to answer the phone.

But, of course, she did.

"Hello?"

"Hi, Valencia."

"Hi, Mom." Valencia sat down hard in one of the chairs around the kitchen table. She leaned against the shared wall between her and her neighbor's apartment, listening to the music blaring from their place.

"Valencia, I'm calling to see when you're coming to visit Grandma."

"I didn't say I was," said Valencia, caught off guard. When had the question gone from "Will you?" to "*When* will you?"

"I know, Valencia." Her mother sounded like she was using a metronome to keep her voice at a steady pace. "But I'm saying you really need to. She's taken a turn for the worse. She barely even knows who any of us are, and if you put this off too long, you won't have a chance to say goodbye."

"Mom, you know why I can't come."

"No, Valencia. I know why you *think* you can't come."

Valencia took a breath. She remembered in high school when friends would talk about having screaming matches with their mothers, yelling awful things at them and then uttering cutting remarks as they stormed out of rooms and slammed doors. She couldn't imagine any of it, speaking to her mother in anything other than a calm, respectful tone. Her mother was the kind of soft-spoken woman who did not *demand* respect of anyone but compelled everyone to give it. Even her teenage daughter. Their disagreements had always been quiet, reasonable, discussed in depth, resolved, and then dissolved.

But now . . .

"*Excuse* me?" Valencia's voice sounded strange to her ears. Angry. Cutting.

"Valencia, everyone else in the world can drive on highways. You are not kept off of them by anything other than yourself."

These words echoed like a thunderclap in Valencia's head. She didn't say anything for a long time. "Mom. You *know*. You know what happens. You know how I get . . ." She tried to hold on to the anger because it felt good for a change, but it was slipping, like it always did, into other, more painful emotions. She had always been bad at anger; it was a fire she often saw springing up in other people, but it died in her chest before it caught, doused by hurt or confusion.

Her mother wasn't backing down; she sounded like she was also fighting a war between anger and hurt. "Valencia. You are on medication. You have all the help and support you could ever want. You have—you've *always had*—an easy life. And at some point, you need to just get over—"

"*Just get over . . . ?* What?" The anger reignited, and Valencia willed it to grow.

"Your grandmother—your *grandmother*—my *mother* is . . . dying, Valencia, and—"

Valencia could not help but say, before slamming the phone into its cradle as hard as she could, that she loved her mother. It was one of those things where if she didn't say it, she knew her mother would be in a car accident or fall down some set of stairs, and she'd spend the rest of her life regretting that she hadn't said it. So she said it, and she said it sincerely, and then she hung up on her mother right in the middle of a sentence about *her* mother dying.

In her career as a telephone debt collector, Valencia always marveled at the way disconnecting a phone line stopped a conversation. It wasn't like slamming a door, where either party could keep screaming through it. It wasn't like saying, "This conversation is over," which only worked if you were more stubborn than the other person. It wasn't even like turning around and walking away. It was the only situation she could think of where you could literally turn a person's voice completely off. It was also, she thought now, feeling guilty, grossly disrespectful and inconsiderate.

In the silence after she hung up on her mother, she realized the anger that had caused her to do so was actually self-loathing; the two burned the same but were intrinsically different. Her mother had voiced something Valencia knew to be true and hated about herself: she did have an easy life. She had support, she had access to help in any form she needed it, and she could afford to pay for it. She was privileged in every way. And yet, here she was. Afraid of everything. Sad about everything.

She leaned against the wall again, feeling low notes against her head.

Valencia wasn't sure who lived in the apartment next door, but whoever it was, they sure loved that song.

They played it over and over again, all day long; sometimes it got louder or quieter. At first it had annoyed her how paper thin the walls were, but over time it had become comforting. There was someone there. Someone close. Who it was didn't matter at all, but if she were forced to guess, she'd say it was an old person, because whoever it was had lots of visitors but never left the apartment.

Valencia knew the song by heart. It was a haunting song; it began with a simple melody, single notes that repeated themselves over and over, gaining momentum, gaining more notes and chords underneath them, building into a flurry of angry, minor-sounding scales in the middle and settling back out again. It was a story, and in that story, everything resolved. She liked that about it. Everything should resolve. Maybe art was people's way of making up for life, which never resolved.

She wondered what the song was about. It was about something because everything was about something. She wondered if it was about love. Probably. Not easy, happy, pop-song love, but the complex kind, the classical music kind. The kind of situation where a person falls in love with someone they can never be with, for whatever reason. Or the kind where a person has fallen in love with, say, two people, just all of a sudden, and can't be with either one of them for a multitude of very complicated, very personal reasons.

Maybe she would stumble across the song's meaning on her search for its name and composer—she needed to know these things because she needed to have it with her when she boarded the airplane. It was familiar, and she thought that if she had it playing in her headphones as the plane lifted off the tarmac, she could close her eyes and pretend she was in her apartment on a very windy day.

She rummaged around in her bedroom closet for her old tape recorder and made a short, low-quality recording of the music coming through the walls because she was too shy to knock on her neighbor's door and ask. Despite the volume of the music, the resulting recording was barely audible and full of other sounds—slamming doors, kids playing on the front lawn below her window—but you could make out the basic melody. That should be enough.

She headed to the store on Third Street that sold piano books. It had been there for years, but she'd never been inside. It smelled like moldy paper, and when she walked in, a bell tinkled above her head, and a cat shot out the front door under her legs. An old woman was hunched over the counter at the front, peering through the bottoms of her glasses at some paperwork. Valencia approached her timidly.

"What can I do for you, dear?"

"Um." She pointed. "I'm so sorry—I think your cat got out."

"I don't have a cat."

"Oh." Valencia stood for a moment, staring after the cat and wondering if there had actually been a cat or if her mind was playing tricks on her. For how often she tried to fool herself into thinking and feeling absurd things, for how impossible that was, she worried sometimes that her grasp on reality was the actual illusion, the actual lie. How many black cats that were not there did a person have to see to be considered unwell? She averted her eyes from the door in case she saw another. Or in case she saw Charlene standing there, glaring at her. She shuddered and pushed the tape recorder across the counter harder than necessary. "I have a question," she said, trying hard not to stumble on her words. "My neighbor always listens to this song—I hear it through the walls— and I'd really like to know what the name of it is. It's, um . . ." She wanted to convey its importance in a way that the old woman would understand. She wanted to say something profound, something that would resonate with this music lover and make her see how urgent the whole business was. *Sometimes I think it's about me? It's comforting? It's basically the only constant thing in my life that I'm not sick to death of?* "I like it," she said at last. "It's really, uh"—*there has to be an adjective for this*—"nice."

"Well," the woman said humbly, "I don't know that I'll be able to tell you, but I can sure try." Valencia pushed the play button, and they both leaned in to hear the song over the sound of the rattling air conditioner and a different piano tune played over the shop's speakers. It took exactly seven notes for the shopkeeper to recognize what she was hearing. Her face lit up, and she smiled knowingly. "Oh, this is a favorite of mine! It's Rachmaninoff's Étude-Tableau in G Minor. It's part of one of two sets of studies he wrote."

Valencia loved this old woman, whose face glowed as she spoke. She wanted to be this happy and inspired and kind when she reached old age but worried she'd just be a more severe version of herself by then.

The same way you'd get wrinkles on your face from making the same facial expression over and over, she thought, you could probably get wrinkles on your brain from thinking the same thoughts and feeling the same feelings over and over.

The woman leaned heavily on the counter with her elbows and slipped off her glasses, clutching them with both hands. She tapped them on her pile of papers and squinted at Valencia as she spoke. "Someone asked him once what had inspired the studies, since you can so clearly hear that he was telling some kind of very beautiful story, and he just said, 'I don't believe in the artist that discloses too much of his images. Let them paint for themselves what it most suggests.' I've always loved that."

Valencia loved it, too, because she'd always imagined the song was about her, and this information made her feel like she had the composer's permission to do that. She was listening to it the way he meant her to. It was about love, after all. The complicated, possibly sort of requited to some extent but completely impossible and undeserved kind.

A cup of coffee, a stir stick, and two little white packets of sugar were all neatly lined up on her desk when she arrived at work the next morning. Each item was perfectly squared and evenly spaced. Valencia very much enjoyed neatly lined-up things. Louise said it was neither an obsession nor a compulsion; she just liked neatly lined-up things. Lots of people did.

Who had done this? She looked around, and Peter caught her eye from his cubicle, lifting his coffee cup as if to say "Cheers!" *Morning.* He mouthed the word because he was on a call, then swiveled his office chair to face his computer screen again.

Valencia smiled, but it was a self-conscious smile. He'd thought of her when he was getting his coffee and gotten her some too? He'd known she took only sugar in her coffee? He'd meticulously placed the items on her desk so that all of them were equidistant from each other and so that the square sugar packet was exactly parallel to the stir stick? Maybe it was a message. The kind a man would send to a woman he thought was pretty or smart. *Here's your coffee. I've been watching you. You sure are picky about a lot of things. I love you, and will you marry me?*

She knew she shouldn't let him say things like that, even in her imagination. In fact, she wasn't sure she shouldn't relocate to a different part of the building. Unbeknownst to him, she was spending more and more time thinking of reasons they could never fall in love. It was becoming all consuming, as though he were pursuing her, like the annoying male lead in a movie who would not take no for an answer, forcing his love interest to come up with excuse after excuse why they could not be together. Asking and asking and asking. Flirting and casting longing sidelong glances.

Only, in real life, the only thing he ever asked her was if she was "okay." He kept his distance, respecting her apparent need for space. It was only the thought of him that pursued her.

She wanted to stand behind his chair and clear her throat. "Peter!" she'd announce. "I don't want space!"

And he'd stand, too, throw his arms out, and say, "Oh, good! I don't want to give you space!"

And she'd say, "Great!"

And he'd say, "Would you like to have dinner with me?"

And she'd say, "No! Of course not! I'd be a lot of work in a relationship. I'd be a punishment, and what have you done to deserve that?"

She couldn't even daydream properly anymore.

He was laughing at something the person on the other end of the phone was saying. He was always laughing. She wondered at his ability to be so lighthearted and happy at this job. She could often hear his booming voice bouncing off the walls of his cubicle when he was on a call. "No, no, no, thank *you*, sir!" and "No, no, no, thank *you*, ma'am!"

and "So glad I could be of help today!" and "These things happen, dude. You're on track now, though!" It was never smarmy or insincere; he just had this way of putting people at ease, of making them feel like he was on their side. People, even the people who normally hated debt collectors, seemed to love him. He was genuinely nice.

And that was why he'd gotten coffee for her, she realized. Because he was nice. Men like him didn't get coffee for women like her for any other reason. He wasn't trying to romance her. He wasn't even trying to be her friend. You didn't need to be someone's friend to bring them coffee; you just had to know they existed—which was a little depressing to think about, since this was the first time in four years that anyone had brought Valencia coffee.

The last person had been Sarah.

Sarah was an effervescent nineteen-year-old who'd worked at West Park for a very short time. Debt collection had been a between-semesters summer job for Sarah, a means to an end, and she'd moved away when she quit to study in Europe somewhere. They hadn't kept in touch, and this had been mostly Valencia's fault. Valencia was horrible at keeping in touch. She hated talking on the phone.

Sarah's leaving accentuated Valencia's staying. It made her remember being nineteen and thinking she'd work there for a little while longer and then head off on some great adventure and begin her life. All these years later, she was still at West Park. At some point, she'd started blaming it on Charlene's death. Sometimes it felt like everything could be linked to Charlene's death and to Valencia's culpability. Even the things that had happened before it, like maybe what she'd done was so heinous that she'd begun her punishment before she had even committed the crime.

"Do you sit here?" someone asked, and Valencia realized she'd been standing, looking at the back of Peter's head for an embarrassing amount of time. She glanced over and saw that the man who normally sat in the cubicle to her left had been replaced by a woman in a scarlet blazer with hair the color of airport coffee. She was hanging on to the divider between their cubicles, holding her hand in such a way that the enormous rock on her left ring finger was on display.

"Yes," said Valencia. How long had this woman been here? "Is that your desk now?"

"I guess," said the woman. "It's where they told me to sit. So we're desk neighbors, hey?"

Valencia nodded. This woman was intimidating in a different way than Peter had been. She was very glossy, polished—not like a model or an actress, but like the women who worked at the perfume counter in department stores. With perfect fingernails and silky hair and a face full of makeup that seemed difficult to move.

The woman smiled, and Valencia saw that her teeth behind the perfect lipstick were quite crooked, like someone had pushed them all to the front of her mouth. "I'm Grace," she said. She didn't seem to mind that her teeth were crooked. Her confident smile said, *I like them like this.*

Valencia was surprised to feel her heart dip back into her chest. She hadn't noticed its ascent to her throat at the thought of Peter's attention—not only his attention to her but also his attention to symmetry and ninety-degree angles.

"I'm Valencia," she said, sounding like a perfectly normal person. She coaxed her face into a smile, feeling proud of herself for ticking all the boxes. Maybe Peter had been a gift to her, the gift of a practice meeting so she could do it right and make an actual friend.

She scooped up the coffee cup and cradled it in both hands like they were cold even though it was summer. She held the cup up the way Peter had earlier, and the gesture seemed to be acceptable in place of a handshake. She often noticed that women, generally speaking, were less likely to aggressively pursue a handshake than men. A man would've stood there for a million years with his hand out, ignoring her cues just as purposefully as she sent them out.

Grace beamed. "Valencia," she repeated. "I'm glad they put me next to you. I get so nervous starting new jobs, but this place seems all right." She looked at the photograph on Valencia's wall. "I didn't know what to expect. I told my fiancé I was going to be a debt collector; he thought I was insane. But, I mean, it's not like I'm going to be here forever. I'm saving up a little extra for the wedding, and then I'll go do something else. Or nothing! I'll be, like, a housewife." She laughed, and the laugh came from the very back of her throat and threw her body like the kickback from a shotgun. It was surprising, and it wasn't, and Valencia liked it. "Just kidding," she said. "I'd rather die." Valencia leaned in, furrowing her brow. This woman was fascinating. She had a funny way of speaking that seemed a little put on. She tossed her head a lot, like an actress in a shampoo commercial. Or a horse.

"So, what do you guys do around here for fun?"

"We don't have fun," said Valencia. "We're debt collectors."

"Right," said Grace, laughing and looking around the room. "Which is hilarious, by the way. If you'd told me a year ago I'd be a debt collector someday, I would've thought you were crazy. It's just temporary, though. Could you *imagine* being here forever?"

Valencia opened her mouth to reply, but absolutely nothing came out.

CHAPTER SIXTEEN

When I awoke, my roommates were gone. The sun was shining right on my face like it was trying to wake me up, my locker door was wide open, and my jacket was missing. They'd left my backpack, probably because there was nothing in there that anyone would want unless one of them had forgotten a toothbrush. I was thankful I'd thought to sleep with my purse.

I felt like I'd been asleep for days. Maybe I had. Anything was possible. I imagined going to the front desk and having the manager present me with a bill for three hundred nights. I sat on the edge of my bed and stared at the wall for a while, thinking about suicide.

Not mine, of course—the girl's. I wondered why she'd done it and if she'd survived and if I could've stopped it. I even considered the absurd possibility that she hadn't meant to jump, that she'd slipped.

At that point, I hadn't yet been to a funeral; I hadn't ever really thought about death. I had a friend when I was a kid who talked about it all the time; she was obsessed with it and cried during class sometimes because she worried about her parents dying while she was at school. Her existence seemed sad to me, thinking about death all the time. (But then, I didn't—and still don't—think *not* thinking about death ever is any better, to be honest. Pretty much everything in life is about balance.)

Eventually, I became hungry. I wondered if it was wrong to be hungry when someone had died. I felt guilty about it. Nevertheless, I changed my clothes, brushed my teeth in the shared bathroom, and headed out again. A woman with neon-pink hair smiled at me. I remember thinking she shouldn't be smiling; I remember feeling offended on behalf of the dead girl from the bridge. I stared at her until she looked away. The world tilted sideways, and I was in motion again.

My feet walked across the city without much direction on my part. They took me to Central Park. I felt impressed, at the time, that my feet knew how to get somewhere so iconic. (But now I know how big Central Park is compared to the rest of Manhattan, and also how close it is to the hostel to begin with. How had I missed it in my wandering the night before?)

I crossed the street and entered the park with a great sense of purpose and also none at all. At points, I thought I saw the girl in the green jacket, and I realized, finally, that I was looking for her. I kept checking newspaper stands to see if she was mentioned. She was not.

I stood on a rock. I walked down a path. I bought a pretzel from a hot dog cart. I saw a horse pulling a carriage. I crossed a bridge. I went under a bridge. I sat on the edge of a bridge. *Who built all these bridges?*

The park felt so still, despite the multitudes of people it contained. Still, yet alive, buzzing. Like a sedentary giant with an active imagination. Just as it had the first time, the tipping earth delivered me to a very specific place and leveled out.

I stood on a great terrace. There was a fountain, a lake with turtles in it, a tunnel with music pouring out of it. That was where all the people were. It was the heart of the giant.

There was a wall in front of me, a temporary structure covered in colorful envelopes. A man sat on a folding chair with a table in front of him containing a massive stack of envelopes and papers and pencils. He was slouching, like he was self-conscious of the space he took up, even sitting down. He glanced around, making eye contact with random people in the crowd, smiling nervously. He didn't notice me at first, but when he did, his smile broadened. In this magical setting, he seemed like a funny little wizard. Was he the one playing the game, rolling me here? Maybe he could move time backward, give me another chance to talk to the girl.

"Hello," he said.

"Hi," I said. He flinched, like I'd lunged at him, and it made me jump too. We both laughed, and this seemed to put him at ease.

"Would you like to participate in a social experiment?" he asked.

I would. "What kind?" I asked.

"The fun kind," he said. "It's open to anyone who wants to participate, but it's preferable that you be in the city for at least a couple of days or more." I decided right then that I would extend my trip for no other reason than to participate in an unknown, fun kind of social experiment with this jittery little man.

The man was wearing a bow tie. He was sweating.

"I call it the Music Boxes Project," he said. "Like mailboxes, but not." He paused, searching my face for approval. "The way it works is one person takes a paper and writes a bit about themselves. An honest introduction. It has to be honest, but aside from that, it can be anything they like. They'll put the paper in one of these envelopes. On the outside of the envelope, they'll write their favorite song lyric. Anything that means something to them. They'll leave it here with me, and I'll tack it to the wall."

I nodded. His speech was well rehearsed; he gave it like a timid—or terrified—game show host. As he made reference to a piece of paper or a pen or the wall, he touched that thing with a trembling hand, looking to me constantly for confirmation that he was explaining it all well enough.

"These envelopes will hang here for people to read. If a person comes along and sees a lyric they connect with, or that they also love, or whatever, they are welcome to take that envelope and 'meet' the person inside. They will then write their own introduction and leave it in the envelope for the first person to find when they come back. From that point on, it's out of my hands." He grinned at me, proud of his project. He flinched again, but it was subtler this time. "Some people have exchanged phone numbers or met for coffee; others have chosen to remain anonymous and just communicate for a little while through their music box." He paused. Cleared his throat. His shoulders jumped almost imperceptibly.

"In short, you may either start a new envelope or look through the ones on the wall and see if there's one you'd like to answer. You are not allowed to choose more than one, and you are not allowed to change your mind after you've chosen. I also ask that you let me know if or when you leave the city so I can take your envelope down. Does that all make sense?" Now he looked anxious, almost apologetic. "It's just kind of a fun little experiment—a chance to connect with someone based on shared sentimentality, or humor, or intellect. I've found that people who share a love for the same music often have many other things in common as well."

I nodded and scanned the wall. It was beautiful; I felt sad that this man should feel the need to apologize for it, call it "just" anything. So many languages were represented there, letters and symbols I'd never seen before in my years growing up on the Saskatchewan prairies. The ones I could read contained lyrics from across all genres, and the writing ranged from shaky just-learning-to-print to pretty, looping script.

Even the choice I had to make here—to add my own envelope to the already-full wall or to answer someone else's—said something about me, I thought.

I decided to start a new one, so I took a paper, but then I stared at it blankly for a few minutes.

"This is hard."

"No," said the man with the bow tie, giving his head a few extra shakes. "Just write an introduction. Like you've met someone—in a park." He smiled. "A line that says something about who you are. Your age, your name if you want, physical features, a hobby. Short and sweet. Or long winded, if that's how you are. Just be honest."

I wrote a few sentences about myself. I wasn't sure if I was being honest. I reread them and asked for another paper. The man told me almost everyone did that. He wouldn't let me have one, though. "I don't want you to polish it," he said. "I want whatever you've written initially to stay there." He grabbed the paper from me and, making a show of averting his eyes to assure privacy, folded it in half and slid it into an envelope. He kept his fingers stretched apart like a musician performing close-up sleight of hand. "Now this," he said, "is the hard part. What are you going to write on your envelope?"

But it was actually the easier part for me. I'd had the same song stuck in my head since yesterday afternoon. I took the envelope back from him and leaned over to write the words from the Cake song Conor had sung the day before during my perfect moment.

He grinned and thanked me, clumsily, and tacked my envelope to the wall. "Come back any time and see if you have a message."

I visited an art gallery I can't remember the name of but didn't like it as much as the graffiti on the sides of the buildings that you could see for free. I had supper at a pasta place in Little Italy. I went to a Broadway show and cried through the whole thing. I looked for the girl in the green jacket everywhere, even though I knew it was a ridiculous thing to do. I knew I wouldn't find her.

When I came back to the wall the next morning, the man with the bow tie wasn't there. His chair and table were folded up and chained to the wall. I found my envelope anyway and peeked inside. I saw only one piece of paper, and I was disappointed for a moment, but then I realized that if someone had left me a message, they would probably have kept my paper, and this one might be theirs, not mine.

Sure enough.

I marveled at this as though I'd won something. Yes, there were a lot of people in New York, but there were also a lot of envelopes on the wall. Some of them had very compelling lyrics on them. Some of them were written in fancy calligraphy or had pretty doodles around the edges. What were the chances of someone singling mine out, and so quickly? I wondered if they'd been disappointed or excited when they'd read my introduction inside. I wondered if they were around my age, or if they were a child, or an elderly person. I wondered what we had in common, since we both, presumably, knew and liked the same particular song. I unfolded the paper and went to sit on the side of the fountain.

The note was even simpler than mine but much more exciting. It read, simply, *I rode my bike right into a woman yesterday while this song was playing and didn't get a chance to ask her name or properly apologize. What are the chances you're her?*

After writing my reply and returning my envelope to the wall, I sat there by the fountain for three hours. I'd forgotten to be hungry, forgotten to be cold. An older lady walked past and tsk-tsk-tsked at me for not wearing a jacket. To be fair, I was shaking like I was sitting on a washing machine instead of a stone fountain. Not from cold, but from anticipation and nerves. She came back fifteen minutes later with a blanket and wrapped it around my shoulders. I refused it at first, but she was insistent. She seemed like the type who was used to taking care of someone but didn't have anyone to care for now. I thanked her, and she walked off, happy to have been helpful. In recent years, I've begun to understand that feeling.

The man with the bow tie came and set up his table and chair in front of the envelope wall. He didn't seem to see me or recognize me like I thought he would, but he'd probably talked to hundreds of people the day before. How memorable did I think I was, anyway? I guess I just knew that what was about to happen would be important. I knew it with the same certainty that I'd felt when the ground had pitched forward and delivered me to this magical city. And it wasn't just a feeling or a guess. I *knew*. Maybe I assumed that all of the people around me would intrinsically know, too, just from being in my presence. As though you could tell someone's life was about to change by looking at them. I tried to remember if I'd had that sense about the girl on the bridge.

I watched another busker set up beneath the arch of the great structure in front of me. To my left, a group of preschool children, all holding hands, made their way onto the grass for a snack. Tourists posed for pictures, a man dressed as a mime performed a comedic routine in the center of the square, a couple stumbled past me, laughing so hard it was a wonder they could see where they were going.

There were so many voices bouncing off the curves of the architecture, so many heels on the cement; the water from the fountain provided a steady whoosh to fill in any tiny sound gap that might have remained. It seemed louder the second hour than it had the first, but by the third hour I thought it felt silent, like watching television with the sound turned off.

It was in this roaring quietness that I saw him out of the corner of my eye, and I felt the corners of my mouth stretch out to my ears.

I watched him walk his bicycle toward the envelope wall. He shook hands with the man behind the desk and pointed at my envelope.

I leaned forward, afraid that he would see me before I was ready to be seen, like I was eavesdropping.

I watched him rest the bike against his hip and open the envelope. He was still wearing his bike helmet; his hair poked out the bottom a little. His hands shook. When he saw the note inside, he grinned. The man with the bow tie said something to him, and he nodded happily and pumped his fist in celebration.

I think there's some kind of magic in witnessing how someone feels about you without them knowing that you are there. His face lit up as he pulled the letter out of the envelope, and his eyes widened as he read my response.

Chances are good. Coffee? Now?

I was so spunky back then.

He looked up, scanning the crowd. I held my blanket up to my chin for a second while I steadied myself, and then I let it fall back. I had relished the moments of being hidden and observing him from a safe distance, but now I was ready for him to see me.

We met for the second time. He held his hand out a little awkwardly, and I took it, and we engaged in a handshake that lasted for a long time because neither of us seemed to want to let go.

While he shook my hand (and shook it and shook it) he apologized, again, for the bruising on my face, which I'd forgotten about but which probably accounted for the extra kindness and the pitying glances I'd been receiving on the subway. I told him he needed to stop apologizing, and he apologized for that too. I noticed at some point that we were not technically shaking hands anymore, but still, as we stood there talking, our hands hung in between us like the knot in the middle of a tug-of-war rope, and neither made a move to let go.

He told me how he'd been riding through Central Park and come across this Music Boxes Project and how my envelope caught his eye. He said he'd known it was mine before he even opened it because of the song and the busker and our strange first meeting. "It's been that kind of week for me," he said.

I knew what he meant.

Without discussing it, we started walking. We walked through the trees, over all the bridges, and back out into the skyscrapers. We wandered down side streets and main streets and back alleys. He pushed his bike, the helmet slung around the handlebars. We must have passed famous landmarks—buildings and places from various movies and television series I'd seen and loved—but I didn't notice any of them. I was somewhere I'd always wanted to be, and all of a sudden, maybe for the first time in my life, I didn't care where I was at all.

We walked all day and through the night and out of it into the next morning, until I felt dizzy and delirious and like I had sand behind my eyeballs and in the bottoms of my feet. Still, it didn't register that I was tired; I thought, *This is it! I'm in love!*

We asked each other questions and told stories; we spoke recklessly, the way you do when you're not tongue-tied by nerves or vanity or fear. He was moving from stranger to friend at an incredible rate; the more I knew about him and the more he knew about me, the more the chasm closed. I told him everything. I told him things that would be awkward to tell someone I knew, but I also told him things that would be awkward to tell a stranger. The lines were blurring fast.

And this time, when I told the story of how I'd come to find myself in New York, it was met with a satisfying amount of interest and fascination. There's nothing like a date with a silly, self-absorbed man to make you appreciate a good, you-absorbed one.

"Do you travel a lot?" I asked him after we'd exhausted my story. It struck me that he might do trips like this often and was just pretending to be impressed by my one spontaneous day. I half wished I hadn't admitted that this was my first time on an airplane.

He was eating a hot dog, and a big drop of ketchup fell on the front of his shirt. The wind blew through his straw hair, and it looked, for a moment, like a miniature wheat field right on the top of his head. "It depends who you ask, really," he said, shrugging. "Ask my mom if I've been anywhere, and she'll go, 'Oh, heavens, yes, that boy never sits still!' But really, she just means that I go camping with my friends a lot."

I laughed. His impression of his mother was dramatic but full of affection. I thought he probably joked with her like that in person, too, and liked the thought of a man who said the same things behind his parents' backs as he did in front of them.

"Anyway," he went on, "I don't put too much stock in being well traveled. What good is going anywhere if you can't find joy in staying still first, right?"

I nodded, but I wasn't sure if I had ever really found joy in staying still; it was always only that I had nowhere to go.

(I think about that conversation a lot these days. I'm eighty-seven years old, and I've been still for years. I have a girl—you—to do my laundry and vacuuming. I couldn't *go* if I wanted to. The health insurance companies won't cover me to travel, and my lungs won't cover me to walk through the park. I have more health issues than I do dollars. But whenever I feel stuck, I hear Mr. Valentine tell me to find the joy in it. He still talks a lot for someone who hasn't said a word to me in almost fifty years.)

I didn't realize we were going to cross the Brooklyn Bridge again until it loomed in front of us. I hadn't told him about what had happened the night before; it had begun to feel unreal, like a dream—an awful dream, but one that faded as the day went on. Now it not only felt real, but it also felt like the scene was replaying. Like we would get to that spot on the bridge and the girl would be there crying, and I would have a second chance to do the right thing.

If only.

We paused to look at the statue; she hadn't moved an inch since the last time I saw her. I imagined a big stone tear grinding its way down her face and landing in the water below with a crash that made waves, pushing the girl's body gently onto the shore.

CHAPTER SEVENTEEN

Valencia had nothing in common with her new desk neighbor. Grace was like a blown-out photograph. She was bright, almost brash, not oblivious to her imperfections but unaffected by them. She was exciting, aspirational.

Still, Valencia wasn't sure about existing in such close proximity to someone like Grace. It was a bit terrifying. But then, it reminded her that things existed that were terrifying but somehow also *good*. And Grace certainly didn't seem bad—just extreme in every way.

In the end, it only took a few days for her to win Valencia over.

On her second day of work, she popped her head into Valencia's cubicle and said, "Hey, Valencia, can you remind me what the shorthand is for when you contact a customer but don't collect a payment?"

And Valencia, who had not been asked for help in her whole career at West Park, was happy to feel needed. "S-W, C-H," she said slowly, importantly, "N-P, C-B, T-M-R-W." *Spoke with cardholder, no payment, call back tomorrow.*

"Thanks, lady," said Grace, disappearing like a gopher down a hole.

She needed more help after that. And then she began to compliment Valencia on various things, like her earrings or her shoes. And then she began asking Valencia questions about herself and about the other people who worked at West Park. Of course, amid the questions and the compliments, she said plenty about her own life, her opinions and her fiancé and her hobbies. She was not terrifying, as it turned out. She was just wonderful.

The result of this, together with the daily phone calls from James Mace, a growing collection of silly but impressive drawings from Peter—which she kept in her purse—and the specter of air travel looming in her nearer-by-the-second future, was that the rest of June and the first part of July flew by. Time had never done anything but crawl for Valencia; it had never even walked before (she had, at points, wondered if it had lain down and died). This new speed was exhilarating.

It was now mid-July, the sweltering, sticky part of the year, and the women were sitting in Grace's car in the West Park parking lot—where everyone could see them—listening to rap music with all the windows down and the volume cranked up.

Valencia felt conspicuous with the bass reverberating through the soles of her feet and up her spine. It felt rebellious somehow, to be making so much noise, and it was a feeling that could not be described as delicious or thrilling, just itchy. Uncomfortable. She was thirty-four, not sixteen. She was able to acknowledge, with no regret, that she had missed her chance to be unapologetically loud in public. You could only really do that for as long as people thought you were too young to know better.

She couldn't claim to have ever known better; she could only claim to have been too distracted by certain facets of adolescence to even notice others. The distractions were, in no particular order, the impending death of herself or her loved ones, hygiene, Don, and schoolwork. Charlene, too—mostly—at the end. Rebellion hadn't even crossed her mind. It had not been in the perfectly ordered schedule she kept tacked to the wall beside her bed.

Her schedule had been like a string that held her limbs on; if something disrupted it, like vacation or illness, she'd come all apart. Her parents had worried about her, even pre-Charlene. She knew because she'd overheard them worrying once when they thought she was asleep.

They had been in the backyard and must not have realized their voices would carry through her open window, or that it was open in the first place, or that she was awake. Her dad had sounded angry, which didn't necessarily mean he was. "But maybe we should push her a little," he'd said. "Challenge her on this stuff. It's not good that she's so stuck in all these ruts. I caught her sanitizing the bottoms of our shoes again last night. At four in the morning."

Her mother hadn't sounded upset, but she'd replied quickly, almost before he was done speaking, which meant that she was. "Well, I agree, but I think if we push her at all, she'll just snap. She's like a glass twig, that girl. Maybe if we let her do her . . . routines . . . she'll slowly start getting better at some point."

Her father had burst out laughing, and it had frightened Valencia because it had sounded wrong—hollow, sad, and angry, like a scream or a sob disguised as a laugh. Like a little girl in a white dress in a horror movie. It was the ghost of a laugh she'd recognized and loved. "Yes, Meg, yes," her father had said, still laughing like that. "That is exactly how to deal with this. Ignore it. See if it gets better. Let our daughter stay up all night sanitizing our house and counting things and slamming doors and turning lights on and off and on and off and on and off." He'd sounded deranged, and Valencia hadn't known what to do, so she'd shut her window.

She'd kept her window closed at night after that. She'd tried hard from that point on to give the impression that she wasn't so fragile because she felt bad for making them worry.

Many years later Louise would draw the lines and connect the dots and patronizingly explain to Valencia that many of her compulsions to do with guilt and self-monitoring had sprung up in that time, her anxieties the seeds and the secrecy and suppression the soil. "Interesting," she would say, using a tissue to scrub at some newly discovered stain on her desk. "Don't you think so, Valencia?" But Valencia did not think it was interesting. She'd already made the connections. Louise seemed to operate off the assumption that Valencia did not engage in introspection of any kind, ever—which was, of course, absurd. Valencia almost exclusively engaged in introspection.

Sitting in Grace's car, Valencia drew a line from the memory to the shame she felt now.

She felt like a beggar, standing on a street corner with her hat in front of her on the sidewalk. Only instead of coins, her coworkers magnanimously tossed her their spare judgments as they passed by. She sat straight up with both of her hands in her lap—she had at first tried to slouch into her seat, cool and casual like Grace, but slouching was, apparently, an art, and Valencia had been cursed with one of those mothers who always said, "Sit up straight!" at the slightest bend of her spine. When she tried to slouch, she looked like she was sick or old, anything but relaxed. She'd have to practice slouching at home, in the mirror.

Grace, who always kept her metaphorical hat on and didn't accept any kind of personal assessments from strangers, was undaunted by the people walking past, like it didn't occur to her to even wonder what they thought of her. She wanted to spend her coffee breaks in the car, listening to music. If it was nice outside, she rolled the windows down. If her favorite song came on, she cranked it up. Her life was simple, very cause and effect. Lots of basic decision-making. She was probably able to open bathroom doors and shake hands with handsome men whenever she felt like it and probably didn't think of those things as luxuries. What a carefree way to live, only having to worry about problems that were actually problems, only having to think about things that were worth thinking about. The thought of this kind of freedom was staggering to Valencia.

The car rumbled beneath her, and she side-eyed the stereo. Here was yet another way that she and Grace were not the same. Grace liked music that sounded bossy; she liked music that was loud like her, music that marched. Valencia liked contemplative songs about love and existence. How was it possible for two people to have completely opposite reactions to the exact same combination of notes and vibrations and pitch and rhythm and timbre and texture? It was like a science experiment. You plugged in all those controlled variables—and there were *so many* of them—and the listener was the dependent variable, the one that changed everything. The whole experiment hinged entirely on the listener.

"Fifteen minutes is too short for a coffee break," Grace said, digging in her purse for lipstick. "I could use a *real* coffee. Not the gross bean water they make here."

Valencia examined the dash in front of her, which was covered in dust. She reached up without thinking and touched it, leaving behind a black spot. It was like pushing a button; her mind promptly supplied her with an image of a plump, spidery dust mite, grossly magnified. She was sure she could feel the microscopic creature in the grooves of her fingerprint, multiplying and crawling up her arm and into her ears. It felt like someone was shuffling a deck of cards inside her rib cage.

She realized that Grace had asked her something, and she hadn't answered.

"I'm sorry. What were we talking about?"

"Are you okay?"

"Oh. Yes. Yes, I'm fine." She would be fine; she just needed to get there. *One, two, three, four—*

"Okay. Let's go." Grace buckled her seatbelt and backed out of her parking spot before Valencia registered what she'd said.

"Go? Go where?" She stopped counting—and breathing—for a moment.

"To get coffee. I told you I need a coffee." Grace hit the steering wheel; the horn honked, and Valencia jumped. "You know what? Let's just not go back to work today. Let's play hooky. Valley! I have the best idea: let's drive somewhere out of the city, to some small town on the Number One, see if we can find a weird little small-town bakery." Grace pulled out of the parking lot and took the corner fast.

Breathe. Breathe. Five, six, seven, eight, nine. "That sounds fun, but"—*ten, eleven, twelve*—"I can't." *Thirteen, fourteen, fifteen*—

"Why not? We're adults. No one'll even notice."

Sixteen, seventeen, eighteen. Valencia usually felt better by eighteen. Eighteen felt complete, like the closing of a circle or ending a song on the right note. It was a hefty number but not too high—like twenty. Seventeen and nineteen were odd, and odd numbers felt wrong— barbed and jagged and dangerous. She had discovered this helpful number sometime back in her teen years, and it had never failed her before. She always felt better by eighteen.

This time, Valencia did not feel better by eighteen. She felt worse.

"No, no. Thank you, but I can't." She felt the dust mites in her lungs, on the inside of her legs, in the tips of her toes. The muscles behind her ears and all the way down her neck began to bunch up, and her stomach lurched. *Relax, just relax . . .*

"Come on, girl. You need this. A good cruise on the highway with the windows down—"

"I *know* what I *need*, Grace. Take me back! Now!" Valencia hadn't screamed in a very long time, and she'd certainly never screamed *at* someone. But her heart was pounding in her ears and her chest was cramping sharply, sending sparks across her shoulders and down her arms. Was she having a heart attack?

But she knew it wasn't a heart attack. It was a different kind of attack. She sat back in her seat, breathing deeply through the pain.

Grace pulled into a parking lot, and the women stared at each other for a moment.

"I'm so sorry, Valley," said Grace slowly. "Are you okay? I shouldn't have . . ." But she trailed off, and it was clear that she wasn't completely sure what she was apologizing for.

Valencia felt miserable. "No, I'm sorry. I have . . . a hard time with spontaneity."

"That might be an understatement," said Grace, but she didn't sound angry. She patted Valencia's knee, and Valencia looked at her, surprised. "Do you want to talk about it?"

"About what?"

"About, I don't know, *it*. What's on your mind?"

Valencia could not possibly explain about the dust mites or her fear of highways. "My grandmother died yesterday," she lied. Grace hummed and nodded and said she was sorry to hear it. It wasn't that big of a lie; her grandmother was going to die any day now.

"Was it . . . were you expecting it? I mean, was she sick?" Grace asked gently.

"No," said Valencia. "She stepped on her cat and fell down some stairs." Valencia didn't know where this came from—some colorful quadrant of her brain that wasn't getting enough exercise.

Grace turned the car around and drove back to work, and Valencia apologized for letting her emotions overtake her, and Grace said helpful things about how grief makes people act in strange and uncharacteristic ways. Valencia did not say out loud that this was about as characteristic as it got with her. Instead, she told Grace about her grandmother's cinnamon buns and was even able to muster up some tears for the show.

The tears were genuinely for her grandmother, even though she was not dead yet. But they were also for herself. She wanted to go on a road trip. It was such a shame that road trips required a person to drive on roads.

"I had to put my dog to sleep yesterday. I wake up this morning to an empty house, to the reminder that my best friend died yesterday, and then *you* call. And you want to take the only thing I have left.

My money. You worthless. Piece. Of garbage." The voice sounded flat and thin and cold, like a layer of ice on a lake. It sounded like its own entity—like it wasn't attached to a body. It was too thin to have breath behind it.

"I am so sorry about your dog . . ." Valencia couldn't keep her voice from breaking, and it frustrated her. She wanted to sound like she didn't care about this anonymous person. She wanted to be a professional and say, "Ma'am, I'm sorry about your dog and the unfortunate timing, but this money doesn't belong to you." But she didn't want the person to think she was heartless.

She'd always cared too much about the opinions of others. She had considered that this aching need to be liked made people like her less, that it would be stifling and repulsive to those she came in contact with, so she tried not to care so much—like a drowning person trying not to swallow so much water, as though trying would override the body's natural instinct to gasp for air. It was a cycle that left her lungs full of water they couldn't use and unable to take anything good in.

She was relieved when James was the next caller.

"I was wondering: Do you play any instruments?" he asked without even saying hello first.

"Used to," she said. "I took some piano lessons when I was eight or nine. I don't play anymore—but I read a book on musical theory recently. It was very good."

"Musical theory, huh? Whew." He said this like it was strange to read a book about musical theory. "What made you pick that?"

She wanted to say, *Why wouldn't I pick that?* But she could tell he needed a better explanation. "It was the part of piano lessons I liked the best as a kid—music is a whole other language, you know?"

"Well, yeah," said James, "but isn't that language just Italian? *Fortissimo? Crescendo? Allegretto?*"

"But I mean all the symbols, and the notes. The key signatures. The rests. I enjoy the fact that I can interpret a sheet of music more than I ever actually enjoyed playing the notes on it."

He laughed. "That's a good way to look at it. Would've made theory classes more interesting, probably, if I'd thought of it like that. Like code."

"You play?" For some reason this surprised her, though she didn't know why. Maybe because in her school days it had been the girls who'd played piano; the boys had played drums or guitar.

"Yeah," he said. "A bit."

A bit could cover a wide range of expertise, depending on who said it. She wondered if he were a concert pianist or something like that, saying *a bit* to be modest. Or maybe he could barely plunk out "Heart and Soul" but did so whenever there was a piano in the room, to the chagrin of everyone else present. Maybe that's what he meant by *a bit*. She hoped not.

"A bit?" she said. It felt important to know.

"I play at retirement homes," he said quietly.

"What?"

"My grandmother lives in this one down the street from me, and I go over and play for her and her friends. And I guess"—he chuckled, or sniffed, she couldn't tell over the phone—"I guess word got out, because I got a phone call from another home and then another. I have a circuit."

Valencia's face flushed, and at first she couldn't figure out why. Then she realized she was embarrassed. She would never be able to admit to this man that her own grandmother was on her deathbed and she hadn't even gone to say goodbye. She cleared her throat, trying to dismiss the thought.

"I bet they love it," she said. "I sure wouldn't mind if someone came and played piano for me."

"Well, someday," he said, and she wondered if he meant someday he would play the piano for her or someday she would be a decrepit old lady in a retirement home, and some other young man would come play piano for her. She decided that, were he attempting to allude to future plans and, therefore, to them having some kind of future in which said plans could be carried out, it would probably detract from the moment to ask him to clarify. She further decided that it was nice to just assume that he meant what she hoped he meant and to leave it at that.

CHAPTER EIGHTEEN

Mr. Valentine took me to the airport two days later. I needed to get back to real life, whether I wanted to or not—though I did entertain the thought, briefly, of just disappearing from it altogether. Staying there.

He said he'd come visit me.

For the next few months, we talked on the phone and sent letters and postcards. My workplace had just gotten the internet, and I acquired my very own email address, to which he sent short notes from his work computer: questions about my day and funny stories from his. As nice as that communication was, I liked the letters best. I liked being able to hold something he'd had his hands on just a few days prior—even if a mailman had touched it in between.

One day, I went to work, and there was no email waiting for me. I sent one, but no reply came. Concerned, I sent another a few hours later. Still nothing. Before leaving for the day, I sent a third.

I was in a terrible mood by the time I got home. I was concerned, but I was mad, too—and ashamed of my neediness. Maybe he was just sick that day; he didn't have the internet at home and wouldn't be able to tell me. Still, when you're in that beginning part of a relationship, it's hard not to be a little clingy, a little ridiculous.

I stomped up the stairs to my place and dropped my keys when I pulled them out of my coat pocket. From where I stood, fumbling to find the right key, I could hear the door buzzer inside my apartment. "Give me a second," I mumbled. It was probably someone trying to sell something, and I didn't care very much if I missed them. It was, considering my mood, probably in their best interest if they missed me.

It buzzed again, louder and longer, like the person outside was really leaning on it.

"Hold on!" I yelled. Mrs. Dziadyk from across the hall was just leaving her apartment with her ten-year-old son, and she looked at me with concern. I wasn't generally a loud tenant, someone to stomp up the stairs or yell into my empty apartment.

I made it inside, cheeks blazing from cold and embarrassment, just as the buzzer sounded for the third time.

I held the button down and barked into it. "What?" I exclaimed, fully expecting the person outside to say they had the wrong apartment number or to ask me if I'd like to buy some makeup.

"Will you marry me?"

I stood there for a moment, stunned. I couldn't think of what to say. "Who is this?" I asked, breathless. I knew who it was, though. People did not often propose to me, even back then.

"Me," Mr. Valentine crackled back.

"Oh," I said. And then I started laughing, and I couldn't stop laughing, and through my laughter I said, "Well, then, *yes*. Yes! Sure."

"And may I come in?" he asked.

And I said, "Well, okay."

There was a season of silence. A time of paperwork and planning and months and months of waiting and being stuck, him on his side of the border and me on mine, while the government sorted us out. We were stuck with a purpose, though, and I thought often about his words on the Brooklyn Bridge. I tried to learn to find the joy in staying still, and I think I succeeded, for the most part. But staying still is much easier when you know it's only for a short time.

All of the legal things we had to work through were like the elastic of a giant slingshot, which stretched and stretched and stretched until we thought it might snap and break, but then it—finally, suddenly—let go, and it flung him over the border and into my waiting arms. This time he didn't knock me off of my feet in the literal sense, but somehow, I still felt winded.

We got married at ten o'clock on a Tuesday night, a strange time for a wedding, maybe, but I'd always wanted a nighttime wedding. I wanted something that felt like a big secret. I always drove past churches and parks on Saturday afternoons and saw wedding parties getting their pictures taken. I didn't want that. I didn't want people to even suspect.

You only need two witnesses for an elopement, so we had my Mrs. Davies and her Mr. Davies. They stood with us at the very front of the church instead of sitting in the pews. I walked in to the only song Mrs. Davies knew how to play on the piano—"You Are My Sunshine"—wearing my favorite sundress. We said our vows and exchanged rings; the service was all of five minutes long. When the pastor pronounced us husband and wife, the little assembly cheered, and Mr. Davies yelled, "Kiss that bride!" This was met with four shouts of approval from all of us. Mr. Valentine's voice was the loudest. And then he kissed me, and everyone hugged, and we ran down the aisle and out the door and on to our next adventure.

I always thought marriage would be like the end credits rolling on a romantic movie. I thought the world would stop tilting for good, and we'd come to rest in each other's arms on the balcony of this little apartment and live happily ever after in comfortable quiet. And, for a little while, it did. And we did.

"Let's move to the living room," says Mrs. Valentine. "This chair is not comfortable for my bony old bum."

Anna smiles. "Okay."

"Besides," says Mrs. Valentine, "my living room floor is so nice and clean, bless your heart."

They sit on the couch beside each other. The chair across the room feels haunted to Anna; she can't shake the image of Mrs. Valentine talking to it so expressively, especially knowing who she'd been talking to. She looks away from it. "Oh, Mrs. Valentine, one question before you start again."

"Yes?"

"Did you ever find out what happened to the girl on the bridge?"

"Ultimately, no. Did that part of the story bother you, dear?"

"Well, yeah. I mean, I just want to know what happened to her. Before and after she jumped."

"It bothers me too." Mrs. Valentine furrows her brow. "A question for you, Anna: Do you think I bear some of the responsibility?"

"Of course not," Anna answers quickly.

"But I didn't tell her not to jump."

"You didn't know she was thinking of it."

"But I could have stopped her."

"But . . . that's just not worth thinking about."

Mrs. Valentine grimaces. "Well, worth thinking about or not, I do all the time."

Both women are quiet for a moment. Anna shifts in her seat. "So, you got married," she says finally, hoping that it's okay to leave the girl on the bridge, at least for now. "Then what?"

Mrs. Valentine smiles sadly, then sincerely, and Anna feels as though she can see her mind clicking from one topic to the next, like a TV changing channels.

When we'd been married for about six months, I found a word in the fridge, scrawled on a paper in pencil, folded in half, and balanced neatly on top of the milk carton. I read it out loud as Mr. Valentine pretended to inspect the cereal on his spoon. "Cappadocia?"

He looked up, a neutral expression on his face as though he had no idea what I was talking about. "Pardon?" He loved to be facetious.

"What's this? What's—where is—Cappadocia? I assume it's a place?"

He shrugged. "It's just fun to say." He took an extralarge bite of cereal and said the word with his mouth full. "Cappadocia."

A few days later, I found a paper tucked into my makeup bag. "Arashiyama," it said in Mr. Valentine's neat capital letters.

I found "Trolltunga" under my pillow and "Príncipe" in the shower, and one night as we sat on the balcony, I discovered "Fogo Island" tacked to the wall behind my head.

"What's this all about, anyway?" I asked. He shrugged. "Hey!" I hissed. I threw Fogo Island at him, and it fluttered to the floor between us.

"Just good words," he said. "Names that are fun to say. And . . ." He took a big gulp of coffee and squinted hard at Friesen Street. "Well. I've always thought that it would be fun to plan a trip based entirely on the names of the places, not reputation or travel guides or popularity. Just . . . like: Trolltunga." He said it like the word was an explanation in and of itself, but then he saw it needed more explaining. "It means 'troll's tongue' in English. Don't you want to go there? And when everyone else is talking about how they went to Florida to sit in front of water for a week, we'll say, 'We went to Trolltunga!' We'll say it just like that. 'Trolltunga!'" He threw his fists out to the side and shouted the word so that it echoed off the roof of our little balcony and made me flinch. I shushed him, but I was laughing.

"And did what? What does one do in Trolltunga?"

"Who knows? That's the exciting part. We'll make a list of places with good names; we'll go and go and go—until the money runs out."

"What money?"

He looked a little sheepish. "I've been saving up for this. For a long time. I have a bank account for it, for traveling. I got an inheritance from my grandparents when I was a teenager, I had a part-time job all through high school, I put all my birthday money in it . . . and so on." I raised my eyebrows, and he nodded apologetically. It was one of those wordless conversations we had sometimes.

You shouldn't go around having secret bank accounts.

I know. I'm sorry.

After a moment of contrite silence, he cleared his throat and swallowed more coffee. "I've wanted to do this since I was twelve. That's how long I've been saving up names and money. Now that there are two of us, it'll probably have to be a shorter trip, but it'll be a better trip, too, so it balances out."

Even before I could consciously decide, I felt the familiar pitch of the earth beneath my feet.

CHAPTER NINETEEN

August appeared all of a sudden. It was like a magic trick. *Abracadabra! August!* The anniversary of both Valencia's birth and Charlene's death, separated by twenty-one calendar squares. How was Valencia supposed to celebrate one in the shadow of the other?

Charlene had been twenty-four. Valencia's mother had called that August 3, pretending she wanted to talk about something else, and then she'd paused and blurted the news out, and Valencia had said, "Oh. That's terrible," and that was all. Because Valencia didn't know if her mother knew whose fault it was. Did anyone?

August had become, over the years, a tangible thing—not just a concept, not just a unit of time. It came in the night, on July 31, and hung in the air, evenly separated into smoky crystals like a thick, soupy fog. It was weighty and sludgy and disorienting and hard to walk through. She breathed it in and choked on it. She tried to make peace with it and failed.

Valencia always woke up on August 1 feeling like everything inside her was liquid, even the bones. She felt like if she let herself start crying, her body would cave in as it emptied out, and she'd end up as just abandoned skin and clothes on the ground in the parking lot at work. Someone might step on her, and they'd look down and say,

"What's this?" and someone else would look over and say, "Oh, that was Valencia. She was very upset, and she cried all of her insides out."

This year, it was all bigger and worse. August 3 was two days away. She still hadn't picked a destination for her trip and had been adamant with herself, with James, with Grace, that she hadn't bought a ticket yet because there were so many options, that she was having a hard time narrowing it down. Now she realized she'd been lying again. She hadn't bought a ticket because she wasn't going anywhere. The proof was in her work schedule—she hadn't asked for time off. August 3 would come and go, and she would remain in her chair, talking on the phone, and then she would turn thirty-five a few weeks later.

She stood beside her car, taking deep breaths with her eyes shut, counting to eighteen. She opened them just as Peter rolled up on his bike. He smiled brightly and slowed to ride beside her as she walked toward the building, his front wheel wobbling as he lost momentum.

"You okay?" The usual question. Not just the usual question from Peter; her mother asked her this question every time they spoke. Grace had asked it a couple times recently. For a moment, she held on to this: there were people in the world who, to varying degrees, cared that she was okay. She couldn't help but smile.

The voice within her countered, *Or you just look like a wreck all the time, and people don't know what else to say to you. Care is a very strong word to use here. Concern is good. Fear, maybe.*

"Yes, just tired. It's early," she said, looking at him out of the corner of her eye. His face was red again. "Thanks, though." He shouldn't have to feel bad for being so nice. What did it matter if it was pity or care? It was attention. She was not—had never been—the kind of person who needed constant, stupid amounts of attention, but everyone needed a little of it. And when it came from someone like Peter, it counted for extra. Her mother had to care about her by virtue of being her mother. Grace was the kind of person who could not help but care about every-one. Peter . . . well. Peter just counted for extra.

"Yeah, no problem." His front wheel shook again, "It's r—, it's r— uh." He put a foot down to keep from toppling to the side. "It's really nice out today, hey?" She felt her smile reach her eyes. When he spoke to her he stuttered and stumbled over his words and became exactly as awkward as she was. She'd always worried she had that effect on people, and this felt like proof—that her shifty eyes and thick tongue were contagious somehow. That her visible discomfort in social situations made everyone around her equally uncomfortable and unable to connect with her in any sane way. She was thankful Grace seemed immune to it. James was, too, but presumably this was only because he couldn't see her.

Peter dismounted and chained his bike up; she paused to wait for him because she thought she should after he'd waited for her. He turned to her and smiled. "Shall we?" he asked. She wondered if he'd forgotten to take his helmet off or if he usually left it on until he went inside. She nodded.

They walked in silence through the front doors, together but separate. Their faces fixed forward, eyes wandering to the sides now and then, in perfect synchronized step with each other but refusing to acknowledge it, all the way to their cubicles, where he gave her one more smile before sitting down. From behind her, she heard him say, "Oh, my helmet!" and looked back in time to see him fumbling with the clip beneath his chin. He caught her looking and gave a nervous laugh. "Forgot I was wearing it," he squeaked.

She turned away, but the image of his face caught in her mind in the way that only unpleasant things usually ever did. Without meaning to or expecting to or even wanting to, she burst out laughing.

It felt incredible. She couldn't remember the last time she'd laughed—it had been sometime before Charlene died. She thought of all the times she'd almost laughed on the phone with James Mace, like her heart had wanted to but she hadn't remembered how. She hardly knew the "how" of it now; it was just happening without her, like sneezing, like her body was trying to get rid of an irritant.

She turned again and saw that Peter was laughing, too, oblivious to the significance the moment held for her. They were laughing at him, but they were laughing together, and he seemed overjoyed by it.

She laughed harder and harder until she realized she wasn't laughing anymore; she was crying. Sobbing. Peter looked terrified now; he reached for her but stopped, maybe remembering her aversion to touch or maybe just not wanting to touch her.

"I'm sorry," she said, her voice garbled. "I am . . . I'm just . . ."

"Tired?" he said, like he knew she would need help thinking of a normal-sounding excuse.

She nodded thankfully.

He pulled a Kleenex out of his pocket and offered it to her, and without thinking—no small thing—she took it from him and pressed it against her face.

He smiled at her. "It's clean," he said. "I promise."

"Thank you," she said. She would go to the bathroom and wash her face in a moment, but it helped to hear him say that. It was a little miracle that he knew he should.

"West Park Services, this is Valencia. How may I help you today?"

"West Park Services, this is James. How may I help *you* today?"

"Mr. Mace," she said, so relieved she almost started crying again but trying to sound playful, like him. She'd gone to the bathroom and composed herself as much as she could but was dreading that first phone call of the day. This was a second miracle, on the very day she wanted thousands of miracles. But who was she to ask for thousands of miracles? Two was a lot of miracles for someone who didn't deserve any. "Can I help you make your payment today?" She still asked him this sometimes, to keep her guilt at bay. She tried hard not to think of the interest he was accruing by leaving his account untouched for so long.

He laughed softly, as though there were other people still asleep nearby. "Not today. How're you doing?"

"I'm fine," said Valencia. She always said she was fine when he asked.

"Okay," he said, "then I have something for you."

"You have something for me," Valencia repeated. She looked around the room, half expecting him to appear from behind a cubicle wall.

"Okay, bear with me on this one; it's a little ridiculous. But, as with pretty much everything, it's less ridiculous if you just go with it. Okay?"

"Okay."

"Okay. So, background: When I was a kid I wanted to be a lexicographer—before I really understood what a lexicographer was, I wanted to be one, just because I liked the word. I couldn't appreciate the irony at the time, but I do now. It stuck, too; in junior high when all my friends wanted to be police officers, I wanted to write dictionaries. I've always had this fascination with words—not grammar, necessarily, not always the correct usage of words in sentences—just the words themselves, how it feels to say them or the mental pictures they conjure. I collected them, like other people collect stamps or whatever. I'd fill pocket notebooks with words or write them on sticky notes and tack them to the bulletin board in my bedroom. Then I moved out on my own and words took over my whole apartment, just because I could let them. There are sticky notes everywhere—on the windows, on the kitchen counter, on the walls, on my bedside table. It's kind of a dumb hobby, but you need a good, dumb, eccentric hobby, I think. I heard somewhere that eccentric people live longer."

"Okay," said Valencia, picturing her own life stretching on and on ahead of her, even more vast and endless than she had previously supposed. *I'm so eccentric I might be immortal*, she thought miserably.

"Anyway, all that to say: today I picked a few words off the walls and decided I'm going to read them to you. It's like . . . a lexical bouquet. Please enjoy." He cleared his throat in an exaggerated manner. "Number one: *pyrophoric*. Capable of spontaneously igniting in the air."

Valencia leaned onto her desk and placed her chin in her hands. She was touched; she'd never received a bouquet of any kind before. She thought of him sitting in his apartment like it was a field of wildflowers, selecting the most beautiful words with her in mind. She pictured a piece of confetti fluttering down from the sky and bursting into flame with a soft pop. *Pyrophoric*.

"*Efflorescence*," he said next. "The state of flowering. Or—I like the second definition better—an example or result of growth."

He went on like that.

Gossamer.
Evanescent.
Chrysalism.
Lilt.
Erstwhile.
Pyrrhic.
Eunoia.
Velleity.
Enouement.
Paroxysm.

As she sat in the place where she was going to die, looking at the painting of the bird on the hat and listening to James Mace read his list of words—twelve in total—a smile spread across her face, and she wondered, briefly, if you could marry someone over the phone, could have a successful long-term relationship with someone that way. She wouldn't have to meet him, ever.

Wouldn't have to touch him.

Couldn't meet him or touch him.

He was easy to talk to because he couldn't see her, couldn't see her compulsions playing out, didn't make that concerned face at her.

She frowned. Because now she was thinking about laughing with Peter. Passing pictures back and forth. Him giving her a Kleenex, being able to read on his face that he cared—and he did care, she knew that now. Because she had *seen* it. And as hard as she'd always worked at convincing herself that she didn't want that or didn't deserve it or that it was safer not to have it, she couldn't help but wish for it now and then.

"So that's that," he said, interrupting her thoughts. "Was it weird? It was weird, wasn't it?"

"Yes, and I loved it," she said. "I'd take a bouquet of words over a bouquet of flowers any day." There was a tremor in her throat as she said *flowers*, a bit of the laughter from earlier left over in there, maybe. A tiny bolt of lightning that traveled down her spine.

"Cool," he said, sounding relieved. "And now tell me: How are you today, actually?"

"Fine," said Valencia, even though she knew he knew she wasn't.

"Okay," he said. "You just sound sad today. No pressure to tell me all your secrets, but I'm a listening ear if you need."

A listening ear sounded nice. Louise knew about Charlene, technically, but Valencia wasn't even sure Louise remembered. Louise heard so many people's stories in a day. Valencia could tell James Mace, and she wouldn't have to see judgment on his face, or disappointment. It would be like taking the story out of her head and throwing it into a hole, wouldn't it? And the last time he'd asked her to open up, he'd proved himself a worthy confidant.

"A friend died in two days," she said finally. "I mean . . . that makes no sense. Two days from now is the anniversary of her death. Several years ago now."

"Ah," he said. "I'm sorry."

"No, don't say sorry to me. It was my fault."

James Mace didn't respond. Valencia noticed her hands were quivering and that she hadn't taken a breath in a while.

She decided she wasn't going to say any more, but when she opened her mouth to tell him that, the whole story tumbled out instead.

CHAPTER TWENTY

Charlene moved to the city halfway through eleventh grade and found herself, unfortunately, in my classroom. She came in right before the bell rang on her first day, clutching her backpack in front of her instead of wearing it. She'd outlined her eyes in black and her lips in red, as though with thick crayons, and she'd sprayed her very short brown hair into a sticky, immovable clump, even though it probably would've sat obediently on her head like that, like a taxidermied squirrel, without any extra help. She stood just inside the door, licking her lips and rubbing them together and waiting, it seemed, for someone to come talk to her. No one did. She probably felt hopeful that day, anxious to make friends, maybe to try out a new persona or get rid of an old reputation. She rubbed one of her eyes and suddenly looked like she'd been in a fistfight.

My best friend was a rich girl named Bethany. Bethany was beautiful. She'd already dated all of the boys in our grade by the time we hit high school—lots of them more than once. She was mean, too, but we were all mean. Every one of us. (I hate when people talk about high school like there were good people and evil people, because that's not how it works. It's like the rest of humanity: there are nice people who are mean sometimes, and there are mean people who are nice sometimes.)

Bethany hated Charlene right away. I didn't know why, and she never outright said she did, but you could tell. A look, a comment that could be taken a number of ways, a tone when she spoke to Charlene that she usually reserved for the English teacher, who she also hated. Sometimes she made Charlene cry, and then she'd act shocked and irritated, like she didn't have a clue why Charlene was being such a baby. It made Charlene look stupid, and that was all it took for everyone else to hate her too.

We made a monster out of her in our minds. The Charlene I remember was very ordinary. She certainly wasn't stylish, hadn't grasped the rules of hair and makeup yet, but she wasn't garish or shocking in any way.

But the Charlene we loved to hate had a tiny head. She had massive hands and huge red ears. We picked her apart, *tore* her apart, and re-created her. I've always wondered if she saw herself the way she was or the way we told her she was in whispers she was meant to overhear, in notes she was meant to intercept, and, eventually, in plain, impolitic English as she walked down the locker gauntlet every morning. The torture of Charlene was like a quiet spring rain that gradually became a torrential downpour.

We were all really good at justifying our behavior or disregarding it completely.

She was kind of asking for it, you know? She was kind of a know-it-all. She kind of looked at you like she was better than you. She was dumb, and she didn't pick up on things. Those clothes, that hair, that lipstick. She had a weird laugh . . .

Besides, other kids got picked on, too—I got picked on. Even Bethany got picked on sometimes.

Everyone was mean; everyone was a teenager. Being a teenager was hard.

But maybe deep down we all knew there was a difference. The difference was that Charlene was never allowed up to breathe. Everyone got dunked, but we held her under. And I was the one who killed her, because I was the one whose hand was on the back of her head when she ran out of air.

It was the Christmas party in our senior year. Our whole class was there because it was also a farewell party for a girl whose family was moving to the States. Charlene was there too. The outright bullying had tapered off at the beginning of the year, maybe because we'd grown up a little, but more probably because Charlene had shrunk into a tiny little ball of a person that made her a harder target to hit. She didn't speak up in class, and she didn't hang around in the hallways at recesses. She had headphones on and a book in front of her face at all times. You couldn't catch her eye, no matter how hard you tried. But she was at that party, and I still don't know why.

A bunch of us were in the kitchen. The kid whose house it was had two doctor parents, so the kitchen was the size of my house's whole main floor. Some of the girls were clustered around the bar making drinks; people were coming in and out of patio doors that led to the backyard, and the music was turned way up. There were people everywhere, on the floor, on the counters. Charlene was sitting in a corner scowling. Like she didn't want to be there. And it bugged me, for some reason. Why was she there if she didn't want to be?

I was sitting on a barstool talking to a friend when the patio door slid open and my ex-boyfriend walked in. He wasn't in our class, but he was good friends with a lot of the guys who were. I figured one of them must have invited him. We'd broken up—he'd dumped me—two days before, and I was still deep in the postbreakup grieving process. He'd said he wouldn't be at the party. But there he was.

I saw him scan the room, pointedly avoiding me. Then he walked over to Charlene. I heard him introduce himself and ask if he could sit with her. Suddenly, it was like she transformed in front of my eyes. Her slender frame, her short brown hair, her delicate features on that perfect little head—she was gorgeous. I hadn't noticed, but someone else had.

The night wore on, and he didn't leave her side. He drew a smile out of her, and then another, and then he had her laughing. I hadn't seen her laugh since she was new to our school. I couldn't take my eyes off of them. I was miserable.

At three a.m. there was something exciting happening in the backyard; I never found out what it was, and I didn't care at the time. Most of the boys and some of the girls filtered out there to watch, and Charlene was alone again, but now she looked happy, content in her corner, waiting for Don to come back. That's when Bethany called over to her. "So, Charlene. What's with you and Don?"

She shrugged. "Nothing. I just met him."

"No, no, you met him six hours ago. I saw this happening. You guys are, like, *old friends* now."

Charlene was cornered. Everyone in the kitchen was suddenly in the conversation. She looked at me, and I realized then that she *knew* she'd been sitting there flirting with my newly ex-boyfriend. It didn't occur to me before that she would know. She'd been so absent, so ghost-like at school, that I kind of forgot she would be aware of what was going on around her, what was going on with her fellow classmates.

The worst part was everyone else was looking at me too. They wanted to know what I thought of the whole thing. *Charlene. Charlene is the one Don has chosen to replace you. Two days later.*

I hated her so much right then, and I know now how irrational that hatred was. But in that moment, it was like she'd done it on purpose. Like she'd stolen him from me. Like there'd been a chance of us getting back together before she'd sneaked in.

Bethany leaned forward and raised her eyebrows at me before turning to Charlene. "Do you like him?"

Charlene shook her head. "I seriously just met him," she said. But she was blushing.

"You know he, like, *just* dumped Vee, right?"

Charlene nodded uncomfortably, biting her nails. "I swear I'm not trying to start anything."

I couldn't take it anymore. This was humiliating. "Whatever, if you are," I said. "I don't care. He's probably just trying to make me jealous. I mean, why *else* . . ." I stopped. I hated myself for saying that. I was not usually someone who said horrible things out loud. I laughed at horrible things other people said, and that was bad, too, but I think I felt morally superior for not being the ringleader. The other girls in the kitchen snickered, and Charlene stood up and slunk off to the bathroom. Anyone else would've stormed away, but Charlene didn't have fire like that in her anymore; she'd been under water for too long. She had blotches around her eyes, and her mouth was puckered.

I was on the verge of tears too. Bethany grabbed my arm and hauled me out of the kitchen, toward where Charlene had gone. "Come here, hon," she said. She always called me pet names like hon and dear, and it was infuriating, especially in that moment.

"Where are we going?"

"I don't know. Out." She pulled me down the hallway to the staircase by the front entryway and sat on it, patting the step beside her. "Breathe, Vee," she said as I slumped down. "You look like you're going to blow up. He's just a stupid guy. It's just stupid Don. And stupid Charlene. Stupid Charlene with the tiny head."

I laughed when she said this, in spite of myself. It felt good, even if it was not good, to unite against someone else when I was feeling awful. "Stupid Charlene with the tiny head," I mumbled back, consoling myself.

"Char, Char, hit her with a car!" chanted Bethany suddenly, swinging her arms around like she was leading a choir. She had been drinking, a lot. I burst into a fit of giggles at the rhyme. In that moment, it was the funniest thing in the world to me.

"Throw her in the water, where all the fish are!" I yelled back, watching Bethany's eyes widen at my clever addition. She doubled over.

"Yes!" she howled. "*Yes!*"

So I kept going because it felt so, so good. "Hit her with a shovel, on her stupid head! She's better off not here, better off dead!"

The rhyme was mean, but it wasn't how I felt. No matter how mad I was, it wasn't how I felt. I knew somewhere inside that I wasn't mad at Charlene; I was hurt by Don, and I was jealous of Charlene, and I was embarrassed by Bethany. But I was a stupid teenager who couldn't work all that out at the time. My brain landed on Charlene like a tire in a deep rut on a dirt road, and I pushed the pedal all the way down.

I would find out later that Charlene had more issues than a bunch of idiot kids making her life miserable at school—she had an abusive, alcoholic father who picked fights with her over ridiculous things and a very sick mother who didn't stand up for her. When I found those things out, I wished I'd known—like I'd have treated her better if only I'd known her homelife sucked so much. But what kind of person did that make me, if I needed a good reason not to make up a song about murdering someone?

Bethany, still laughing and clutching her belly, shrieked, "I am going to *puke!*" She swung herself off the staircase in the direction of the bathroom, stumbled forward, and shrieked again as she ran into Charlene, who'd just come out of it. She froze, then lunged toward the bathroom again. Charlene stood there for a long time. Her face wasn't screwed up anymore; now it was frozen and white. That was when, in hindsight, I knew I'd killed her.

"Better off dead," she said in a flat voice. I wasn't sure if she was talking to me or not. "Maybe." And then she turned and walked out the front door.

According to the news the next day, she visited her house briefly before driving down the road to the train bridge. She left her car parked at the bottom, climbed up, jumped off. A bystander had seen it but hadn't been able to stop it. Or hadn't even tried.

She lived the next six years as a paraplegic and passed away due to complications—I don't even know what kind of complications—on August 3. She was twenty-four. My mom called me that morning and pretended like she was calling about something else, but at a pause in the conversation she said, "Oh, I have some sad news. Do you remember that little girl who was in your class for a little while in high school? The one who jumped off Cherry Hill Bridge? Charlene?" And I acted like I didn't for a moment and then said at last that maybe I did, and she said, "She died this morning. There were complications, and she hasn't been doing well for the past few months; I guess she finally slipped away."

And I said, "Oh. That's terrible."

CHAPTER
TWENTY-ONE

"That's not the same as killing someone," James said. "It wasn't your fault, what she did." This logic was simultaneously maddening in its simplicity and also what Valencia desperately needed to hear.

She sighed. "I don't know." She wished she could suck the whole story back in. She'd thought it was going to make her feel good to get it out, but it wasn't any better on the outside of her brain. It was worse. It felt even more real than it ever had.

Neither of them said anything for a minute. Then James said, "*Oh. August third.*"

Valencia didn't say anything.

"You planned your trip for the anniversary."

"Mmhm."

They were both quiet again. She could hear her pulse in her ears. James broke the silence. "Not to change the subject—"

"Oh, please do."

"Have you decided where you're going?"

"Yes," she lied.

"Oh, wow," he said. "That's so great. So cool. I'm glad you're doing this. Especially now that I . . . you know . . . know more of the reasoning behind it."

"Me too," she said. She was thinking about everything all at once. August. August 3. James Mace. The bouquet. Turning thirty-five. You didn't get a bouquet of any kind for someone you didn't like, did you?

"So?" he said. "Where are you going?"

You didn't call someone every single day if you didn't think of them in that way, did you? He knew about her anxiety, her OCD, and he was still there. *Charlene.* He knew about Charlene, and he was still there. He was still talking to her; that was unexpected. Airplanes. That gorgeous velvet voice.

"New York," she said. "I'm going . . . coming . . . to New York." It was a declaration. It was almost a marriage proposal.

"Oh," he said. She thought he sounded disappointed, and that surprised her.

"Oh?" she said.

"Uh," he said, "I . . ."

"Maybe I'm not?" she said. She couldn't help the quaver in her voice.

"Well," he said, "I just don't think . . . I didn't realize . . ." He didn't sound disappointed anymore; he sounded terrified. "You can't."

"I *can't.*"

"Listen, Valencia—"

"Never mind," she said, and she hung up. She had thought she knew what it meant to be humiliated. *Apparently not.*

Someone was tapping on her shoulder, so lightly that she might have missed it if her nerve endings had not all been on alert, all reaching outward, looking for some kind of explanation for the sudden switch in emotion. The fingertips felt like a spider crawling across her sleeve, and at first she thought that's what they were. But when she turned, it was Florence, the secretary.

She couldn't remember the last time she'd spoken to Florence—probably when she started, to sign whatever papers needed signing and fill out whatever forms needed filling out. She'd been old, Valencia had thought, but she looked younger now, even though over a decade had passed. Her hair was shorter, dyed to hide the gray, and that must have been all it took. She smiled, crinkly eyed, at Valencia and pressed on her shoulder. She spoke softly, sweetly, and in one big breath without any pauses, but with sharp staccato breaks between each syllable.

"Hello Valencia sorry to bother but I have a message for you your mother phoned and would like you to call her back as soon as possible please at this number." She handed Valencia a sticky note with a number written inside a bubbly heart. "She said to tell you it was urgent."

Valencia didn't have to call the number to know what the call was about.

She must have looked as shaken as she felt because Peter appeared at her side instantly, asking if she was okay and if he could get her some water and looking concerned, and then Grace was there too. Valencia spent a few minutes trying to reassure both of them that she was fine, just a little tired today, and then Norwin appeared at her side and sent them both back to their cubicles in a display of authority no one had ever seen from him before. "Valencia," he mumbled through the straggly hairs of his unkempt beard, "you look sick. Maybe you should go home."

Valencia looked up at him in surprise. "I'm fine," she said. But tears streamed down her cheeks for the second time that day, and this time she couldn't stop them.

"No, I don't think you are," he said and then, more firmly, "Go home, Valencia." He looked so sincere and concerned that Valencia couldn't refuse.

As she pulled out of the parking lot, it occurred to her that she hadn't actually called her mother back. Her mother, whose own mother had presumably, finally, passed away. Valencia should have stopped at the office on her way to her car. Her mother would be sitting by the phone, crying, waiting for her daughter to call. And now she would have to wait at least fifteen minutes more. Fifteen minutes is a long time when you're grieving, because every one of those minutes is stretched out to hold all the regrets and memories and sadness inside of it.

By the time she got back to her apartment, she was running a fever. She knew that her brain and body were connected, but it still always amazed her that her thoughts and feelings could manifest themselves physically so quickly. That sadness or anxiety could gather in the pit of her stomach and somehow *become* vomit.

She made it up the stairs to her place and headed straight for the phone, which suddenly seemed to be at the end of a long, spinning, slanted tunnel. When her mother picked up—after three excruciating rings—her voice was small and sad, and Valencia felt disoriented, like she was a mother calling a daughter and not the other way around.

"Valencia?" said her mother. "Did you get my message?" As though Valencia might have just happened to call out of the blue.

"Yes," said Valencia. Her mother didn't say anything back to her for a long time after this, and Valencia wondered if she should remind her mother that the message had simply been to call home, that there had been no actual content. "Is everything okay?"

"Valencia, Grandma's gone."

Valencia couldn't think of the right response. *I'm sorry. I'm so sad to hear that. What do you mean, gone?* What was she supposed to say?

"Are you coming to the funeral?"

This should not have been a difficult question, but Valencia was having a hard time processing it; she had not been given enough time in between *Grandma's gone* and *driving on the highway.* It felt unfair, like she had been handed a box of bricks and then asked to run up twenty flights of stairs. She blinked stupidly at the fridge.

"Of course you're not," said her mother, still playing the part of the daughter, her voice juvenile and bitter. "Of course you're not—I should've known."

This was twenty more flights of stairs. Valencia wondered for a moment if she'd said something out loud without realizing it. Had she *said* she wouldn't be going to the funeral? She heard herself whimper into the phone, aghast at her inability to speak to the one person she'd never had trouble speaking to before.

"When I die, Valencia, are you going to bother to come to *my* deathbed? Would you *drive* to my funeral? Do I mean enough to you?" Her mother was having a full-on meltdown. She was berserk. Her voice, which had once tiptoed so carefully to Valencia, was kicking at her now.

And then the line was silent, buzzing quietly, and Valencia realized her mother had hung up on her. And she had not said "I love you" first. And Valencia had not had a chance to say it either. She dialed her mother's number, desperate at the very least to say the words, for her mother to hear them, but no one picked up.

She called over and over and over, letting it ring until the answering machine kicked in each time. Finally, she left her three-word message on the answering machine, hoping that would be good enough.

She wandered into the living room and put a movie on. She watched it all the way through, and when it was over, she began it again. She slept through most of the third viewing, but by the fourth she'd begun to care deeply about the characters, having spent so much time with them.

They had so many problems, these fictional friends, but they were problems that would never happen to anyone in real life and resolved every ninety minutes, like clockwork. They were problems with a great soundtrack—one that all but drowned out the piano music from next door. They were fireworks, dazzling and dramatic, but also carefully planned out and perfectly executed, a thrill, a display of danger that wasn't actually dangerous.

Real people's problems were just boring and messy and cyclical—they never actually resolved. They morphed, repeated, and grew. Sometimes they seemed to disappear and then came back in other forms.

Valencia called in sick to work at some point when she was sure a night had passed. She said she had food poisoning. Salmonella. It was something she'd always worried she'd contract—it was the reason she had never cooked chicken in all of her adult years. The phone began ringing at persistent, reliable intervals—it was her mother, she felt sure—but Valencia just lay on the couch with her eyes closed. She didn't think she could stand to hear that screeching, out-of-control version of her mother again, didn't know what to say to her.

At one point, Grace stood in front of Valencia's door and knocked for thirty-five minutes straight. "Valley!" she yelled. "My knuckles are turning purple!"

Valencia finally let her in, but only because she couldn't concentrate on the movie over the thought of Grace's knuckles shattering on the wood. When she opened the door, the women stood there looking at each other for a long time. Grace probably thought Valencia was too out of sorts to remember her manners and invite her in, but Valencia was only thinking about how long it had been since she'd allowed another person into her apartment. She wasn't sure she could handle it. But Grace finally just stepped around her friend and sat on the couch, and it was done, quick like ripping off a Band-Aid. She watched the rest of the movie with Valencia in silence.

When it was done, Valencia started it over again, and Grace didn't move except to slouch into her seat a little more.

Grace was so good at slouching.

Together, they sat through the movie twice before Grace spoke. "You need to eat something," she said, pressing the pause button on the remote. Valencia took it from her, trying to inconspicuously clean it with a Lysol wipe. Grace didn't notice. "*We* need to eat something. What do you have for food?"

Valencia shrugged. She felt heavy and stupid. "Uh . . . I'm not super hungry. I don't think I have anything in the fridge. Milk, maybe." *Most definitely past its expiration date.* "Dried pasta in the cupboard. Cereal?" Who let her live by herself?

Grace smiled, and the smile was kind, not condescending. She reached for the cordless phone on the coffee table and ordered a pizza with cheese and pepperoni.

Valencia was not as sneaky, this time, when she wiped the receiver as soon as it left Grace's hands. She was feeling more and more itchy at the thought of someone in her apartment but was trying desperately to suppress it. She would be okay. She would clean later. She would Lysol wipe every single thing. *One, two, three, four, five six seven eight nine ten eleven twelve thirteenfourteenfifteensixteenseventeeneighteen.*

"What a long day," Grace mumbled, pulling her feet up underneath her on the couch. Valencia wasn't sure why Grace's feet needed to be on the couch. She tried not to stare at them; she didn't want to be rude, but she also didn't want feet on her couch. She shook her head, and Grace looked at her strangely. "What?"

Valencia shook her head again. Grace was too good at reading facial expressions. "Nothing."

Grace shrugged. She pulled her hair back into a ponytail and secured it with a purple elastic, but she had so much of it that it immediately began a slow descent to the nape of her neck. "I'm so ready for the weekend."

Valencia looked up in surprise. "The weekend? It's not Friday yet." Surely she hadn't missed that much of the week. She looked at her wrist and then at the clock on the wall, then again at the feet on her couch. She couldn't remember what she was looking for. "Is it?" All of a sudden, she wasn't sure. Those feet. Would Grace still want to be her friend if she pushed her off the couch?

"Well, no," said Grace, oblivious to the storm brewing in Valencia. "I'm just ready for another. Does your apartment always look like this?"

Grace's voice was fading into the background with the piano music; Valencia was preparing for her next therapy session with Louise, where they would discuss how to handle having other people in her apartment, but this question got her attention.

She had forgotten what her apartment looked like. It had been so long since someone else was in it and she'd been made to look at it through their eyes. Now she hated what she saw. The junk mail was piling up on the coffee table along with books and magazines and water glasses and coffee cups and half-empty plates. A yellow legal pad on the couch between them with "Things You Should Never Ever Say Out Loud: An Essay by Someone Who Has Said Them All" scrawled across the top. A pair of dirty socks was balled up in a corner, crumbs underneath the dining table. Crumbs on the dining table. Crumbs on the couch. Dust floating in a sunbeam. She felt her face heat up and wondered what *she* looked like if she'd unknowingly neglected her hair and face and body the way she'd neglected her apartment. "Yeah," she said, "I'm really sorry—"

"Oh, don't be! It's just . . . it's not what I expected. I kind of figured your place would be spotless, like really, really clean. You know, because of your germ thing."

Valencia blushed. She hadn't told Grace about her "germ thing." She hated these reminders that it was exactly as obvious as it felt. She tried to raise her eyebrows, like she didn't know what Grace meant.

"Your Lysol wipes at work and stuff," said Grace. "I just kind of thought you were a neat freak."

Valencia glanced around the room. Her room. Her mess. Her germ thing. "I honestly don't know," she said finally, unable to fully understand herself. "It's all mine, I guess? My germs. They don't freak me out. I don't know why. I feel like I know what's all here . . ." Her gaze rested on Grace's feet, still tucked beneath her on the couch. *Those* were a different thing entirely, and, again, she didn't know why.

"Interesting," said Grace, like a therapist. Like Louise. *Interesting.*

Grace leaned over and squeezed her friend's shoulder. This wasn't a therapist thing. This was a Grace thing. Valencia tensed; why did Grace have to be so touchy-feely? "So, the pizza will be here in ten. Is that enough time to tell me what's wrong, Valley?"

"I'm just sick; I think it's the flu," said Valencia.

"You're a big fat liar," said Grace.

"I know," said Valencia miserably.

Grace settled back down into the couch. "Tell me," she demanded in a voice she usually reserved for work. "I didn't come here just to watch a movie ten thousand times. It's not even a very good movie."

Valencia considered this. She'd already told Grace that her grandmother had died—before her grandmother had actually died. She couldn't very well tell her friend her grandmother had died *again*. And she definitely couldn't admit that she'd been so afraid to leave the city that she'd stood her grandmother up on her deathbed. But if she said she was upset about James, would she then have to talk about Charlene again? This was a problem she kept encountering as she got to know people—they kept wanting to know her back.

She squinted at Grace and shook her head, but Grace just scratched her knee and waited. She must have known, the way she knew everything else, that this was going to take a while.

"Well," Valencia began, "I've been talking to a guy—"

"A guy! A *guy*? What guy?" Grace acted as though she'd been waiting her whole life for this. As though there was exactly one guy on earth, and he'd been in hiding from the female population for years, and Valencia had been the one to find him.

Valencia could feel her cheeks warm. Her eyes landed on Grace's feet again, and she spoke without thinking. "Um . . . can you please take your feet off the couch?" Valencia was shocked at herself, but even more shocked when Grace did so with no reaction of any kind. "I—thank you."

"Valley! Tell me about the guy!"

Valencia felt as though she'd discovered a superpower she didn't know she had. "Thank you. Seriously. I wasn't trying to be rude—"

"Valencia." Grace's eyeballs were coming out of her head. *The guy! The guy!* Somehow, she was shrieking without moving her mouth.

"Right. Sorry. Okay. It's this guy named James." James. For the first time, she contemplated his name, thought through how she would present him to Grace. She felt like it was important to make a good impression on his behalf, even if he had broken her heart. She didn't have enough friends to be a bad one herself.

James. The name made a good impression. It suggested strength, a no-nonsense personality—he was not, after all, called Jim—he was *James*. Buttoned-up. Professional. And the *way* she said it filled in the rest of the blanks.

"Who's he? Does he work at West Park?"

"He's . . . a cardholder?"

"What? Oh! Like you met him on the *phone*?" She leaned forward and grabbed Valencia's wrist. Valencia didn't like that. "This is amazing, Valley. Tell me everything. Now."

"That's kind of all there is," said Valencia, sensing a way out. "We talked a few times. Well. We talked every day. He was really . . . I . . ." She stalled. "I liked him, I guess? But I don't think he's going to call back anymore."

"You had a fight? Or what?"

"Yes," said Valencia, lying again, relieved not to have to tell Grace about Charlene. "It's just over. I was going to go meet him in New York, but when I told him about it, he got all freaked out and told me not to."

"He told you not to?" Grace was melting into a puddle of sympathy and empathy and contiguous sadness.

"Basically, yes."

This was all the explanation Grace needed. She squeezed Valencia's shoulder, and the pizza came, and they watched the movie again even though Grace was right; it wasn't very good at all.

The next thing Valencia knew, early morning sun was puddled on the floor, and the room was cool and the air damp; the window over the dining table was open, and a car alarm blared outside. Piano music wailed through the wall, and Grace was asleep, drooling on Valencia's couch. The phone rang. Valencia answered it before she remembered she didn't want to.

"Hello?"

"Hi, Vee."

Valencia almost dropped the receiver. She glanced at Grace, still fast asleep.

"Vee? You there?"

"How do you know my number?" said Valencia. *He shouldn't know my number.*

"Yeah," he said, as though agreeing with her. "It's kind of a funny story . . ." He paused and said something else that Valencia didn't catch.

Grace started to stir. Valencia nudged her shoulder with an elbow. She was shaking. When you worked at a job where you regularly received death threats, you didn't want to be found so easily—it didn't matter who found you; the point was *you'd been found*. She'd had nightmares about this since she started at West Park.

"Valley? You okay?" Grace asked, yawning and rubbing her face, but she already had her other hand on Valencia's knee and was trying to peer into her eyes. "You're white. Who's on the phone? Are you okay?"

"Vee? You okay?" James sighed. "This was a bad idea. Maybe we should have this conversation in person."

Valencia hung up the phone.

"Who was that?" Grace asked again.

"Him," said Valencia.

"Him? *Him* him? What'd you hang up for? What'd he say? What's wrong?"

"Grace! He called my home phone number! How did he get that? Can anyone just get my phone number? How easy is it to find out other information about me? Like my address? He said he wants to talk in person." He may as well have been breaking her apartment door down.

"Valley, Valley, chill. Why does it matter if this guy knows where you live? I thought you were the one who wanted to meet in real life?" Grace looked concerned but in a bored way. Worried about Valencia's feelings but not the situation. She got up and went into the kitchen, pulled the pizza box out of the fridge, brought it back to her place on the couch.

"Don't people say stuff to you on the phones at work? About how they're going to hunt you down and kill you? And Norwin always says to me, 'It's okay; they don't know what country you're calling from even—they can't trace us; they can't find us—you'll be fine.' But obviously . . ." Valencia was pacing the floor.

Grace shrugged and rolled her eyes. "Yeah. But they wouldn't. Who even thinks about their debt collector after the phone call is over?"

Valencia thought of a man who had threatened to torture her. If James Mace could find her, that man could too. "We're just annoying voices to them. What are the chances of someone actually following through on that kind of threat?"

People always asked that: *What are the chances? What are the chances of being struck by lightning? What are the chances of a car crash? What are the chances of someone robbing the exact bank you're in at the exact time you're in it?*

Slim. But these things still happened. And if a thing had happened or could happen, it could happen to Valencia, and things like chances wouldn't matter then. The fact that there was a chance in the first place was important. Why was this so hard for people to understand? People gambled, didn't they? *There is a chance.* Valencia would explain this to her friend. "Grace," she said. Grace raised her eyebrows and waited for more words, but there were no more words. Valencia leaned forward, willing understanding to pass from her to her friend. Grace leaned forward, too, her forehead bumping against Valencia's.

"Valencia. Dear. Hear me when I say this: you are being irrational. He probably called the center and asked Norwin for your number, and Norwin is a stupid man. I love Norwin, but he's an idiot. You said you had a fight? So that means this guy actually cares about you. If a guy doesn't care about a girl, he doesn't chase her down. He breathes a great big sigh of relief and finds another girl he hasn't had a fight with yet. Haven't you been paying attention to this movie? I mean, you've watched it enough times to get the basics on human relationships."

Valencia's heart fluttered. Grace was the irrational one, but maybe irrational thought was the key to sanity. Maybe you had to choose one or the other.

"You're right," she said, even though she knew her friend was wrong. "You're right. But what do I do?"

"Call him back."

"No."

"Okay, *I'll* call him back."

"I don't have caller ID."

"Ever hear of a little thing called last call return? You just push star, six, nine, and it calls back the last number to call you." She squeezed Valencia's shoulder again. "Okay. It's ringing . . ."

Valencia froze. She heard a muffled click and a tiny, faraway voice. A woman's voice. Grace frowned and jumped off the couch.

"Hi," said Grace, suddenly sounding cautious and unsure. "Is James there?"

The tiny voice uttered a single syllable.

"James?" Grace said again.

Two syllables.

"James, uh . . ." She snapped her fingers at Valencia, whose mouth was hanging open. "James . . . Mace! Is James Mace there?"

And more syllables, apologetic. Grace smiled into the receiver. "Okay, sorry to bother you." She hung up. "But how is that even possible?" she asked the phone, ignoring Valencia.

"What, he wasn't there?"

"Did I do something wrong?" Grace stared at the keypad in confusion. "Star. Six. Nine . . ." She looked up at Valencia, and her usually expressive face was perfectly blank.

"What, Grace?"

"Oh, uh." Grace returned the phone to the table by the couch. "I guess that's just a dead end? We should probably get to work."

"I'm not going to work, Grace. Who was that on the phone?"

"Yes, you are. Get dressed."

"I *am* dressed. Still." She gestured at the black dress pants and button-up top she'd been wearing since Monday. "Tell me—who was that on the phone?"

"Valley, I don't know. It was weird. It was some home business, and a woman answered. She's never heard of anyone called James Mace.

And you can't wear that. I can't smell you from here, but I'm positive you stink."

Valencia sat straight up, confused. "What does that mean then?"

"Your guess is as good as mine. Girl, your shirt's all rumpled."

"Did you call the wrong number?"

"Valencia! Stop this. Go change."

The two women sat in silence. Valencia shook her head. "What does it mean, though?"

"Valley," said Grace in a voice that was probably meant to sound reassuring but had something else laced around the edges. "I think it means last call return has failed us. I think that's all it means. Okay, let's go. At least brush your hair. I want to grab a bagel on our way."

"I'm not—" Valencia started to say that she was calling in sick again, but then she stopped. "What day is it?"

"Um . . . the third. Why?"

"No reason." Valencia was hit with a rush of adrenaline, like she used to have before she went on medication. It was exhilarating. Her heart started to pound. Come to think of it, she usually took her medication by this point in the morning. Had she taken it yesterday at all? She couldn't remember.

This feeling was probably unrelated. It was like an ocean wave, but not the kind that would knock the wind out of you or bash your head against rocks. It picked her up, gently but quickly.

Valencia would go to work after all. She had something she needed to do. "Okay. Okay, I'll come."

"Good."

"Grace? Are *you* okay?"

"Don't worry about me, Valley. I'm just hungry."

Valencia frowned. Grace was lying. But why?

CHAPTER
TWENTY-TWO

"Trolltunga!" Mr. Valentine extended his fists in the air again, but this time his booming voice didn't echo off anything. It shot straight out into space and never came back.

We were there. Having a picnic on the horizontal rock that did, indeed, jut out from the side of a mountain like the tongue of a great stone troll. We were more than two thousand feet above the lake Ringedalsvatnet, and it had taken me a lot longer to warm up to the idea of such great height than it had taken Mr. Valentine. He'd marched right out to the tip of the rock like an awkward, unfashionable model on a runway and screamed, and then he'd just stood there, completely still for at least five full minutes, looking absolutely tiny in the face of such a wide expanse of space and air. Finally, he turned to me, and I shuddered to think of his back to that fatal free fall.

He said, "Yikes, right?" He was like a little kid, giddy with excitement.

After a lot of coaxing, I crawled out to him on my belly like a big lizard, and my stomach dropped as though I was already falling. I was acutely aware of gravity trying to suck me down into Ringedalsvatnet, pulling me against the granite, threatening to break the chunk of rock right off the mountain. There was so little beneath me and so much beneath that.

We stayed like that for a while, me on my face, him surveying the Norwegian valleys and mountains and lakes like they were his kingdom and sporadically yelling, "Trolltunga!" I think he would've stayed there forever, drinking in the scenery and breathing the mountain air. Eventually, I was able to sit, and we unpacked some sandwiches. We'd hiked for eight hours to get there, and I knew I had to be hungry, even if right then my stomach occupied the narrow space in my gullet.

I got better with heights. The next three years were a blur of them—and also depths and widths and lengths.

Metaphorically speaking too.

We brought the scraps of paper with the names on them in the front zipper pocket of my backpack, and when we were done with a place, we just picked a new one and headed there by whatever means necessary. It was an exhilarating way to live; I wished we could live that way forever.

Príncipe came up next. It turned out to be a small, almost completely forested volcanic bump just off the west coast of Africa. We stayed in a little hut right on the beach, and Mr. Valentine spent a lot of time on the island looking through a bird-watching book. I spent most of mine standing on the beach contemplating the ocean.

It was more than I'd expected it to be. More water, more shades of blue, more force, more calm. Growing up, water was something I only saw in taps, in my glass at the dinner table, in a puddle on the street, or in a ditch in the spring. It had never impressed me much, but now it took my breath away.

I stood at the edge of the ocean the way Mr. Valentine had stood on Trolltunga, with my face up and my eyes wide, watching the waves stretching out and breaking apart, then falling back into themselves, seamless again like skin. It was a different kind of height—deceptive. I couldn't see the bottom, so I couldn't comprehend how high I was. I tried to wrap my brain around how much life was swimming around in that emerald-blue sink, how many other living things were touching the water that reached up and fell on my toes. I stood there for so long that my skin burned and blistered and even my eyeballs felt tender and itchy.

We drew the next name right there on the beach as the sun set. "Fogo Island," said Mr. Valentine.

"Where's that?"

"Canada, actually." I brightened at this, and Mr. Valentine laughed at me. "Are you homesick already?"

"No! No. Not at all. But familiarity is nice." We sprawled out on the sand and looked up at the sky. "Then again," I said, "this sky looks pretty familiar."

"Yep," Mr. Valentine agreed. "We could be in a Saskatchewan wheat field right now." He was right; the water sounded like the rustling of wheat stalks, and the sky was the same one I'd grown up under, amazingly. We were far from home, but we were still home.

We left the next morning for our forty-eight-hour trip back to Canada. At one point, we had a short layover in the London airport. Mr. Valentine fell asleep on a row of chairs at gate 41, and I sat on top of our bags watching people: A flustered-looking man and a woman with a screaming child. A group of laughing, bleary-eyed flight attendants. A couple of rich-looking young women with brand-new luggage and hiking shoes that hadn't been broken in yet.

And then, out of the corner of my eye, I saw someone familiar—or at least, I thought I did. Her hair was longer now, but still dark, bluntly cut. She wore a bulky green jacket that hung down almost to her knees, a denim skirt peeking out from underneath. She was in the same boarding line as the women with the new luggage, but she was there alone, bouncing on the balls of her feet in nervous anticipation and biting her nails. I couldn't see enough of her face to know for sure that it was her, but I was overcome with the desire to find out. I needed to know that she'd been rescued from the water and was now enjoying her life, traveling through the London airport, same as me. I stood, but she was already showing her boarding pass to the woman at the desk and then disappearing down the walkway.

CHAPTER
TWENTY-THREE

Valencia lay on the living room floor in her little apartment, arms stretched above her head, staring at the ceiling. In one of her hands, she clutched a printout of James Mace's personal account summary, including his full name and home address. She was listening intently to the music coming from the apartment next door, thinking again about Rachmaninoff's original intentions for the song. Had he written it about beauty or pain? She couldn't tell. Valencia wondered if he'd been an exceptionally sad person or an excessively happy one—she was sure he was an extreme person, either way. Was the song about falling in love or falling out of it?

Or maybe he'd been insane, and the song was about him. Insanity could sound like love. Maybe that was why he didn't want to disclose his images, or whatever. Better to be thought of as passionate or heartbroken than crazy.

At the moment, she could relate to all three possible Rachmaninoffs. She held the paper with James Mace's address straight up in the air in front of her face.

She'd gone into work, found the information, printed it off, and come right back home the second Grace's back had been turned. For some reason, she felt that Grace wouldn't approve of her plan.

She wasn't thinking straight; it was like she was watching her thoughts flash across her mind's eye like fireworks. They were loud and bright, and they were giving her a headache. One thought, specifically, kept nagging at her—she needed to call her mother. But what would she say? How could she apologize for her behavior? And then, the funeral: How was she supposed to drive to the funeral when she hadn't been able to drive to her grandmother's deathbed? Would anyone forgive her? No. And they shouldn't. She'd just add it to her debt. She'd live a few extra years and spend them at the debt collection agency. It was fine; it was all fine. It was an absolute mess, but it was fine.

She needed to take her medication—everything was so bright and colorful right now. Even the anxious thoughts were not so much upsetting as loud, like they were screaming at her on the other side of chicken wire but couldn't get at her. It would be a shame to dim it all down again. Why had she shut out this part of her for so long? It was *loud*, to be sure. Almost—*almost*—to the point of discomfort, but, again, it had been so long since she'd felt anything so vivid. Maybe it just took some getting used to. Maybe it would be different now.

She couldn't keep a thought in focus for long enough to properly think her way through it—it was too noisy—so she pushed her fingers against her forehead and made her decision without thinking anymore. She stood up. She grabbed her passport, her keys, and her wallet. Stuffed some clothes into a backpack, slipped into her jacket. For the first time ever, she was going off script in real life.

She was either crazy or in love. Like Rachmaninoff.

Two hours later, she sat at the airport in her usual spot, ripping up the piece of paper with James Mace's address on it and letting it fall on the floor at her feet. Did normal people have usual spots at airports? People who didn't go to airports to pick other people up or go on trips themselves? She'd been sitting there for hours watching the planes come and go, trying not to cry.

She'd come with all the resolve she could muster and felt so proud and brave. Urgency had outweighed her fear. She'd thought that maybe she could show up at his door—maybe he did want her to come; maybe he'd just been surprised when she'd told him her idea. It was like in that movie she'd watched on repeat for the past few days. It was like every romantic movie: People never meant what they said. They said they wanted to end the relationship or be left alone or for the other person to be free of them, but what they actually wanted was to be chased and caught and loved.

Wasn't she a prime example?

She'd never done anything so impulsive before, and she'd felt free for the first time that she could remember. As she'd crossed the polished airport floor, she'd sworn she could hear the piano music floating through the air. The low minor chords had hung over her head like heavy rain clouds; she could almost feel the notes hitting her face. She'd gripped her backpack straps with white knuckles; she could feel her heartbeat pulsing through her whole body. She was doing this, finally doing something that meant something. Fireworks.

But as she'd approached the ticket counter, she'd fallen apart. It had started with a single thought: What if her plane fell out of the sky? And then she was picturing it and feeling it and hearing it, and she couldn't breathe or think or move. She'd known all at once that this was as far as she would go. She'd taken a running leap, but her feet had melded to the ground, and her whole body had landed in a slump. She was, at the very most, a toppled statue.

Stuck.

She was not brave. She was not free. She was just manic.

Now the thought of getting back into her car and driving felt overwhelming. All the people. Her grandmother's funeral. Louise. Her airways constricted, and she couldn't feel her hands. She set her backpack on the ground and made her way to her spot. She needed familiarity.

A flight attendant brought her backpack over with a stern expression and said, "Ma'am. You really shouldn't leave your bags unattended in an—oh, are you okay?"

Valencia forced a smile and lied. She was good at that. "I'm fine. I just got some bad news. I'm sorry. I need a moment."

The flight attendant patted her on the shoulder and reminded her that she should keep her bag with her at all times. Then she walked away.

And what next? She couldn't sit there forever. She looked down at her hands in her lap. They were red, dry, and scabby from constant washing in scalding hot water. Old lady hands. She stared at them for a million years. Two million. Three million. When she looked up again, Grace was standing in front of her.

"You okay, Valley?"

"Yes," said Valencia. "No. How did you know I'd be here?"

"I checked your apartment first and then the hospital. And then I remembered you saying you did this sometimes. It was the last place I would've thought of, so I'm glad you're here. What're you doing?" Grace stepped forward, and a man bumped into her on his way past. She saw the bag, lying beside Valencia like an obedient dog. "Are . . . are you *going to him*?" She whispered it with her eyes wide, almost reverently. Grace would appreciate this kind of grand romantic gesture.

But Valencia suddenly felt like she'd fall asleep if she blinked her eyes. There must have been an adrenaline release valve somewhere in her body; it was all gone. "Yeah. No. I mean I was." Her words melted into one another. "I don't know why," she mumbled, looking at the floor. "I thought I'd show up at his door. Isn't that insane? That's insane."

"Not insane," said Grace. "I have to admit, though, I'm worried about you. You know I care, right? I'm not trying to pry. Did your fight with this guy affect you this much, or is there maybe something else?"

Valencia felt like Grace was expecting her to burst into tears or take offense or something, anything, but all of her emotions had evaporated like water in a pot.

"I'm fine," she said. "Should we go back to work?"

Grace sat beside her friend, her dark eyebrows huddled together under her hair, as though having their own discussion. Valencia beheld her obvious care, mystified. Feelings were like a foreign concept all of a sudden, a different language.

"No. Talk to me, girl. What's going on?"

Valencia shrugged with her whole body. Okay. Talking was fine. Talking was whatever. Sleeping, though—sleeping would've been a better thing.

"Do you think that woman who answered the phone when you called was James Mace's wife?" The question floated out of her mouth, and she almost looked around her to see who had spoken it.

Grace looked mortified. "He has a wife?"

"Not that I know of, but . . ." Valencia thought about how quietly he talked, like he didn't want to be overheard, and how abruptly he ended their conversations sometimes. It certainly would explain why he didn't want her showing up at his house in New York. She wondered if she should feel mortified too. Betrayed, maybe. Sad?

No, just tired.

But Grace was laughing now. "Oh, well, then no. Of course not."

"How can you be so sure?"

"Because if he had a wife, and if I talked to his wife that day, she'd have heard of him. Right?"

"Oh. Right," Valencia said. *Unless he was using a fake name when he called.* "What was that look on your face after you hung up? When you called the number back on my phone?" Valencia felt like she was having a conversation through someone else's mouth, knowing that person cared very much about the subject matter but feeling nothing herself.

Grace looked profoundly uncomfortable. She squirmed in her seat and zipped her jacket. Then she unzipped it and jammed her hands in the pockets. She squinted at Valencia like Valencia was the sun. She shouldn't have been so concerned about what Valencia was going to think; Valencia already knew she wasn't going to care. "Well. I didn't hear the phone ring. I was asleep."

"Yeah. And?"

"Well. I didn't hear anyone on the other end of the line when you were on the phone either."

"So?" Valencia yawned.

"And how is it that I could call back literally a minute later and he'd already be gone? That the person there would never have heard of someone who supposedly *just* called from that number? And how is it that this person calls *you* every single day at work on a phone line with hundreds of extensions? Did you ever give him your extension, or is he just calling the inbound line and randomly getting you every time?"

Valencia's forehead crumpled, but she was still more confused than upset. She felt like she should've been upset at Grace's use of the word *supposedly*. She tried to muster up some outrage but got bland discomfort instead. She watched a woman pass carrying a sleeping toddler and dragging a suitcase—not the kind with wheels, the kind that was meant to be carried. Then she understood what Grace was worried about. She tried to play the part of the insulted, indignant friend. "I feel like you're suggesting I lied to you about him."

"No! No . . . I mean I don't know if I'm *suggesting* anything. I'm just . . . *confused* about the whole thing. I'm just trying to understand how this is all possible. And I'm worried about you, like I said. I want to help."

Valencia stared, unsure how to take this. Her brain was putting the pieces together, and the slow processing must have seemed like brewing anger.

Grace grimaced and let out a huff of air. "I just . . . like, I guess it crossed my mind that maybe the other day when I asked you what was wrong, you said it was a guy so you wouldn't have to tell me what was actually up. Like maybe there is no James Mace—maybe you just didn't know how to tell me what was really wrong? Or who had really called you. Or something. I just feel like there's something I don't know about all this. Which sucks, because I'm your friend. I know I haven't been for a long time, but still: I care. I don't want you to have to pretend with me."

Grace squeezed Valencia's shoulder again. She looked concerned that she'd said the wrong thing. And she had, kind of. But maybe she'd also said the exact right thing. Maybe there was no James Mace. Maybe Valencia *was* a liar. Maybe she was lying to herself. She *was* crazy, after all.

"Grace, could you hear the piano music in my apartment?"

"Huh?"

"Never mind. Grace?"

"Yeah?"

"Do you know Peter? From work?"

Grace shook her head. "I don't really know anyone from work, other than you."

"Okay."

CHAPTER TWENTY-FOUR

The currency was the only thing about Fogo Island that even remotely felt like Saskatchewan. It was a tiny blip on the map off the shore of Newfoundland. We took a ferry out and rented a bedroom in a rustic saltbox home right on the ocean. Despite having all the same properties—mainly, lots of water—as the ocean we'd left behind in Príncipe, this one couldn't have been more different.

Fogo, we were told, means "fire," and I assumed the island got its name from the smokelike fog that made it seem like the island was burning all the time. I didn't like it. It felt suffocating, especially after the wild openness of our last locale.

Our host at the bed-and-breakfast was a whiskery old fisherman named Serge, who had tiny, sad eyes. He was quiet and mostly stayed out of our way the first few days we were there. He seemed like the kind of man who had a secret.

Four days into our stay, Mr. Valentine came down with some kind of stomach bug and was confined to our bedroom. I stayed with him for the first few hours of his illness, but when he fell asleep around noon, I decided to get out and take a little walk.

I headed for the water. I picked my way across some rocks to the edge, where the surf crashed at my feet. The oppressive fog hadn't lifted since our arrival, and I could see it wasn't going anywhere, so I sat down in it and let it settle on me. I imagined I was in a cloud in the sky, above everything. I closed my eyes and heard . . . piano music?

It stopped as soon as I understood what it was, as though I'd scared it away. I stood, perfectly still, and listened as hard as I could but still couldn't hear it—had I imagined it?

But just as I was about to give up, there it was again. Seven low notes, and then nothing, and then the same seven notes again. Not like someone was practicing a song they knew but like they were learning one, or writing it. There was a ghostly quality to it, floating through the fog, stopping and starting like an apparition. I followed it back across the rocks, alongside the water, and then into the trees.

I came to a clearing, where I found a small, white, one-room church, surrounded by a picket fence, a dilapidated graveyard off to the side. Some of the graves were on the inside of the fence, and some were on the outside. A wooden sign with no words stood out front. The fog settled on the roof, and I shivered.

The seven notes again.

I saw that the front door of the church was ajar, propped open with somebody's shoe. I took this as a sign of welcome, so I peered inside.

There was Serge, our host, bent over the piano in great concentration. He played the notes again, and I noticed one was different this time. He erased something on the paper in front of him, wrote something else. He didn't seem to be in a hurry. He played the new melody again.

"That's pretty," I said, and he jumped, turning to face me. He didn't seem frightened, just flustered. Embarrassed, maybe.

"Thank you," he said quietly. "It's not finished."

"Can I hear the part that is finished?" I asked.

He smiled. "You have," he said. "That's all there is so far."

"Oh," I said, and I felt embarrassed too. "You just got here?"

"No," he said. "I've been here for hours."

"Oh," I said. I thought I saw a mouse moving under one of the pews, but I wasn't sure. "Is it . . . going to have words?"

"No," he said. "I don't know how to write words. I just know how to write music. If you write the music well enough, you don't need words anyway."

I nodded.

"Is it a story then?" I asked.

"Yes," he said.

"What about?"

"If I tell you that," he said slowly, "then you won't be able to hear your own story in it later on when I finish and play it for you."

"No offense," I said to him, "but at the rate you're going, I'm not going to be here when you're finished."

He laughed, and it was a better laugh than I thought could come out of him. "True," he said. "Since you put it that way." He sat back down on the bench, and I, unsure of myself and unsure of what I thought might be a mouse just a couple feet in front of me and unsure of what he wanted, took a single step forward. Serge cleared his throat and smiled at me. "It's about my wife and daughter," he said.

"That's nice," I said.

"They died in a car accident twenty years ago," he said. "They were on their way to my daughter's piano recital. It was winter, and the roads were bad. I was supposed to be with them, but I was sick that night so they went without me."

I frowned. I wished I hadn't said, "That's nice."

"It's not about that, though," he said quickly, reassuring me again. "It's not a sad song. It's a song about when they were alive, written as though they still are. I write all my songs about them as though they're still here. A little creative license—a little revisionist history."

"Well, that *is* nice," I said, feeling a familiar burn behind my eyeballs.

"Anyway," he said. "I think I'm going to work on the second phrase."

"I should get back anyway," I said. "I'm sorry for intruding."

"It's not an intrusion at all!" said Serge, smiling warmly, though his eyes remained sad. "I do love playing my songs for other people. What good is a story if there's no one to hear it? I hope you come back again, and I'll play you a finished one."

And I said I would, and I did.

CHAPTER
TWENTY-FIVE

Like maybe there is no James Mace.
   Like maybe there is no James Mace.
   Like maybe there is no James Mace.
Absurd.

The way Grace had meant it was that Valencia was lying as a cover for something else. Valencia knew that wasn't the case, but maybe it was something very close to that. Maybe Valencia was being fooled as well as Grace. Maybe she'd imagined James Mace into existing simply because she needed him. She'd heard stories like this before, but they were always about other people, people very removed from her. People in the news. People in other cities. People in movies. People who heard voices and believed in fabricated realities. *I could be one of those people.* Valencia thought about the stove and the endless confessing of sins to her ceiling at night and the sanitizing and all of the other things that made her feel like she had begun to fray at the edges. And what about those labels Louise kept sticking to her?

She pictured Louise adding yet another word to her notebook. "These things often come in little package deals," she'd said once, as though a mental illness were a thing you'd buy in bulk to save some money. "People who have OCD often also suffer from anxiety and depression, for example." *Like, isn't that just the most convenient thing? Buy one, get two free! Bundle and save your sufferings!*

Valencia's body confounded her. It was a haunted house in a neighborhood full of people who didn't believe in ghost stories and inhabited by a skeptical woman who had to work a little too hard to convince herself the creaking floorboards were nothing more than the old house settling.

How could a person not understand what was going on inside their own body? It was because she was horrible at communication, simple as that. Why would she be any better at talking to herself than she was at talking to Peter?

Peter. Was Peter even real? Grace had not ever met him, though his cubicle was just steps from hers. How was that possible?

She held as still as she could and listened. She closed her eyes and tilted her head back and tried to think without drowning out her thoughts. *What's going on in there?* Someday, she might have a heart attack and just go on living like nothing had happened because her insides were so bad at communicating with her outsides.

She let out another giant breath, realizing halfway through that she'd forgotten to take air in first. If she weren't already sprawled on the living room floor, she would have collapsed. The piano piece from next door was starting again. She raised her arms straight up in the air and focused on her fingers. *If James Mace isn't real, maybe I'm not either.* That might not have been the worst thing, because if she wasn't real, Charlene either hadn't existed or wasn't dead. She clapped her hands together, and the sound made her jump. "Who knows?" she said out loud. To the ceiling. To the stove in the other room. To the person next door listening to the piano music. "Am I real?" she asked no one, and no one answered. "Are *you* real?" she shouted. Still no reply. "Is there even any music playing right now, or am I completely insane?"

"I'm worried you were right," she said to Grace the next evening. August 6. Grace's bare feet were on the coffee table. She was painting her toenails fire-engine red to match her lips. Valencia had been drumming her fingers on her kneecaps, counting beats to keep from thinking about feet on coffee tables. It wasn't helping at all. She wanted to burn it.

"About what? Which thing? Oh! Oh no, I'm sorry; I forgot about the feet thing." Grace swung her feet to the floor, keeping her toes suspended in the air. Valencia exhaled, relieved, and immediately set to work disinfecting the surface and then washing her hands. Grace watched with a mixture of fascination and confusion. She waited for Valencia to finish and sit back down before asking again. "About what?"

"What?"

"I was right about what?"

"Oh. About me making James Mace up."

Grace looked bewildered. She screwed the cap on her polish, even though she had three toes left. She wasn't slouching anymore. "You made him up?"

"No. I mean, not on purpose."

"How do you make something up not on purpose?"

"Well." Now that she was saying it, it sounded stupid. "I mean I didn't know I was? Like a hallucination? That's like making something up without realizing you are."

"You think James Mace is a hallucination." Grace was not asking a question. She looked unimpressed, like she still thought she was being tricked.

"Well, *you know*, the kind of hallucination that . . ." She pushed out a big puff of air. She didn't want to say the word, but it was one she'd thought of from time to time. "You know. That a schizophrenic person has? I don't know if there's a better name for it."

"A hallucination." Grace was caught so off guard she didn't seem to know which questions to ask.

"That's what I said. He could be."

"You think you're schizophrenic."

"No! But, I mean, I could be. I'm a lot of other things."

"I'd know if you were schizophrenic."

"*No*. You wouldn't. I mean after a while you might—but it *has* been a while now . . . maybe we're both finding out at the same time."

"You think you're imagining James Mace because you're bonkers?"

"Sure. Okay." But Valencia cringed at the word *bonkers*. It sounded cartoonish and flippant.

"But you're not bonkers. I honestly feel like I would know if you were bonkers." Grace thought Valencia was being ridiculous. Valencia could tell. She wouldn't come out and say it that way, though, because Grace was the kindest person in the world. Even if she thought you were being ridiculous, she'd say you were being something else that meant ridiculous but sounded like a compliment. Grace must've owned some kind of special thesaurus. "You're being ridiculous," she said, unscrewing the cap of the nail polish and hunching over her feet once more.

Valencia frowned.

"Valley," said Grace after a minute, without looking up but as stern as Valencia had ever heard her. "First of all, I don't think you imagined James Mace into being. I know that's a thing that happens to other people, but I don't think that's a thing that happened to you. But also, just so you know, if that *was* what happened here, I'd still be in your face right now telling you that I love you and that I'm here for you. Okay?"

Valencia nodded.

"I should never have said any of that. I didn't think you were, you know, flat-out, maliciously *lying*, just avoiding something else. The whole thing is a little far fetched, but life is far fetched sometimes. I think you should come back to work, for real this time, and call this James guy. His number's in the dialer, and you still have unfinished business. You'll always regret unfinished business. That's what I always say." Grace was always saying she always said things she'd never said.

Valencia sighed.

But the next morning she showered, put on a clean outfit, and went to work. Grace looked relieved to see her, and Norwin's face scrunched up the way it did when he was as close to a smile as he got. But Peter wasn't in his spot. Instead, there was a bald man in a brown suit. He had a moustache and a head so shiny you could see the ceiling fan in it. "Hello," he said when he noticed her staring at him. "I don't believe we've met—I'm Gary Greggs." He was like a commercial for scalps. His head was enormous. He reached out for a handshake.

Valencia struggled to retain her smile. She ignored his hand without trying to be subtle. "Hi," she said. "Um, where's Peter?"

The man seemed undeterred. He was one of those robots. "Did he used to sit here? He must have quit. Or transferred." He said it conversationally, with a smile on his face that didn't waver.

Valencia felt a flicker of annoyance, which could very well have been her heart shattering into a thousand pieces. Her pain gauge was broken.

The day carried on, and she floated through it like she wasn't there. She still hadn't taken her medication and was beginning to wonder if it didn't matter. But then, she was beginning to wonder if anything mattered, and maybe that was a sign that the medication did—but the thought of taking it, just putting it in her mouth and swallowing, seemed too hard. Everything seemed too hard. Everything seemed grimy; she scrubbed her mouse and her computer monitor and her keyboard and her hands and each one of her pens, in that order, on repeat, and it never felt like enough.

James Mace didn't call. She hadn't thought he would, but this was the first workday all summer she hadn't heard from him, so it was notable.

At quitting time, the clones of West Park shuffled in quiet, uniform steps toward the front doors. Instead of following, Grace rolled her chair into Valencia's cubicle, eyes glittering. "Let's do this thing," she said. Valencia wasn't sure how to tell her that she already had all the proof she needed. James Mace was not real. Neither was Peter.

Instead of saying anything, she nervously settled in her chair and searched for James Mace's file while Grace stood to keep watch. Pulling up someone's personal credit information for any purpose other than assisting them in making a payment, and doing so without their explicit consent, was one of the few things the women knew they could be fired for—possibly arrested too. Valencia couldn't remember. She tried not to think about it. Fines and jail time were scary enough. But if finding a new job was a feat now, it would be absolutely impossible with a criminal record.

"Are you spelling his name right?" Grace had abandoned her post, unable to keep her eyes from the glowing computer screen. *0 search results for "James Mace."* She frenetically tapped the screen with a long, fake fingernail. "Try spelling *Mace* another way."

Valencia backspaced, typed in *Mase*, and waited for the machine to register the command. "I'm sure I remember seeing it on the screen the way I spelled it the first time. I printed his information out and took it with me to the airport."

"Oh—well, then, where's the page you printed out?"

Valencia shrugged, embarrassed. "I ripped it up." She leaned forward and buried her head in her hands. "I've heard stories about this kind of thing. Brains are awful."

Grace shook her head. "No, brains are awesome. It's almost like you want him to be fake." Valencia wondered if there was some truth in this. If James Mace were to end up being a figment of her imagination, a symptom of a mental disorder, or even just a stress-induced apparition, that would mean she hadn't actually told anyone about Charlene, that it was still her dirty little secret. It also meant that James hadn't rejected her. While the average thirty-four-year-old woman would be terrified at the thought of being so mentally unstable that she was engaging with imaginary love interests, Valencia was more afraid of rejection or disapproval from an actual person. She would rather be crazy.

0 search results for "James Mase." Grace tapped her foot on the floor and drummed her fingernails on the chair and clicked her back teeth together. "Well," she said, ticking like a demented bomb. "Well. Well. I don't know. I don't know."

"It's like this story I saw on a talk show once, where the guy thought his daughter was still alive, even though she'd died a decade earlier." Valencia's voice sounded calm, and she felt calm, but she wondered if she should be panicked. Her emotions—the right emotions—were shelved, too high to reach. "He sat in restaurants and talked to an empty chair and even yelled at her in public sometimes. And then he got arrested because he took someone else's daughter home with him from the grocery store. I'm him."

She felt a dull ache behind her eyes, but it wasn't enough to create tears. She smiled to see if she could—and she could. *That Valencia. So happy all the time. What is her secret?*

"You're not, Valley. Don't jump to the worst possible explanation. If he paid his bill off completely this morning, his file would already be gone. Or it could've been sent on to another agency; that happens sometimes. So that's probably what happened here, too, hey?"

Grace sat beside her friend and put a hand on her back. Valencia's eyes filled with tears, and her face was all blotchy, but her wide smile stayed plastered across the middle of her face like a piece of duct tape on a broken vase. The skin around her mouth quivered, threatening to crumble, new cracks forming and splintering and traveling upward and outward until her entire visage broke.

CHAPTER
TWENTY-SIX

We left Fogo Island after a month of quiet, stretched-out days.

From there we went to Turkey, where we rode in a hot air balloon through Cappadocia, a breathtaking land of fairy chimneys and church ruins and houses carved from the soft rocks of volcanic deposits. The sky was filled with hundreds of balloons, silhouetted against the warm glow of the sunrise. The needlelike volcanic spires below looked especially threatening in contrast. I imagined a sudden wind blowing us all down into the sharp rocks, imagined the incredible sound of all those popping balloons, and found that the thrill in my belly this time was less one of terror and more one of excitement. The realization made me proud.

I was becoming brave.

From Turkey, we headed for Chefchaouen, a city of blue-rinsed buildings in Morocco, and then to Svartifoss, a waterfall in southeast Iceland. We visited Aogashima, a volcanic island in the Philippine Sea, and Arashiyama, a district in Kyoto. We walked through the eerie green bamboo groves and took the Saga Scenic Railway from Arashiyama to Kameoka, even though Kameoka wasn't written on a piece of paper in my backpack (we met a man on a bus who told us about the breathtaking journey and encouraged us to go, so we did).

That was where I think I saw her again—but again, I'm not sure.

We were in a crowd of people boarding the train, and she was sitting on a bench. She was wearing that green jacket again, and I noticed that before I noticed her beneath it—mostly because it was conceivable that a person here might have the same jacket as a person in London, but not that the same person *in* the same jacket might be in London and Kameoka and New York, at all the same times as me. Unless, of course, they meant to be. But she didn't even seem to notice me, so that couldn't have been it.

I stopped, willing her to turn her head toward me. She was gazing off to her right and, again, I couldn't see enough of her face. Mr. Valentine tugged on my sleeve. "Come on," he said gently, wondering why I didn't move. A man behind me ushered me forward with a sharp elbow, and I stumbled into my husband. When I looked back again, she was gone.

Hvitserkur came out of the bag next. If life were like music, those years were almost all sound: sixteenth and thirty-second notes, fortissimo, staccato, echoing off the walls of some great hall, played furiously and flawlessly by the finest orchestra in the world.

We took planes and trains and boats and buses and bikes. We rode the underground funicular in Turkey and a chicken bus in Central America and a totora boat in Peru. We learned how to navigate smoggy cities where no one spoke our language and, strangely trickier sometimes, smoggy cities where most people did. We did a lot of looking: up at skyscrapers and statues and monuments, down at swimming things and valleys and dusty streets. We explored tropical rainforests and endless deserts, stood on many more mountains and beaches, crawled through tight, suffocating tunnels, and stood in fields that stretched ahead of us forever. One day, our feet would sink into fresh snow; the next our toes would be burning on hot sand. We saw animals of all kinds, swam with brightly colored fish, and listened to strange squawks and clicks and screeches from the trees above us in jungles. We kept an eye on our bank account, which was always steadily dwindling but, miraculously, had a ways to go.

All this while still getting to know each other.

(Just like a sunrise is a sunrise, no matter what country you're in or what's between you and it, be it an ocean or a mountain range or a desert, so is a person the same person no matter where in the world they are—they're the same person, but you see them differently in different places. It's hard to get used to someone when the backdrop constantly changes.) I kept discovering new things about Mr. Valentine. Sometimes these things were big and important; sometimes they were precious and little, things that would only matter to a person who was in love. We were exploring worlds—the actual world and the worlds that were each other.

And it was the strangest thing: I'd be in a marketplace and look up just in time to see that green jacket disappear around a corner. I'd be on a street curb and catch a glimpse of it in a bus. I'd ride a bike past a café and think I saw it in the window. The face of the person in the jacket was always turned away, and I couldn't decide if my mind was playing tricks on me or if I was being stalked across the globe.

I began to lose track of time—not that I didn't know what day, month, year it was; I mean I stopped worrying about myself against the backdrop of hours and days passing. When I'd been at home, working and taking care of my ailing grandmother, I'd often thought about my "childbearing years" or about my "fading youth"—the sorts of things you're "supposed" to worry about as a young woman (not as a man). But I didn't think about those things while we were traveling, and I think that was one of my favorite parts of that time.

But one rainy night in Britain as we hung our wet socks on the radiator in our hotel room, I realized something, right in the middle of a sentence about something else. I stopped abruptly, squinting at Mr. Valentine.

He squinted back at me. "What? What's that look for?"

I sat on the bed, thinking.

"What?" he asked again.

I shook my head, shushing him, and he sat beside me.

"I think," I said after a long time, after I had done a lot of counting and was sure, "I'm pregnant."

Mr. Valentine's mouth opened, just a little. He lay back on the bed and put both hands on his face.

"Are you okay?" I asked. "Are you upset?"

He pulled me down beside him, so my shoulder tucked up into his armpit, my head on his chest. "Wow," he said, his voice hoarse, and I felt the word rumble beneath my ear, like it hadn't even come out of his mouth, like his heart said it. *"Wow."*

We lay there in reverent silence for a few moments, trying to comprehend it.

"How are you feeling?" he said at last. It felt like a ridiculous question after such a huge revelation, but it also felt like the bigger, more appropriate questions were ones we'd have to work up to.

"Okay," I said. "I have felt a little . . . off. I thought I ate something weird." That had happened more than once on that trip. "I'm excited, I think. Mostly, I feel scared."

"What?" I couldn't see his face, but he sounded surprised. "Scared? Of what?" I didn't answer, and at last he said, uncertainly, "Of the, you know . . . *having* the baby?"

"Well," I said, "I'm sure I'll be scared of that later." I thought about this for a moment, then sat up and stared down at myself, picturing myself *having* a baby. "Actually . . . yes, I am scared of that now. Thank you."

He laughed.

"But aren't you scared too?" I said. "About the part *after having* the baby?"

He looked at me blankly. "Scared of what? Of it biting me or something?"

"No, of . . . everything. Of literally *everything*. Of us dying and leaving the baby alone in the world. Of the baby dying. Of something else happening to the baby. Of making the wrong decisions for the baby. Of—"

Mr. Valentine was sitting up, too, now. He put his arms around me and smiled. "Oh yeah. I guess I am afraid of all of that."

We looked at each other for a long time. He put his hand on my belly. He looked like he was trying to be sympathetic but was entirely too happy.

I tried to be brave, like him. "But I guess if being scared of something stopped you from doing it, you'd miss out on everything."

He raised his eyebrows, nodding. "All the really good stuff anyway. Like our baby."

"Wow," I said. "Our baby."

I reached for my backpack.

"What're you doing?" he asked.

"One more?" I said hopefully. "I want to do one more. I need some time to wrap my head around this. We need to go home, get a doctor, grow up, all that. But one more first. Okay?"

He nodded. "That sounds like a good plan."

I unzipped the pocket with our place names inside. "Okay, so where is . . ." My fingers brushed against so many little strips of paper we hadn't drawn yet, and I felt torn for a moment, thinking that this would be our last trip for a while, thinking that I would have to stay still—thinking that so much would change when we got back home. Inward movement versus outward movement. Silence versus sound. Stuck versus free. Could I stay still now that I knew what it was like to go? "Salar de Uyuni? Did I say that right?"

Mr. Valentine shrugged. "I doubt we've said half of these right." He took the paper from me and examined the words, trying to say them himself. "Yoo-nee? E-oo-nee? Oo-you-nee? We should name our baby this." I closed my eyes, smiling, listening to him talk. I pictured a little boy, a miniature version of Mr. Valentine. His hair, his eyes, his smile, his sense of humor, his way with words. Maybe my nose. I've always liked my nose. "We should name all of our kids after places we've been," he continued. His voice was deep and sleepy. "We'd have to have lots of kids then. Five at a time. You up for that? What a crazy thing, to think of my characteristics mixed with yours and all the little permutations possible—hey, are you sleeping?"

I wasn't, but I thought I might be soon. I didn't try to swim back toward consciousness to acknowledge his question. There was nothing I liked better than falling asleep to the sound of his voice. I just smiled and let myself sink.

"And that's one of the ways that vacation is so different from real life," says Mrs. Valentine, standing up to stretch her limbs, popping and creaking and groaning like someone's walking on top of her. She shuffles across the room and turns the music up a single notch. "You go on a trip knowing that you're going to see a certain sight, and then you're going to come home and most likely never see it again. You know as you stare out across a desert or dip your toes in an ocean that this is the last time for this specific experience, at least for a long time, and that you need to soak it up and treasure it and remember everything about it for later. So you pause and make sure to properly take it in."

Then she sits down again, fixing her gaze firmly on Anna, and smiles, breathing heavily. "But in real life you go around thinking that everything good is going to last forever, and it takes you by surprise when it doesn't. And when you suddenly realize that it has happened for the last time, it's too late."

CHAPTER
TWENTY-SEVEN

Valencia sat in the parking lot, staring at the call center. It was like a jail, a cement block that had hardened around her like all of her other prisons; she was locked inside so many prisons. The only way to escape was to break through.

She put her car back into drive and pushed the gas pedal all the way to the floor and hunched over the wheel, like the woman in that movie about all the dogs. There was a screeching sound—tires? People?—and a rush of heat that sounded like waves crashing, except the water was fire and glass.

Valencia opened her eyes to see the shattered front doors magically piece themselves together again. The horrific sounds muted all at once. She tried to compose herself, tried to relax, but ended up winding herself up tighter and tighter and tighter. She pictured car crashes and houses burning and holes opening up in the earth and someone in the back seat with a knife. Everything was her fault; everyone was angry at her, terrified of her, trying to hurt her. She picked at her lip until it started to bleed.

If she stopped picturing or picking, her mind started to unspool, to ask unnecessary questions and shout accusations.

This was it. This was why she needed those pills from Louise. She'd forgotten how bad this part was. She'd only tried quitting medication cold turkey once before; it was all coming back to her now. The initial spike of mania had been uncomfortable but also dazzling. It had made her feel like quitting had been the right thing. And the brief numbness that followed had been fine; it was sad, and then it was boring, but it wasn't unmanageable. But this—this was unbearable. It was a combination of the two. Lack of motivation. Disinterest in . . . in *living*, essentially. And at the same time, somehow, everything felt heightened, every sense, every emotion, every worry. Everything seemed real, not just the real things. This is what she'd had to learn when she'd first started seeing Louise: separating reality from unhealthy, irrational thought patterns, understanding what to be afraid of and what to work through. Now it was all muddled; everything blurred together.

She wished James Mace was with her in the car, real or not, to read her word bouquets and calm her down. If he wasn't real, could she just summon him? *How does one summon a hallucination?*

She started to think about that guy again, the one who'd believed his daughter was still alive. He hadn't been walking around the city thinking about how crazy he was. He'd probably just thought he was hanging out with his daughter. He'd probably quite liked his life, and was that a tragedy? People always talked about him as though he should've known better or something. As though he'd chosen it.

Would people treat her that way? Whether this was her reality or not, she suddenly felt like she needed to know the answer.

She found herself looking around, wondering what was real and what was an illusion. It was a slippery slope. If she couldn't trust her mind to know rational thing A, how could she trust that it knew rational thing B? She touched the steering wheel to see if it was real but doubted her fingers. If she couldn't trust her ears, how could she trust her fingers? She began to solve simple math problems in her head, because somehow that felt like proof that she was still real, still with it, still smart and sane.

Five times three is fifteen. Fifteen times three is forty-five. Forty-five times three is one hundred and thirty-five. One hundred and thirty-five times three is . . . well, even sane people wouldn't just know that off the top of their head, would they?

Would they?

Breathe.

She felt hyperaware of her fragility, which prompted a feeling of looking down from a great height. Like she'd lived on the edge of a cliff her whole life and just now saw a drop-off that had been there the whole time.

She remembered the Monday after the weekend of the party, as kids had filtered into the hallways and the news about Charlene's jump had spread. No one had commented on how Charlene was doing, just what she'd done.

She remembered Bethany standing by her locker, looking smug, as Valencia had come around the corner on her way to homeroom. "Who *does* that?" Bethany had said loudly, even though her audience was small. She'd caught Valencia's eye. "Honestly. Even if she broke her leg or something, I won't feel bad for her. She probably just did it for attention."

It was guilt, or naiveté, that had made Valencia nod her head. It was something to cling to, anyway, the thought that Charlene hadn't actually intended to kill herself but had wanted to make them all feel bad. *Who does that?*

They wouldn't find out how bad it actually was until later that week. Valencia remembered the principal's eyebrows, large and dark and arched downward like an arrow pointing at her pinched, unsmiling mouth. She remembered the way the woman minced her syllables into tiny pieces with her stainless-steel tongue and spat them out like she hated how they tasted. "Charlene," she said, "will not be coming back to school—especially *this* school—ever. She sustained severe, life-threatening injuries over the weekend, and I have no doubt you all know by now exactly what happened. The family would appreciate notes of encouragement and, I would add, apologies—but no visitors, please—as they begin the lengthy process of navigating their new life. That poor girl has either a long road ahead of her, or none at all."

A stupid kid in the back of the class piped up. "Like, by none at all, you mean no injuries?"

"I mean no *road*." The principal spoke to everyone in the room, but Valencia couldn't help but feel like every word was directed at her. Her face and body sagged, and she could feel all the color drain out of her cheeks.

Of course, Valencia had felt guilty then, unbearably so, but she'd still been arrogant. She'd still felt above it, above Charlene, above the idea of being controlled by something as trivial as emotion or fooled by her own mind, above the idea of falling off that cliff.

But now she was the one sitting on the edge of the abyss. She took a deep breath. The thought of Charlene jarred her back into her skin.

For now, she was okay.

Perhaps this was the upside of not having the nerve to go to New York—she didn't have to find out for sure if she was crazy or not. Maybe ignorance truly was bliss; maybe not knowing one way or the other was for the best. Things could go back to the way they were, and she could forget about James Mace, real or not.

Her world wouldn't change. She'd always known she couldn't change it; maybe she'd hoped James Mace would change it for her. Maybe she'd thought she'd fly to New York and visit James, and then she'd drive to Saskatoon and say goodbye to her grandma, and then she'd turn thirty-five and begin living an actual life.

She took another deep breath, and as the fresh air hit her blood, her delirium gave way to immense sadness.

CHAPTER TWENTY-EIGHT

We'd been married for four years when he disappeared. Maybe it sounds cliché to say I loved every minute of our marriage, and I'm very sure that I have a bit of a selective memory about it, but I feel like I did truly love it all.

Mr. Valentine had so many different sides to him. He was complex and funny and strange and romantic and brave and adventurous. He didn't do everything right, and he didn't always know what to say, but he was humble and kind and he cared about me, and he made sure I knew it. He put a lot of effort into our marriage, which probably doesn't sound all that romantic to someone who's never been married. To me, the kind of emotional elbow grease he put in was worth all the candlelit dinners, all the roses, all the slow dances.

The day he went missing was a very good day to start, but my memories of that morning are heavily tainted by what I now know was going to happen. When I try to picture that morning, it's dark, even though the sun was already up. Our hotel room is shadowy, and his face is shadowy. I can't make out any of his features. I feel like I'm going to be sick, and I feel panicked. I know something horrible is going to happen. I cling to him and cry. When I put my head on his chest, I hear his heart ticking like the hand of a clock, like it's counting down the last few precious hours we have together. It's the most helpless I've ever felt.

In actuality, I probably woke up the way I always did back then—slowly. Sorting and separating the dreams of the previous night from the memories of the day before while stretching my legs under the covers. I probably rolled over and kissed him and said good morning, if I said anything at all, and lumbered off to the bathroom to brush my teeth.

It was March, and we were in Bolivia.

We'd arrived the day before and found that we couldn't see the Salar de Uyuni without booking a tour through a company. We got information about the different companies and tour options and what to expect and what not to miss from the desk clerk at our salt block hotel in Uyuni. He was a short, handsome man who spoke fluent English with a thick Spanish accent and gestured with excitement, clearly proud of his country and what we were about to experience. As we turned to go, he thumped Mr. Valentine on the back one last time. "Hey, make sure you use a good tour company." He'd already offered this advice more than once. "Those brochures I gave you—go with one of those. I can't stress this enough. It's a beautiful place but dangerous in many ways, and you won't do yourselves any favors by going with a cheap company that just wants your money."

Mr. Valentine smiled and thanked him, but the man's face grew solemn, and he shook a finger. "I mean it. We hear all the time about men taking these groups out, completely wasted. At best, they will feed you overcooked pasta and tell you made-up stories about the sights you are seeing. It's just not the experience you have come here for. These companies"—he tapped the brochures in Mr. Valentine's hand—"they'll feed you llama and quinoa. They will tell you the rich history of the area and make sure to point out every little thing so that you don't miss the important points of the tour. They will know how to drive to avoid the holes in the *salar*, and they will be sober and responsible. Too many people come to an area like this, themselves tourists, and just see an opportunity to make money. They take unnecessary risks and endanger good people like yourselves." He shook his head and furrowed his brows. "Make sure you watch out for yourself."

We said we would and thanked him for his concern. His enthusiasm took over his features again, and his eyes lit up. "Good, good," he said, nodding. "You are just going to love the Salar de Uyuni! It is spectacular. You will never want to leave. And you picked the perfect time of year to come see it."

The night we spent in Uyuni was a restless one for no discernable reason. I couldn't sleep. Mr. Valentine couldn't sleep. We spent most of the night sitting up in a nest of blankets, legs crossed, foreheads together, talking and laughing about our favorite moments from the last four years. We were saying goodbye, but we didn't know it then. He fell asleep before me, and I missed my last opportunity to doze off to the sound of his voice.

The next morning at about eleven, we met our tour group and began our trip to the Salar de Uyuni, which, it turned out, was not a lake at all. It was something that sounded much more boring but was actually much better: the world's largest salt flat.

We arrived in a convoy of 4x4s, having had our brains jiggled around inside our skulls so vigorously that I soon began to wonder if I was hallucinating. We saw red rusty pools of water and bright-pink flamingoes and the carcasses of old, broken-down trains and railway carriages that had been left to rot after the collapse of the mining industry in the 1940s. Our tour guide seemed to know everything, and he shared his wealth of knowledge along with a good dose of wit. He must have done that trip a million times before.

The little vegetation that existed looked like nothing I'd ever seen before—in fact, everything around us was so strange and alien, it felt like we'd made our way to Mars somehow. I imagined that the rocks flying up under us and striking the floor of the Jeep beneath my feet were meteors, and I closed my eyes as my teeth crashed together. I opened them just as fast though, chiding myself for pretending to be somewhere else when I was somewhere absolutely amazing. When we arrived at the salt flat and clambered out of our vehicles, I could hardly believe my eyes.

Two heavens and two earths, two Mr. Valentines, two Jeep convoys, two groups of tourists. The whole desert was a mirror. It was dizzying. I was almost hesitant to climb out of the Jeep for fear I'd fall out of our world and into the parallel one beneath my feet, or at least into a fathomless pool of water, but our tour guide reassured me, saying that the water covering the salt flat was only a couple of centimeters deep, just enough to reflect everything above it. Mr. Valentine hopped out first and helped me down. We sloshed away from our group, as they all pulled out their cameras and began to take pictures of the sky, of themselves, of each other, as reflected in the glassy expanse. We hadn't brought a camera; Mr. Valentine never needed one. He could experience something and then describe it to you in a way that was better than showing you a picture. It was almost as good as taking you there.

As we looked up into one sky and down into another, Mr. Valentine grabbed my hand. He moved his toe, and his reflection copied him exactly. Ripples emanated out from him, and the sky beneath us wavered, but the one above stayed perfectly still. A tiny break in the illusion.

"There it is," he said, smiling. "It's kind of fitting, isn't it? A mirror. We've been everywhere in the world and seen all of these amazing things, and the last thing we see is us. One last look at us as we are, just the two of us, before we go off on this new adventure."

I nodded, looking at us toward the ground, the sky all around. We looked so small, like we could get lost in all of that space, and I was thankful to have him to hold on to.

The rest of our tour group was far away now, shrieking and running and laughing, but the water around us was so still, and the clouds reflected in it so clearly, that it felt like we were standing in the sky.

Evening was approaching on the salar, but no one seemed in any hurry to leave. I could've stayed there forever, though my lack of sleep from the night before was catching up to me. Suddenly, Mr. Valentine pointed off into the distance. "Does that look weird to you?"

It was hard to tell if his words brought the storm into being or if he just spoke the exact moment before anyone else noticed the strange-looking clouds gathering. The whole sky took on a reddish hue, and the wind started whipping my hair across my face. We noticed the tour guides running around to their various groups spread out across the desert, shouting through cupped hands, "Come! Come!" Mr. Valentine pulled me in the direction of the little line of Jeeps, which were filling with tourists. The wind grew, and I felt panicked, though I wasn't sure what was happening. Everyone seemed so calm, and, despite the wind, so did the sky and the desert. It was an eerie, unsettled calm, though. Horror-movie calm. The wind whipped hard and fast, and the clouds rolled silently in.

We reached the vehicle, and our tour guide helped me up, but when I turned I saw that Mr. Valentine wasn't following me. I yelled for him, but I soon saw what he was doing. There was a hysterical young woman running from Jeep to Jeep, apparently having a hard time finding the group she'd come with. My mouth dropped when I saw her face, which was, for the first time on this trip, unobstructed by her hair or the hood of her green jacket. It was the girl from the bridge.

Mr. Valentine tapped her on the shoulder, led her to our Jeep, and helped her climb into the last available seat, just in front of me. He caught my eye and shot me what was probably meant to be a reassuring smile. The door slammed shut, and I yelped. I tried to get the driver's attention. "Excuse me? Hey! My husband is still out there—"

"Yes, ma'am, we know," he said, speaking to me like I was getting antsy about a long line at the bank. He had his customer-service voice on. "We're not too picky about who goes in which vehicle at the moment. We just want to get back to Uyuni as quick as we can. He'll be taken care of—not to worry about that—but it looks like we're getting a pretty good red rainstorm here, and it's hard to drive around when you can't see where you're going." He was calm, too, smiling even. Everyone was so calm.

The vehicle lurched forward and followed the convoy back in the direction we'd come from that morning. The storm followed menacingly, a wall of red dust, the infamous red rain. The wind screamed as the dark-red clouds finally caught up. It got to us next, beating the roof, engulfing the Jeep. All the windows turned brown. Were we inside the ground?

I knew they'd take care of Mr. Valentine, but I couldn't stop the tears that slipped down my cheeks as I stared at the back of the girl's head. Did she know I was here? How could she not? This couldn't possibly be a coincidence; I'd known that all along. I wondered, in a moment of dizzying lunacy, if I were the one stalking *her*.

The older woman beside me patted my leg. "Don't worry, dear," she cooed. "This young man seems like a very good driver. These storms blow up all the time; that's what they told me. They just don't like to get caught out in them. Never know how bad they're going to get or how long they'll last." She had a thick accent. I was pretty sure she was from the southern United States. I glared at her daintily freckled hand on my knee. I wanted to yell, "Who are you, anyway? If you weren't here, Mr. Valentine *would* be!" But instead I said, "I know." Even though I didn't know.

When we got back to Uyuni, which had been untouched by the storm, I exited my vehicle and waited fitfully for Mr. Valentine to emerge from one of the others, forgetting the girl in the green jacket in my urgency.

He didn't emerge.

Even after the last vehicle pulled up, I figured, I hoped, there was still the possibility that it wasn't the last.

I stood there and waited forever.

I don't need to tell you in great detail about the months that followed. There was a team sent into the desert to find him days later after the storm let up. I was told the embassy sent a helicopter, but then I was told by some locals that this was probably only a comforting lie. There was an investigation into the company whose negligence led to his disappearance. And then there was nothing more anyone could do. There was just me.

I stayed in Bolivia for a month afterward. Sometimes, I traveled out into the desert with a tour group to look for him myself. Sometimes I stood in the middle of the salt flat. It dried up shortly after the big storm, as it always did that time of year, into a great white wasteland. Sometimes I just wandered around the little town of Uyuni with tears running down my face. I think I became somewhat of a spectacle, but I couldn't bring myself to care at all.

After a while, my mother flew down to Uyuni and brought me back to Canada. She wanted me to stay with her, but I wanted to go home. I went back to our apartment, which was exactly as we had left it, and I sat on the floor and dumped all of the little papers out of my backpack and read every one, like they were clues, like they'd tell me where he was. Because grief makes you believe strange things; it makes you look for sense where there is none.

I gave birth to our baby, a boy, seven months after Mr. Valentine disappeared, and it was kind of like having my husband given back to me, in some ways. It amazes me, the many ways you can have someone given back to you.

I don't believe he's dead. He's missing, and missing is so much less final than dead. I'm sure he's safe and sound, but without his memory—perhaps he hit his head?—somewhere nice. He knows he's waiting for someone but doesn't know it's me. Someday, he'll recall our street name, our phone number, something, and he'll come find me. It's wishful thinking, but wishful thinking was what got us together in the first place. Wishful thinking is fine.

We met twice; we fell in love twice—once with the idea and once with the reality of one another. We were happily married for four years, the four best and most adventurous years of my life. He gave me a son. One day, he disappeared, and I never saw him again, but I'm still waiting, and I still have a great deal of hope. That's our whole love story.

As for the girl in the green jacket: I never saw her again after that. It could've been that she stopped following me or that I was just too distracted looking for Mr. Valentine to look for her anymore.

CHAPTER
TWENTY-NINE

"Valencia," said Louise, who was slouched in her chair picking at a thread in her skirt, looking disappointed but also distracted, "we have talked several times about the importance of taking your medication *consistently*. Not every other day, not only when you feel like it. Can you tell me what happened?"

Louise's slouch was nothing like Grace's. Grace was all angles and jutted-out shoulders and attitude; she looked like a model on a magazine cover. Louise just appeared to be deflating.

"I don't know," said Valencia. "I forgot one day, and then it felt . . . stupid, almost, to start again."

Louise nodded. She wasn't angry. She probably heard this a lot. "Okay, I hear that a lot," she said. She rubbed the piece of thread and glared at it. "But still. You have to override that feeling. It's like cutting a cast off before the bone is healed. You need to trust that doctors—that I—wouldn't keep you on medication if you didn't need it. And you do. I think you know that."

Valencia nodded back.

"Well. I don't want to beat a dead horse. Do you have anything else you want to talk about today?"

"No," said Valencia instinctively, but desperation made her pause and tell the truth. "I mean yes. I do. It's just that I don't think the medication is working—or maybe it is, but it's not enough, or not the right kind. I think I'm having hallucinations. I think I started having them before I went off my meds."

Louise had thin lips, and when she concentrated on anything, they vanished. "Hmm . . . ," she hummed through the line where her lips should be. "Interesting. Visual hallucinations? Auditory?"

"I don't know?" said Valencia. "See, that's just it! I don't know! How would I know?"

"Ah, interesting," said Louise. "So tell me about it."

Tell me about it. Like it was that easy. Valencia was supposed to be able to point to the place in the fabric of her own life where extrareality material had been sewn in without her knowing? "I guess . . . I guess the one thing is that I've been talking to this guy every single day for months, for actual *months*, and then the other day I realized he doesn't exist . . ." She glanced at Louise to see her reaction, but Louise wasn't reacting. "He's a purple monster with buzz saws for teeth."

Louise looked impressed. "Interesting," she said. "Buzz saws?"

"No," said Valencia, embarrassed. "I'm sorry. I was . . . joking. Or something."

Louise didn't laugh. "No monster, or just no buzz saws?"

"No monster either."

Louise looked disappointed again, and Valencia felt mildly offended. "Anyway," said Valencia. "I *am* imagining a guy. And I kind of . . . I sort of fell for him?" She scratched her eyebrow; this was humiliating. "So, I don't know. I think that's as weird or weirder than the monster thing."

"Nothing's *weird*," said Louise.

You are weird, thought Valencia. "Okay, but what does it all mean? How do I know . . . how do I know *you* exist? What about Grace?" Valencia realized she was pleading with Balloon Head Louise. She felt a surge of panic coming up her throat and choked on it. Louise got a

217

cup of water for Valencia, who drank it gratefully, even though it tasted like a swimming pool sample.

"Okay," said Louise, finally making eye contact. "Okay, so let's talk about this. You don't have to be alarmed. We'll figure it out. You think you're having a psychotic break."

Valencia didn't like that. She didn't know what it meant, but it sounded awful. *I'm not loving that phrasing, Louise.* "I don't, I don't know. I don't *think* . . . I don't think it's *that*. I just . . . wonder . . ."

"Is there a possibility that this person is real, or have you proven absolutely that he's not? Has something happened to prove to you that he's a hallucination?"

"Well, little things. Like—"

Louise leaned forward, stopping her with a raised finger. "Okay, one sec." She flipped through some papers on her desk. "I'm going to read something out loud to you." She lifted her chin and frowned at the page in front of her. "'Worries about stove catching on fire if not checked before leaving apartment. Worries obsessively, must check stove compulsively, to the point of making her late for work or having to go home early to check, causes her to be distracted from work, causes panic attacks and acute anxiety.' This is you, correct?"

"Yes."

"And this: 'Worries her mother will die. Often calls her mother in the middle of the night to check on her, believes that if she does not do this, mother will die.' Also you?"

"Yes."

"I have more—shall I read them, too, or would you like me to get to the point?"

"Sure—the point," said Valencia.

"Okay," said Louise, leaning forward the way she often did before she said something that she thought might blow Valencia's mind, an event that rarely happened. "Do you think that, perhaps, schizophrenia might be your new *stoves catching on fire* and *mother dying*? *Airplanes falling out of the sky* and *man with knife in back of car* and *dying of diseases from bathroom doorknobs* and—"

Valencia shifted in her seat and made a noise in the back of her throat to indicate that she didn't want Louise to keep going. "Is that a thing that happens?"

Louise nodded. "Oh yes. It's not uncommon at all for a person with OCD to become obsessed with the idea that they're losing their mind—why would it be? People with OCD can become obsessed with anything. I'd think it more probable than you suddenly up and becoming schizophrenic, to be honest."

Valencia looked down at her hands. "But I *could* be losing my mind, couldn't I?"

"Oh, absolutely. I could too. Any of us could. Minds are more frail than most people realize. But if that's all we all thought about, and if we looked for signs of it around every corner and read into every single circumstance that we were losing our minds, then we all *would*. Part of taking care of your mind is trusting it. Like any relationship." Louise wrote something down. "I know you find it hard to trust your brain right now, but maybe today just choose to trust mine, okay? Don't think too hard about it. Just let your brain relax."

Like Dr. Wojcik, the dentist. *Take a big, deep breath and relax. Try to let your mouth relax. Try to let your brain relax.*

"Okay."

Valencia sniffed. Louise's office smelled different today, less like flowers and more like fruit.

CHAPTER THIRTY

Valencia turned thirty-five. She'd spent the morning of her birthday crafting an essay titled "Thirty-Five Coping Strategies for Turning Thirty-Five" and the afternoon with her mother at the local art gallery. She'd forgotten about the art gallery. It had sliding glass doors and a big white showroom. Not only could you get away without touching anything there, but it was actually forbidden. A completely germ-free afternoon—more sterile than an operating room. When she got home, she added it to her list, turning it into "Thirty-Six Coping Strategies for Turning Thirty-Five." She could reuse it next year.

Her mother had driven over from Saskatoon a few days before. She showed up at Valencia's apartment unannounced, plopped on her couch, cried, talked, cried some more, apologized, asked questions. It was a mess, but it was the kind of mess that needed to be made. "My mother is dead!" Valencia's mother wailed from behind a giant Kleenex ball. "And I'm not going to lose my daughter in the same summer."

And Valencia, who was working with Louise on allowing people to come into her space without devolving into panic, was able to hug her mother and say, sincerely, "It's okay, Mom," and "We're okay" and "I'm sorry" and "I forgive you."

She used some saved-up vacation time, not to go anywhere, just to rest, and now she was back at work.

She didn't look behind her at the man in Peter's chair, and she didn't look forward to James Mace's phone calls anymore (because he didn't call anymore). She looked sideways at Grace a lot because soon she wouldn't be there either, and everything would go back to how it had been. Valencia would be quiet and insignificant and boring, and her story would plod along. This time she would remember to just let it do that.

She fell into a routine again. She drew one last caricature, this one of Peter. It was her best yet. She wanted to hang it on her wall beside the bird, but she didn't want to have to explain it to Grace, so she folded it up and put it in her purse with the ones Peter had given her. She drank a lot of coffee. Wrote a lot of lists and essays. Continued to double-check the stove and developed a new obsession with the cleanliness of her headset. These days she felt much less like she was sitting on the edge of a cliff and more like she was dipping her toes in the ocean. There were a lot of feelings in there, but she couldn't see them all at once, so they weren't so overwhelming. Maybe this was similar to how normal people functioned? It was nice. *Lucky all of us.*

Mornings, however, were tricky.

She still dreaded work, maybe more than ever. There wasn't any kind of medication that could make her love being a debt collector.

It was late September. The early-morning air blowing in through the windows in the living room was chilly, and Valencia shivered. She stared into her cereal and counted the marshmallows. She leaned back in her chair and surveyed the kitchen. The piano music was louder than ever; it was blaring through the walls, flowing through the air, and rustling the pages of the newspaper in front of her.

And then, suddenly, in the middle of the most frantic moment of the song, it stopped. Just like that. There wasn't even an echo. It didn't leave anything blowing around in its wake. It was just gone. As though she'd been imagining it.

Had she?

Louise had told her not to ask herself that question anymore. "It's unnecessary," she'd said authoritatively. "You need to learn to only ask yourself necessary questions."

For the first time in years, there was silence in Valencia's apartment that lasted longer than the time between the song ending and beginning again. She turned her head to the wall and placed a hand on it, and it was still. It had always rumbled like it was a living thing with a heart and internal organs. Now, she was alone, completely alone. It was eerie.

She wished, in this moment, that she knew the name of whoever lived next door. She would've called out, asked if they were okay. She wasn't sure why she thought whoever it was would not be okay. Maybe she (or he?) was just tired of the song. Maybe the landlord got annoyed and wanted it turned off.

But Valencia had made a connection with the person in that apartment. She just knew, somehow, that the music meant something.

She sat in the quiet and gradually began to notice other sounds that she'd never heard before. The refrigerator hummed. The light bulb sang a tiny, high-pitched note. The clock ticked away like a metronome. She didn't like this song; it had no rhythm or story.

She picked up the newspaper and turned to the job listings. She closed her eyes and drew a circle in red pen. Pet shop clerk. *Cleans cages and make sales.* No. She struck through the circle and repeated the exercise. Gas bar attendant. No. Strike. Again. Nail technician. No! Strike! Again! Custodian! No! Strike, strike, strike!

She dropped the pen and paper in despair. She would be a debt collector for the rest of her life, just as she'd always known she would. She would die a debt collector. Staring at a bird. Collecting debt.

CHAPTER
THIRTY-ONE

Mrs. Valentine feels tired. When a person is old and out of shape, talking can sometimes feel the way that running used to—even more so when a person talks quickly and passionately, punctuating each sentence with flailing limbs. Speaking with Anna is the most aerobic exercise she's gotten since she gave up her morning walk a few years ago. She has to stop and clear her throat after almost every sentence.

But Anna doesn't seem to notice (or else she is just being polite). She perches on the edge of her chair, sylphlike and quiet, taking up so little space and making so little noise it's almost like she isn't there. But she's there enough for Mrs. Valentine. She's all in, and Mrs. Valentine loves her for it.

Mrs. Valentine twists her mouth and examines her swollen knuckles, her wedding band, and her engagement ring, which is missing its diamond. She can't get them off and doesn't feel like making the trip to the jewelers to get the stone replaced anyway. It's something she thinks she should do, but she's not planning on it. She lost him without any warning at all, and then one day, not long after, she looked down and noticed that the diamond he'd given her was gone, and it all felt very significant; it felt strange to think of getting one back without the other.

"Thank you for listening to my story, Anna. I feel like I can tell you now: I made it all up."

Anna's eyebrows are the only part of her that moves. She doesn't look as surprised as people usually do. "Like, all of it? Or just the end?" she asks.

"Lots of it. Most of it. There's truth in every story, I think, even made-up ones. It's based on a true story—mine. It's based on real people—Mr. Valentine, the girl on the bridge."

Mrs. Valentine hopes Anna isn't angry.

"Why?" Anna says. "Because you didn't like the way it actually was?"

Mrs. Valentine slaps the tabletop and shakes her head. "Oh no—it was just fine the way it was. But that story and those people are very old. And you know, when you're old you realize that rules about these kinds of things are ridiculous. Playing make-believe in order to make yourself feel better isn't just for little kids. It's like dyeing your hair red—so what if your hair isn't red to begin with? Doesn't matter. You can make it red. Giving your memories a makeover is therapeutic. Telling the stories as though they're fact, even more so—you can make them real in someone else's mind. What's the difference between me telling you something that happened and something I made up? They're both the same to you. They're both real to you. And now, even though you know it's all made up, you'll still think of the whole thing as real—because you don't know any other truth about me. You and I, we have this shared memory of an alternate story line now. And that, I think, makes it as real as any other one." As Mrs. Valentine rambles, she pulls a little bottle of hand sanitizer out of her pocket and rubs some on her palms before taking a cookie from the plate on the table. Then she leans forward and looks very serious. "What makes something real, Anna? Is it the fact that it exists, or is there something else? I remember a man in the news a long time ago who thought his daughter was alive even though she was dead. He was stir-crazy, but he saw his daughter every day, talked to her, loved her like she was there with him. Now, was she real or wasn't she?"

Anna uncrosses her legs. She opens her mouth and closes it again. Mrs. Valentine smiles. And then Mrs. Valentine laughs. And then Mrs. Valentine can't stop laughing, and then Mrs. Valentine cries.

Anna puts her elbows on the table, which surprises Mrs. Valentine. She's never cried in front of her audience; this is uncharted territory. She's not sure what she expected the girl to do—smile politely, excuse herself, leave? But Anna leans in, her elbows on the table like she's waiting for something.

"I made my friend up too," Mrs. Valentine offers. Maybe that's what Anna is waiting for.

But Anna doesn't move. She doesn't even blink.

"I mean I didn't make her up—she was a real person once. She's just dead now, so I have to pretend to have her over. See," confesses Mrs. Valentine, because confessing feels quite good, "when I was younger, I was worried about going crazy, like that man with the daughter, about seeing things, imagining people and hearing voices. Now, I'm not worried about any of that anymore. I do it all on purpose. Memories of people, mostly. I call them up, like ghosts, and we have coffee."

"Grandma Davies?" says Anna in a whisper. She wants to know if Mrs. Valentine knows.

Mrs. Valentine smiles, and her smile says, *No, not Mrs. Davies— let me have Mrs. Davies.* "Oh, Mrs. Davies," she says purposefully. "She thinks I'm a little cuckoo, I'm afraid. Can't quite get used to my more . . . eh . . . blatant eccentricities. Bless her heart. She *is*"—she pauses on this word, this precious present tense—"a wonderful, wonderful friend."

Anna is quiet for a long time, and then she nods. "She sure is."

Mrs. Valentine beams. "You look just like her, Anna. And you have the same beautiful heart. It has been the most wonderful thing, having you here."

Mrs. Valentine's writing desk is a lumpy double bed with a threadbare quilt and two pillows—one yellowing and flat and one almost brand new. Sleep never comes easily, no matter how hard she tries. The space beside her where Mr. Valentine should be is an inky abyss that she can't get used to, even after all these years, so now, instead of trying at all, she works on her stories. She crawls under the covers, closes her eyes, and builds a wall right down the center of the bed, paints murals on it. The dread and loneliness are still there, of course, but they're on the other side of the wall. She makes something nice to look at between her and them, a flowery fish story. She admires her handiwork and then tears it down and starts over.

But that night as she lies in bed, she thinks about the facts as they really were for the first time in years. She shuts her eyes, and they're the sliding glass doors of West Park, closing behind Grace as she leaves work at the end of her last day.

Grace and her husband-to-be were moving to Alberta to be closer to her family. Valencia walked her friend to the front of the building, by the receptionist's desk, and then realized she'd forgotten her purse.

"I'll come back with you," Grace offered, but Valencia shook her head.

"You go. This is good. I don't really want to watch you drive away."

"How very melodramatic of you." Grace thought she was being silly, but Valencia didn't care. James Mace, Peter, and now Grace. They'd all left. Her small world had expanded so much, and now it had condensed back down so rapidly that it pushed the air out of her lungs. She'd had company, even if she was stuck. Now she was just alone, and being alone after not being alone was much worse than being alone before not being alone.

They hugged, and Grace reminded Valencia to RSVP to the wedding, and Valencia made a dumb joke about how Alberta was too far away, and then Grace made a joke that was really more of a suggestion about Valencia moving to Alberta too. Valencia shrugged. "You know what? I might. There's nothing here."

Grace smiled. "No? Not even that cute guy who used to sit behind you?"

"Who, Peter?"

"Oh, *that's* Peter! I didn't know who you meant when you mentioned him. Yeah, what about him? I feel like he looked at you a lot. And he was so sweet the day you had to go home sick; he looked so concerned for you, even though he had no idea what was going on. You should've given him a shot."

"Oh no, I couldn't," said Valencia. It was funny that this was just coming up now, considering Grace's interest in matchmaking and happily ever afters.

"What, because of James?"

"No, because of me. I just don't think I'm relationship material."

"That's stupid; everyone's relationship material," said Grace. "The material that relationships are made up of is people, and *you're* people. What, do you think I'm made out of different stuff than you? Do you think people who worry extra don't deserve to fall in love with other people?" She pulled Valencia into a hug, even though she had to know by now that Valencia didn't want a hug. Then again, Valencia wondered if maybe she did want a hug after all. And she wondered if she was wrong about being relationship material too. And she also wondered something else; she pictured that day her grandmother had died and how Peter had been right there at her side immediately after she'd gotten off the phone with James, looking, as Grace had said, so concerned even though he couldn't possibly have known that she had any reason to be upset.

"Okay, but seriously now, I have to go," said Grace. "My career as a debt collector is officially over. I'll see you at the wedding."

"Maybe sooner," said Valencia. "You never know."

"Aw, you'd drive on the highway for me?"

Valencia laughed. "For you, the future Mrs. Davies, I will . . . try."

And then Grace burst into a fit of giggles over how weird *that name* sounded and made Valencia promise not to say it again, and Valencia kept her promise for forty years.

Grace disappeared through the doors, and Valencia went back for her purse, and a few minutes later, she stood perfectly still just outside the building, catching her breath, and then she looked up, and he was standing there doing the same thing.

"Hey." Peter looked more nervous than she'd ever seen him.

She opened her mouth because she thought she should say hello, and perhaps that she'd missed him and regretted not being able to say goodbye—or, for that matter, much of anything else before that—and maybe even that she was glad to see him, but the words were too big and sticky to get out. They clung to her throat and made it itch, so she coughed instead. She knew she was bad at telling people that she appreciated them or that she liked them, even in a platonic way, or, really, at saying anything at all positive about a person to their face. She was afraid of coming off as needy or clingy. She mumbled a greeting and laughed for no reason. She could feel her mouth climbing up the side of her face, and she held it down with all her might. Her face did strange things when she was nervous. Acrobatics. She had to be very strict with the muscles attached to her mouth and eyes and eyebrows.

He laughed, too, but it was a cautious laugh. He was looking at her like she might burst into flames, like she was a spark and he was holding a can of gasoline.

They were still standing right in front of the sliding doors, a couple of rocks in the steady stream of five o'clock work escapees. Valencia, standing and looking at Peter, felt as though she were at the doors of an

228

airport, looking out into an exciting new city, like there was an adventure out there waiting to be had. She felt that something important was about to happen and that there was nothing she could do to stop it.

She felt a little rush of bravery, the kind that eluded her normally. She felt impetuous. She took a deep breath, and when she let it out, it sounded jagged. She was going to do something amazing, something completely uncharacteristic. She was going to put herself out there. He could reject her—she knew that—but suddenly she understood why people took risks.

She remembered a picture she'd seen in a travel book once of hundreds of hot-air balloons hovering precariously in the air above sharp rocks in Turkey or somewhere. She remembered looking at it and thinking, *Why? Why would anyone do that?* And now it made sense. Though, of course, what she was about to do was ten thousand times scarier.

Shaking, she tipped her head to the side, gesturing slightly to the bench a few feet away. "Do you want to sit?"

Do you want to sit? The scariest thing she'd ever done. A loaded question. A question that asked more questions.

Do you want to sit? *With me? And talk? Will you be my plus-one to Grace's wedding? Will you be my plus-one to our wedding? How many children should we have?* She might need to ask some of these questions out loud in case he didn't catch the subtleties. Men, she knew from extensive television viewing, often didn't.

But for now, he did want to sit. With her. The rest would come later.

They sat. They shifted. They looked at each other and past each other and away from each other. Before Grace had come along, Valencia used to sit alone in this place on her breaks when the weather was nice enough. There was a breathtaking view of the parking lot.

They watched the employees of West Park silently trickle out of the building, a sea of brown suit jackets and moustaches and gleaming bald heads. The cars in the parking lot thinned out. The sun cooled off a little.

And still, they just sat.

Valencia had used up all of her bravery just asking that one question, so she said nothing.

Finally, Peter straightened up and cleared his throat. He looked at her, squinting and screwing up his face, holding up a hand to keep the sun out of his eyes. He looked away again, watching as a blue minivan backed out of its spot. "Okay," he said as it drove away, as though that was what he had been waiting for this whole time. "Okay," he said, his face redder than she'd ever seen it. She worried that he wasn't breathing. "I have something to tell you."

Her hands were shaking, and she wondered why she was nervous when she wasn't the one who had something to tell. He stared at her hands, too, and it made them shake even harder.

"Okay," said Valencia in a tiny helium voice.

"I'm James Mace," said Peter.

Valencia didn't say anything. She'd figured it out a few minutes earlier, but she wasn't going to say that.

"I thought you knew," said Peter. "Right from the beginning, I thought you knew. I called you on your direct line; I used the name of a guy I'd talked to on the phone earlier; he was in the system for a long time. I thought you might even recognize the name. I thought it was our inside joke. I thought it was this unspoken thing: *we both like talking on the phone better*. But then when you talked about coming to New York, I realized you didn't know. I felt awful. I tried calling your house; I tried calling you at work, but someone else was sitting at your desk—they told me you were on vacation, and I didn't know how to get ahold of you. And besides all that, I've just really, really missed you—in person and on the phone. And . . . here."

He reached into his pocket and gave her a paper. She unfolded it. "Me?" She couldn't help but smile.

He nodded. "Your head isn't that big. Your hair isn't that big either. Your ears definitely aren't that big. Actually, your hair is that big. But it's good. It's really good hair."

Peter was holding his hand in front of his face again. Maybe less to shield his eyes from the sun and more because he didn't know what else to do with himself. He sounded frustrated, but she knew the tightness in his voice was probably more nerves than anything else.

She had pulled her legs up onto the bench, and now she hunched over them, her hands covering her mouth so he couldn't see whether the corners turned up or down. He already knew so much more about her than she knew about him.

"One thing," she said. "When you called my house that day, Grace called the number back and a woman answered, and she had no idea who you were?"

Peter laughed and then looked guilty, like he knew he was still on trial and it wasn't safe to do that yet. "That would've been my sister; she lives with me."

Peter rubbed the palms of his hands on the knees of his blue jeans and cleared his throat. "Anyway. I didn't come here to justify myself or ask you to forgive me—I'd love to know you don't hate me, but I can't blame you if you do. But I thought you should know the whole deal. I felt like you deserved that." He stared at the parking lot, as though they were at the top of a mountain looking out over miles and miles of breathtaking wilderness. As though they were on the Brooklyn Bridge in New York, taking in the city skyline.

And then Valencia did another very brave thing. This is how brave things work, after all—they lead to more brave things and more brave things.

She folded the paper and tucked it into her purse next to the one she'd done of him. Looking straight ahead, fixing her eyes steadfastly on Peter's bike, perched on its kickstand next to her car, she reached out her hand and rested it on the bench between them, palm up, fingers open.

He smiled and took it, and they sat there like that for more hours. She looked sideways and saw that the corners of his mouth stretched so far to each side that his face seemed in danger of splitting open. His eyes crinkled at the sides, and his chest puffed up like he was about to burst into laughter—he looked so happy, and she knew it was because he was holding her hand. This made her want to cry, but not because she was sad. They began to talk, and she felt like she was meeting a new person she already knew very well.

She tried very hard not to think about germs. And when the thought crossed her mind that she didn't deserve this or that he didn't deserve her or that it was all unsafe and terrifying, she closed her eyes and recited her poem in her head. *Airplanes are the safest way, the safest way to go. Better to be way up above than on the ground below . . .*

CHAPTER
THIRTY-TWO

Mrs. Valentine pretends to untangle her earphones so she won't have to shake her seatmate's hand; it's a much more believable show these days, the string catching on her large knuckles, her trembling fingers working agonizingly on a simple knot. Maybe it's not a show after all. She nods at him instead, and he takes the hint. "Are you heading home or away?" he asks.

"Home," she says. "After I go somewhere else first."

He looks confused.

"This is home for me," she clarifies. "I was trying to be funny."

He laughs. "So, you're heading out on vacation then? Or visiting somebody?"

"Neither," she says. "It's a business trip."

"Really?" He's confused again. To be fair, she is confusing, even to look at: a brittle, aged woman with flaming red hair. Decorated from head to toe in jangly jewelry and colorful, dressy clothing. On a business trip. "What kind of business?"

She loves that she's in the stage of life where no one bothers to be subtle anymore. People have been making strange faces at her all day, in the taxicab, at the ticket counter, and in the airplane. At worst, they think she's lying about what she's up to—at best, senile. "Another joke," she says. "I'm going on an anniversary trip. With my husband."

"Oh, well, how nice," says the man. "And where's he at the moment?"

"Quite dead, years back now," says Mrs. Valentine.

The man clears his throat. She keeps smiling at him, still fiddling with the cord of her earphones. "Ah," he says. He's young, probably in his sixties. He recovers quickly. "May I ask how long it's been?"

"Fifty years," says Mrs. Valentine, enjoying the look on the man's face. "That's why I thought an anniversary trip was appropriate. We never got to celebrate our fiftieth wedding anniversary, not even close. So, here I am! That, and my therapist thought I should get on an airplane. I'm afraid of them. Terrified."

"Your therapist?" People always react this way when she talks about Louise. Like old people shouldn't have therapists.

"Oh, she's gone now too. The airplane prescription was for a long time ago—I'm just now getting up the nerve."

The man's face is turning red, and the sight of color creeping into his cheeks nudges a sleeping part of her memory. She gasps slightly, but the noise is lost in the sound of the plane engine and all the other wheezing sounds she makes.

"Are you all right?" he asks. It must show on her face.

"Yes." She smiles again. "You remind me of someone."

"You don't remind me of anyone," he says, and she feels this is meant to be a great compliment.

She beams. "Good."

The line of people boarding the plane begins to thin out, and Mrs. Valentine's stomach flutters. She feels calmer than she thought she'd feel, and prouder. Peter was right about this being good for her.

She reaches into her purse and pulls out the caricatures she and Peter made of each other all those years ago. She'd drawn him a bulbous head, a massive mouth, and flattened helmet hair. He'd given her a big pile of fuzzy hair and a tiny little button nose. She smooths them out and sets them on her lap, nudging the man beside her. "This is him," she says in a low voice, pointing. "My husband."

He doesn't look surprised this time. "I like his head," he says, grinning.

Mrs. Valentine looks at the man for a moment and then holds the picture up next to his face. "You know," she says, "you actually look so much like him. It's uncanny."

"My head's not *that* big." The man laughs, and Mrs. Valentine laughs along. She likes him. She's glad he'll be her seatmate for her first airplane ride. He feels familiar, comforting.

A young woman settles into the seat on the other side of Mrs. Valentine. Unlike the man, she doesn't introduce herself or make any attempt at eye contact or conversation. Mrs. Valentine doesn't know airplane etiquette. Maybe it's the responsibility of the person already sitting to welcome newcomers to the row? "Hello," she says, as the man beside her did when she sat down. "Are you heading home or away?"

The girl, who is arranging her carry-on beneath the seat in front of her, looks up and smiles faintly from beneath dark-brown bangs; she isn't trying very hard to hide her annoyance. "Hi. Away."

"Ah," says Mrs. Valentine. The girl also feels familiar to her. All of this familiarity is quite unexpected for such an unfamiliar situation.

The flight attendant, a lady with thick, long braids gathered to one side of her head, begins to give safety instructions over the public-address system, and Mrs. Valentine grips the armrests. The girl to her left has her earbuds in and her eyes closed, but the man to her right pats Mrs. Valentine's arm reassuringly. She smiles at him before placing her own headphones over her ears and pushing play on the ancient Walkman. The piano music blares to life, just as tinny and bewitching as ever. She closes her eyes, too, like the girl. The plane lifts into the air, and she promptly bursts into tears.

I should have done this sooner.

The man mistakes her tears for fear—perhaps, they are, in part—and takes it upon himself to distract her. Unfortunately, the only thing he knows about her is the death of her husband. He waits until she's taken the earphones off to accept pretzels and water from a flight attendant, and then he smiles cautiously at her.

"Do you like to talk about him?"

This was a good question, thinks Mrs. Valentine. Very polite, sensitive. He must have prior experience with old, bereaved people. "Yes," she says. "So much."

"Well, then," he says. "Tell me about him."

She pauses, wondering which story to tell. She has a whole library of them now. Every time she finishes imagining a new version of their story, she likes to tell it to someone—Mr. Baker, the mailman, the grocer. The gardener. A neighbor. A lady on a park bench. Anna. The telling is always like the last stroke of a paintbrush; Mrs. Valentine feels it's necessary for each story to be imprinted on someone's memory. It's almost as good as writing them down.

In these imagined worlds, Mr. and Mrs. Valentine have done everything; they've gone everywhere and had every kind of job and adventure. There are hundreds of versions of him wandering the earth, lost in the desert, held captive in a foreign jail, beleaguered by amnesia, hidden away in the witness protection program, biding his time, missing her as much as she misses him.

Someday, every version of him will come home.

She loves the thought of that. Her mind doesn't treat the real memories differently from the dreamed-up ones; when she closes her eyes, they all look the same. She feels lucky to have lived so many lives. But she decides to tell this man the real story. It feels right. It is, after all, their anniversary.

"Have you ever thought about where you're going to die?" she asks the man.

"All the time," he says, and she smiles.

She begins with the call center and the bird on the hat and Peter, Grace, and James Mace. Louise and the pills. The caricatures passed back and forth, the small wedding, which had indeed taken place in a church late at night. And then she breathes out of her nose very hard and nods her head and silently counts her fingers, the ones on her right hand and then the ones on her left.

The man sitting beside her waits patiently.

Their last conversation did not take place in Bolivia, or on a pirate ship, or in outer space, or any of the other outlandish places she said it had over the years. They were in the bedroom in their tiny apartment, a space so small that no matter where they stood in it, they could reach out and touch each other. It was early in the morning, and he was getting ready for work; she sat on the edge of the bed staring at the white wall in front of her while he buttoned his shirt up. She was apologizing again.

The conversation was one they'd had so many times it had ceased to be a conversation and was now a play they put on for no one. They had their lines and blocking memorized, and they paused in all the right places, and it was starting to become less real, less believable, because it had been done to death. They didn't put as much into it as they once had.

It always started with him asking—stumbling over his words as though they were giant rocks and he had to crawl across them to get to her—if she had thought any more about children. About having children. With him, he meant. Ahem.

And then she'd grow still, and her eyes would close, and she'd say that yes, she did, all the time, and he knew that.

And he'd say he wanted to know if anything had changed, and she'd start to cry and say that nothing had changed as much as she desperately wished it would, and he would walk across the room—two steps—and back and then say something about how he wished he could afford a house with a bedroom that a person could actually *pace* in, for crying out loud. He wasn't mad; he thought this was a funny thing to say. He didn't want her to feel bad—which, she thought, was generous of him. She felt like she deserved to feel bad.

Physically, as far as she knew, she could have children with him. Mentally, she wasn't sure she was up to the task. They'd started to try shortly after their wedding—she was thirty-six, after all, and the clock was ticking (her aunt said that to her). But she'd quickly become consumed with all the things that could go wrong before, during, after the birth, well into the baby's teenage and adult years. What if she miscarried? What if the baby was stillborn or died in its crib? What if it got cancer or what if it got bullied at school or what if it had a peanut allergy? What if the baby's mind was like hers? What if it lay awake at night, every night, for its whole life, picturing horrible things, trying to cry quietly into its pillow so it wouldn't worry its parents?

Her constant worry began to make her physically ill, and at her doctor's recommendation, they'd taken a break from trying. Then she was afraid to start again. And then she was nearing forty. Maybe they both knew there would be no baby. Maybe they'd keep having this conversation until they were elderly people, just pretending they still had a choice.

But on that day, the play had a surprise ending. Where she would usually dissolve into tears and crawl back into bed, leaving him late for work and unsure of how to comfort her, she instead wiped her face with the edge of the bedsheet and announced that she wanted to go on a trip.

"We were having a fight," she says to the man seated beside her. "We had been trying to start a family and had just found out we couldn't." Though this is not the whole truth, it's close enough, she thinks. Not everyone needs to know everything. "I told him I wanted to get on an airplane. It was like dangling a carrot in front of a horse; I knew he wanted to leave the city so badly, but I couldn't go anywhere. He was only stuck by proxy. But instead of getting excited, packing a bag, and driving me to the airport right then, he sat beside me on the bed and said no.

"I got all worked up over it, over everything, really, about how a baby—a whole family—was supposed to be our one adventure and I'd blown it, and now we were both confined to this boring, quiet life forever. And we sat there for a while, and finally, he said to me, 'Valencia, life is just like music. It's made up of sound and silence.' He reminded me of one of my favorite musical terms—*fermata*. It's a symbol, a parenthesis turned on its side overtop of a dot. When it's placed above a rest in a piece of music, it makes the rest last longer; it's called a *grand pause*. Composers often put it right before a really beautiful section. Like everything in music, it's always intentional. *Fermata* emphasizes the beauty of what's going to happen next. He left that morning with a promise that what was next for us would be beautiful, and that afternoon someone fell asleep at the wheel of their car and veered into oncoming traffic. My husband didn't even make it to the hospital."

Mrs. Valentine notices that the girl next to her is listening now. She can't decide whether she minds or not.

She doesn't know how much more she's going to tell the man anyway. She's drifting into even more personal, introspective territory. She thinks of sitting on the floor of her apartment surrounded by scraps of paper with Peter's favorite words, like a manic detective working to crack a case with no actual solution, like he had simply disappeared and she could find him if she rooted through all of his words. Grace sat with her while she worked through all of her questions out loud: Was there something else, something beautiful, that would've happened if the accident hadn't happened? Was she wrong to think the time before the accident was the pause? Or was this the pause? Would the beauty Peter promised her ever come out of this? He'd said the grand pause was never unintentional. Surely there could be no grander pause than death—and yet, nothing was less intentional than a car accident.

The man shifts in his seat, and she worries she's been in her head for too long.

"That's that," she says simply. "Nearly fifty years ago."

"What was the beautiful part?"

"Pardon?" Mrs. Valentine is surprised by the question. The girl seems to lack any embarrassment at having inserted herself into such a private conversation. Then again, she almost has no choice, sitting so close. Maybe this is another part of airplane etiquette Mrs. Valentine is unaware of.

"You wouldn't have told us what your husband said about something beautiful coming after if he didn't end up being right."

"Yes, and he was right," Mrs. Valentine says. "It didn't feel beautiful at first, because it was so awful. It felt like being torn apart and then rebuilt, and that rebuilding was, I'm sure now, the beautiful part. Because the worst had happened! Do you know how much of my life I spent waiting for something terrible to happen? I was obsessed with it, consumed by it. I spent every moment dreading it—and all of a sudden, here it was, and it was every bit as awful as I'd imagined it would be. And then . . . life went on. I realized then how pointless and powerless fear is, and though it didn't go away completely, though my brain worked—still works—the same as it always has, I was finally able to grow. I had never done that before. I'd been shrinking my whole life. Rebuilding, change, growth—those things are so beautiful. Beauty is on a different plane than happy and sad or easy and hard; I'm sure you know that. A song can be sad and beautiful at the same time. Life too."

The three passengers sit together in silence. The pilot's voice announces the plane's descent into New York City over the public-address system. Mrs. Valentine startles. "Is it over already?"

"Afraid so," says the man. He snaps the tray to the seat back in front of him and stuffs his garbage into his Styrofoam coffee cup. "But it was such a pleasure to meet you. I've never met another Valencia—that was my mother's name. I'm James." He reaches for her hand again, and this time she decides to shake it. She is on an airplane, after all. She'll have to wash her hands when they land either way.

The girl is wrapping her earphones around her wrist. She leans across Mrs. Valentine to shake the man's hand too. "I'm Charlene," she says. "Nice to meet you both."

The flight attendant who read the safety speech appears at Charlene's side and places a manicured hand on Mrs. Valentine's shoulder. She looks concerned. "Are you still doing all right, ma'am? Do you need anything?"

"I'm fine, thank you," says Mrs. Valentine brightly. The stewardesses on this airline have been so attentive; they introduced themselves multiple times, constantly interrupting her conversation with James to check on her. She'd expected as much, traveling alone as a senior, but still.

"Okay, just holler if you need anything. I'm right over there. My name's Dee. We can help you off the plane when the time comes, too, if you need, and with any other accommodations once we've disembarked. Okay?"

Dee smiles and pats Mrs. Valentine on the shoulder. Then she buckles herself in beside a young male flight attendant named Jim.

"Is she okay?" he asks.

"I guess," says Dee.

"She's been talking to herself the whole flight," Jim says. "Talking, laughing, crying. Alzheimer's?"

"I guess."

"Poor old lady."

"I don't know," Dee says. "She looks happy, doesn't she?"

Mrs. Valentine sags in her seat beneath her wispy shock of red hair and smiles tearfully down at two pieces of paper taped together. She leans over and shows it to the empty seat on her left.

"I guess," says Jim.

"Do you think she'll be okay?"

"I hope so. She's sweet, isn't she?"

"Yeah."

The plane touches down on the tarmac and rolls up to the gate. The passengers begin to stand and open overhead compartments, but Mrs. Valentine sits perfectly still until everyone else has gone. Then she stands and makes her way to the front.

When she shuffles past on her way out the door, she reaches up and pats Dee heavily on the shoulder. "Bless you, dear; thanks for not giving me trouble about the imaginary passengers next to me. I needed to keep my mind busy. This was my very first time flying! You're a sweetheart, young lady."

Dee feels relieved but even more puzzled. "No problem at all. That's what we're here for. Big plans for the evening?"

"Yes," says Mrs. Valentine. "Such big plans for such an old woman. I'm here for my fiftieth anniversary."

"Oh! How wonderful! Congratulations."

Mrs. Valentine smiles at her.

"Can I help you with anything, ma'am? Do you need a wheelchair or assistance finding the baggage claim?"

"Oh, thank you! I don't have any baggage, but I do need help finding the departure gates. I'm catching a flight out in about five hours."

"Oh, for sure. Where to?"

"Back home. My husband and I are having our anniversary supper in the terminal, and then I've got to head right back. I'm an old bird, dear girl. One night in the Big Apple is quite enough for me."

Dee gives her the now-familiar befuddled look, and Mrs. Valentine wants to reach out and hug her. "Dear girl, dear girl," she says, holding back a laugh.

The pair makes their way down the hallway and into the terminal, where Dee sees that Mrs. Valentine gets through security and safely to a little food court near her gate.

Mrs. Valentine orders what feels like two very extravagant meals of pasta and coffee and takes them to a window to watch the planes land and take off, something she hasn't done in many years. She spreads everything out on the seat beside her, one place setting facing her and another mirroring it. She won't worry about the wasted food; she needs all the tangible props she can get tonight. She reaches into her bag and pulls out an old bike helmet, which she sets on the bench in front of the other plate.

She sips on her scalding-hot coffee and closes her eyes, and when she looks up, there he is, walking across the terminal to meet her. He looks the same as he always did, and she knows he's thinking the same thing about her, which is comforting. He sits down next to her, ignoring the pasta, and wraps her up in a hug and holds her until her coffee gets cold. Then he hands her a little black velvet pouch.

"What's this?"

"Your birthday present," he says.

"It's not my birthday."

"No, but I've missed a few of them. Nearly fifty, I think. Rounding up." He winks at her.

"True." Mrs. Valentine takes the pouch. She notices the couple in the next row of seats staring and whispering, but she doesn't mind.

She shifts in her seat, sending her fork onto the floor. She leans over to pick it up, and the simple motion takes so much effort that Mr. Valentine vanishes for a moment. She wonders if this is how women feel at nine months pregnant: the aching hips and feet, the flesh and fat multiplying on top of itself and getting in the way, the once-simple tasks that suddenly seem preposterous, like picking a fork up off the floor. A familiar sadness echoes in her body at this thought, and she's amazed that it still lives there after all these years of trying to starve it out. She pushes past it as she's learned to do.

She closes her eyes, and the sadness dissipates, nostalgia replacing it. In this alternate reality, the movement reminds her of something she's experienced. In this story, her husband sits beside her, and their son is a polite, inquisitive man named James who treats old ladies with respect. A happy ending in every way.

How lucky she is.

She opens the pouch. It contains a single diamond the same size and cut and carat as the one she's lost. She takes the stone and gently places it in its setting on her left hand. It fits perfectly, like magic. Mr. Valentine grins at her. "I found it in the apartment, under the stove, and wanted to get it all shined up before I gave it back to you," he says.

"Thank you," she says. "It's still so beautiful."

"Like you, Vee." He always says stuff like that.

"Happy fiftieth anniversary," she says.

"Happy?" he says.

"I am. This will all make for a very nice memory tomorrow morning."

Mrs. Valentine slips her headphones over her ears and fumbles for the play button. She watches the sun set behind the airplanes and enjoys an unexpected fireworks show off in the distance, beyond the skyscrapers, as she finishes her pasta. She admires the glint of the imagined diamond and savors the echo of her dead husband's laugh in her head as they sit, hand in hand, watching the airplanes. The real gets all mixed up with the imagined, just as she'd hoped.

ACKNOWLEDGMENTS

Thank you, Barclay. There're a lot of things to thank you for; I could write another book! But I live with you, so if you'd like an itemized list, feel free to come ask for one.

Thank you, Erin, for telling me at the playground that one time that I could write a book. I probably wouldn't have if you hadn't given me "permission" or made writing a book seem so accessible. ("Just write one," I think you said.) I started writing this one that day. I hope you do not regret your advice.

Thank you, Sarah, for being such a steady, reliable writing friend and for becoming the regular kind of friend along the way. I am confident that I would never have written more than three chapters if it hadn't been for your strict deadlines and endless cheerleading. It would be cool to meet you in real life someday.

Thank you, Hannah, Jannaya, Robyn, and Kate for reading my rough, rough drafts and giving such valuable input. It was easy to trust your opinions and advice because I think you're all very cool. Which is why I chose you as readers but also as friends.

Thank you, Dr. Nilofar at the Regina Public Library, for being so generous with your time and feedback and for making me feel like a real writer.

Thank you, Victoria, for being such a wonderful agent and believing so strongly in this book. You have done *so much* for me, and I don't take it for granted.

Thank you, Alicia, for all of your hard work and encouragement and advocacy, for "getting" this book (in more ways than one) and taking such good care of it. I have loved working with you.

Thank you, Laura, for your sharp editorial eye, for reading this thing over and over and over and making it better with every pass. You're amazing.

Thank you, Philip, for the gorgeous cover. I love it.

Thank you, Lake Union, and every person there who helped make this book a *book*. This has been such an incredible experience.

And thank you to all the Regina coffee shops that were my offices. Especially The Naked Bean and Brewedney and Stones Throw.

ABOUT THE AUTHOR

Photo © 2018 Kiersten Taylor

Suzy Krause is a Canadian writer and music lover. Like Valencia, she has worked as a debt collector, and like Mrs. Valentine, she likes to tell stories. She writes about her life at www.suzykrause.com. *Valencia and Valentine* is her first novel.